The Detective Esther Penman Series

The Art Merchant
Vengeance
Pentacle

For updates on all new releases and promotional offers, follow author J.K. Flynn on Amazon and Bookbub, or sign up to the newsletter at **www.jkflynn.co.uk**

VENGEANCE

A Detective Esther Penman Thriller

J.K. Flynn

First Published in Great Britain in 2023 by Chingola Publishing

Cover designed by J.K. Flynn with Bookbrush.com

ISBN: 978-1-7391797-3-1

www.jkflynn.co.uk

VENGEANCE

PROLOGUE

IT HAD BEEN a long day for Carlton Riddell. One of the most stressful of his life. Despite the cold, he felt the sweat on his palms as he hurried around the corner and out of sight of the Marriott Hotel. He was three blocks away from it now.

Still not far enough.

What had happened in that hotel room was all types of illegal. He felt dirty. Soiled in a way that no amount of soap and water would fix. And he'd be facing jail time for sure if he got caught.

But he'd known that before he went in there.

Known it long before he decided to do what he did.

He pushed these thoughts aside as he hurried around another corner, putting one more block between him and the hotel. It was done now, and there was nothing for it but to push on with his plan. Nothing to do but stay focused. If he stayed focused and kept his nerve, he could do this, and with any luck, get away free and clear…

He shifted his briefcase from one hand to the other, glancing over his shoulder to make sure he wasn't being followed as he quickened his step. Even through his heavy overcoat, he was able to smell his own nervous sweat; he'd kept his jacket on the whole time in the room, hiding the damp patches under his pits and between his shoulder blades. He'd been trying to act cool throughout. Despite the icy air that fogged his breath now, he was *still* sweating. Sweating and shivering at the same time.

Finally, he rounded a corner and spotted his blue BMW convertible. It was sitting in the small, off-street parking lot where he'd left it half an hour ago. His journey from the carpark to the Marriott had been a haphazard and circuitous affair, with constant looks over his shoulder, but now that the deed was done, he was sacrificing caution for speed. He wanted to put as much distance as he could between him and Room 513 of Belfield's Marriott Hotel, and he wanted to do it as quickly as possible.

A glance at his watch told him it was just after ten o'clock. The buildings all around here were office blocks and upmarket stores, their windows blank and unlit. The pavements might have been empty, but with Christmas only two weeks away, the streets themselves were awash with festive lighting. It left very few shadows to skulk in. And Carlton wanted shadows. He wanted to fade away and disappear. Whenever he spotted the headlights of an approaching car, he looked down at his feet, only raising his head when it was well past. He tried to convince himself that nobody would be looking for him yet, but there was no way to be sure of that. So he kept his head down and his pace up until he reached the carpark.

Most of the spaces were empty. A quick scan confirmed

the half-dozen vehicles there were the same ones as earlier, frosted over now as the night grew colder. His convertible had started frosting up too, but no matter; a couple of minutes with the blower on would clear it. It was a couple of minutes that Carlton would rather use putting distance between himself and the city centre, but at least sitting into his car would get him out of sight.

As he fingered through his keys to find the fob, he heard the rev of an engine in the street behind him. He spun and was immediately dazzled by headlamps. Squinting, he took a step backwards as a van veered into the lot and skidded to a stop next to him. Panic seized him. He *had* been followed! Someone knew!

There was no time to react as the driver's door swung open and a hulking figure leapt out. A glance towards the carpark exit told Carlton it was too far to run. Dressed all in black, his face hidden by the cowl of a hooded top, the man stalking towards him was a monster. Not tall, but broad and heavily muscled, as if he spent every waking hour in the gym. Carlton found himself backing up instinctively, trapping himself between his own car and the one parked next to it. He gripped the handle of his briefcase tighter and raised it up to his chest like a shield.

"Wh-what do you want?" he spluttered. "Who sent you?" *Maybe he could strike a deal…*

Whether the guy went to grab him or hit him, Carlton couldn't tell, because instinct kicked in and he ducked. He swung his briefcase and caught his assailant on the side of the head. The man grunted and lashed out. It was a wild haymaker, and in other circumstances Carlton might have avoided it—he might even have used a technique from his old rugby days to bring the beefed-up bastard to the ground—but just at that moment his left foot found a patch of ice; he slipped and fell straight into the oncoming fist. The punch sent him tumbling, head smashing against the window of his BMW on the way down. He hit the ground hard.

For a moment, he didn't know which way was up. His ears were ringing, and a dull, star-speckled brown cloud filled his vision. Blood, warm and sticky, covered his face; he could taste the coppery tang of it on his lips. Recovering his wits, his hands scrambled blindly over the stony tarmac for the briefcase. *Where was it? Shit!*

And then fingers gripped his throat. The heavy weight of his attacker was suddenly on top of him. He tried to protest, but it came out as little more than a gurgle, the hands around his throat making it difficult to breathe, let alone speak.

He began swinging his fists, but his knuckles seemed to bounce off that hooded skull to no effect. Sucking desperately for air that wouldn't come, he attempted a jab at the kidneys, tried to bring his knees up, but he had no strength. He was like a kitten trying to push off a mastiff.

And then a shift of the light revealed his assailant's face, veins bulging at neck and temples, spittle bubbling on his lips as he grunted with the effort of choking the life out of him. And Carlton recognised him. Recognised those eyes. Eyes that bored into him with a determination he couldn't remember them ever possessing before. *What? How—*

Desperately, he clawed at that face, but the man drew back, drifting out of Carlton's focus. When he tried again to reach for those eyes, it was as if he was being held at a great distance, or his arms had suddenly grown too short.

A dark cloud began to eat away at Carlton's vision as the

grip on his throat grew tighter. For a long moment, all he could feel was intense pain and heat, as though his throat was full of shattered glass. Then that too faded, and he felt nothing.

Slowly, the sounds of the world dwindled away, and Carlton Riddell's world went black…

1

AN ICY WIND rose over the gravestones, stirring the trees and bushes that dotted the cemetery. Esther hunched her shoulders against the cold, glad of the thick woollen scarf Jean had insisted on pushing on her as she'd headed out the door that morning. Her aunt could be suffocating at times now that Hannah was gone, but Esther couldn't complain; she owed Jean so much, not just because of what she'd done for her over the past few months, but for a lifetime of kindness.

As she stood over her mother's grave, Esther thought about how different Jean and Hannah had been. Sisters by blood, but *entirely* different people.

The grave itself was no more than a patch of raw brown earth, frosted in places where the weak winter sunlight failed to dispel the morning shadows. There was no headstone, just a simple wooden cross with the name *Hannah Penman* and her dates of birth and death carved into it in small, blocky writing. Freshly laid bouquets of flowers lay huddled around the cross, their cellophane wrappings rustling in the cold wind. The headstone was finished—she'd seen it in the workshop—but it wouldn't be put in place until the earth around the grave had settled. Esther was learning new things about the business of death since Hannah had passed away suddenly last week. Although 'suddenly' probably wasn't the right word, not with cancer. Too suddenly for Esther, that was for sure. After years of estrangement, she'd only started getting to know her mum again. One moment, Hannah was being discharged from hospital with another couple of months to live, maybe more, and the next she was gone.

She hadn't cried. Not yet. Jean had done enough crying for the both of them. It was harder on her. She'd been taking care of her sister for almost a year, ever since the cancer really took hold. Even still, she did her best to put on a brave face around Esther. That was Jean all over; she was one of those people who put everybody else ahead of herself.

It was nicer here today, with no one about. Not that there had been many at the funeral the day before. Hannah hadn't had many friends. Some of the people she'd met through Jean over the last few months had shown up to pay their respects. All Jean's friends and neighbours, really, but better than no one showing up at all.

Esther's boss had come too. She'd told Jared there was no need, but she was grateful he'd come in the end. More than just a boss; Jared was her friend. And like her late mother, Esther didn't have very many of those.

Belfield's main cemetery was big enough that the drone of the city felt far away here, deep among the tree-lined walks and the ranks of silent headstones. She preferred standing here today, alone, without people commiserating and trying to make awkward small talk. And yet, despite the peace and quiet, she was finding it hard to concentrate on her mother. She'd come here this morning thinking she would say a quiet goodbye, with no one else to bother her, but she couldn't focus.

She found herself fingering the cast on her left arm. Pulling aside the cuff of her coat, she looked down at the name and phone number scribbled there in blue felt-tip pen. Not for the first time, she thought about ringing that number. Thought about what that might lead to. And, not for the first time, she pushed the thought away. Another person to grow close to was just another person to eventually lose.

She switched her gaze instead to the wooden cross, and the name etched in the damp wood. How many years had she spent hating the woman buried here? And after all those years, it seemed a cruel twist of fate to be given only five short weeks to grow close again, to forgive and mend bridges, before being snatched apart once more.

Esther had been living with her aunt in Sarsbury for the past month. Ostensibly, she'd moved in to help Jean take care of Hannah in her final weeks, but the truth was that Jean—Jean, who had managed to care for her sister for months without any help—had heard about Esther getting attacked in her apartment in Belfield, attacked by a man sent to kill or capture her because of her investigation into a dangerous local drug lord called Peter Darren. And although Esther had arrested Darren since then, and he'd been remanded into the custody of nearby HMP Marshfield ever since, he was no less dangerous. People like Darren maintained a level of influence on the outside even when they were locked up. As soon as Jean learned about the incident, she'd insisted Esther take her spare room. When the chief superintendent in charge of Belfield's district had decreed that Esther was going to have to leave her apartment for security reasons anyway, she'd taken her aunt up on the offer. She'd planned to use the opportunity to help out, to lift some of the pressure off Jean and spend more time with her mother before the end.

But now Hannah was dead, and Esther found herself living in her aunt's house as an accidental lodger.

Thoughts of Peter Darren made her glance at her watch. He was due to be arraigned at Belfield Courthouse this morning. If she wanted to make it, she would have to start moving. She wasn't about to miss this court appearance, even if her new chief inspector was insisting she take a few days to grieve. Apparently she needed some time out. Compassionate leave. But Esther knew what she needed and what she didn't need. She didn't need days on end, moping around the house, or wandering about town, with nothing to occupy her mind.

And she didn't need to spend the day standing at the grave of a woman she'd hardly known, not knowing what to think or say.

She was going to that hearing this morning.

"Sorry, Mum," she muttered to the grave. "I'll come back when my head's not up my arse."

It was then, just as she turned to leave, that Esther spotted him. A man, less than a hundred yards away, standing in front of another burial plot, watching her. Kitted out in an ugly brown overcoat, he was stocky and short, late fifties maybe, with a tanned complexion and a thick mane of dark grey curls. He was far enough away that

Esther couldn't see his eyes clearly, but she didn't have to—she could *feel* his gaze on her.

When he saw her looking, he turned and hurried away.

Heart quickening, Esther scanned the graveyard for other watchers. The place was busy—more like a local park than a traditional cemetery in some ways, with dog-walkers and joggers everywhere—but no one else stood out or appeared to be paying her any attention.

The man in the brown overcoat was following a path into a copse of evergreen trees. She was about to lose sight of him.

Touching the cannister of pepper spray in her pocket—a weapon she kept with her at all times now—she set off after him.

Not bothering to stick to the pathways, she cut across plots of grass between the gravestones. The cemetery had plots dating back to the eighteenth century, with new ones squeezed in among the old; gothic monuments and statues, in marble as well as stone, provided plenty of places to hide from view. She watched as he ducked out of sight behind a crumbling mausoleum.

Darting across the pathway after him, Esther almost collided with a cyclist. She jumped out of the way as the guy made a deft manoeuvre to avoid her. Calling out an apology, she raced on without waiting.

At the mausoleum, there was no sign of the man in the brown overcoat. Esther hopped onto a low wall surrounding a two-hundred-year-old tomb to get a better vantage, squinting against the low morning sun.

Of the half-dozen people in this part of the cemetery, none were the man who had been watching her. The nearest cover—hedges, a stand of evergreen trees and a couple of larger monuments—were all too far away for him to have reached in such a short space of time. The only other possibility was the gateway nearby, a wrought-iron arch in the Georgian railings that bounded the graveyard. To make it out of that gate, he would've had to break into a run himself.

Was that the flash of a brown coat among the cars beyond the railings?

Heads turned as Esther raced down the slope towards the gates. She was trying to look all ways at once as she emerged onto the street. It was a Friday morning and the traffic was heavy, the footpaths choked with pedestrians. But there was no man in a brown overcoat.

She hurried to the next intersection, glancing into the cars parked by the kerb along the way. They were all empty. When she reached the junction, she scanned every crossing street, but she couldn't see him anywhere.

He was gone.

Accepting defeat, she muttered a curse and checked her watch again. She needed to get going if she was to make it to court for the arraignment.

She turned and headed for the nearest bus stop, keeping a lookout for anyone in a brown overcoat as she went.

2

ESTHER FLASHED HER warrant card to the security guard as she stepped into the courthouse lobby. The portly old man, probably ex-police himself, gave her a friendly smile and waved her through the metal detector. She headed for the lifts.

Belfield's courthouse had been rebuilt ten years ago. Gone was the Victorian edifice, with its crumbling walls and musty courtrooms; now the building boasted floor-to-ceiling glass façades street-side and state-of-the-art custody suites below, with access corridors running directly from the courtrooms to the jail cells in the basement. The magistrates' courts and county courts took up an entire floor each, while the top floors were reserved for the higher courts—the Crown Courts—where all the more serious criminal trials took place.

She scanned the Crown Court listings, posted on a noticeboard next to the elevators.

R v Peter Darren
Court 16 – 3rd floor

With a glance at the small crowd milling about in front of the lifts—scumbags in tracksuits, shoulder-to-shoulder with suited solicitors, and barristers in their black gowns and wigs—she decided to take the stairs.

Climbing the steps, she realised she was nervous. It was true that giving evidence at court could be a bit daunting, even for cops, but Esther had long since lost the butterflies she'd felt as a rookie. She wouldn't even be taking the stand today. No, the nerves she felt were nothing to do with giving evidence. It was Peter Darren. The man gave her the creeps, and this morning's incident at the graveyard hadn't helped.

She and Jared had taken Darren down for drug-smuggling and conspiracy to murder six weeks ago, but as the boss of a drug-running operation, Darren didn't get his own hands dirty, which made securing convictions for the big stuff a little more challenging.

It had all started in October, when Esther attended the scene of a murdered local woman called Rachel Gorman. Jack Barry, the man they suspected of having killed her, was found hanging from a tree in the Norwick Forest a few days later, and Rachel's husband Charles had thrown himself from a bridge shortly after that. But Peter Darren was the man behind it all, the organised crime boss for whom Jack Barry and Charles Gorman had both worked. Esther was certain it was Darren who'd ordered Jack Barry to kill Rachel—either because the woman had found something out, or because Charles had crossed some line—but knowing something and proving it in court were two very different things. As expected, the CPS—the Crown Prosecution Service—were wavering on the murder charges. They had dropped the conspiracy charge in relation to Rachel Gorman altogether, and now they'd started vacillating on a final decision around Jack Barry, despite the fingerprints CSI had found at the scene linking Darren to the crime. The fact that police had initially ruled Barry's death a suicide was coming back to bite them now.

Luckily, they had Darren on a whole host of other charges. The financial crime department had offices full of brainy accountant-types who had taken Peter Darren's art gallery ledgers apart and gone through his personal finances line-by-line, adding a string of money laundering offences to the case. With the drugs link, tentative as it was, those charges alone ought to be enough to see Darren go down for years. But Esther wanted him convicted of Jack Barry's murder too. Anything less would feel like a failure. He was obviously a smart man, having not just evaded charges, but having managed to stay below the radar of the force's intelligence department for so long. And smart criminals were the most dangerous. Darren had proven the point. He'd sent that hitman to her apartment, and men like Peter Darren didn't sit idle while in prison. He would have contacts on the outside. She thought about the man in the brown overcoat at the cemetery and wondered if he'd already lined up the next attempt on her life…

As she reached the lobby on the third floor, she scanned the scattered crowd. Scumbags, lawyers, and some scumbag lawyers. Policemen stood out a mile in this company, even without their uniforms. Unlike the criminals—who didn't even bother to change out of their trackies these days, even for Crown court—and unlike the solicitors and barristers in their tailored three-pieces, or their gowns and wigs, all the cops wore scuffed shoes, cheap suits, and ugly ties. Any crim could see them a mile off.

She spotted Jared hovering near the doors to Courtroom Sixteen, chatting with a barrister. Her boss was well over six feet tall, but this man was taller still. In contrast to Jared, he was thin as a beanpole, with sunken cheeks and a hooked nose. His sharp features and stooped stance made him look like a vulture in his black gown and white wig.

Jared looked surprised to see her. "Esther," he said, "I wasn't expecting you to be here." He turned to the barrister. "George, this is Detective Sergeant Esther Penman. Esther, this is George Robinson, lead counsel for the CPS on the Darren case."

The barrister turned to her and flashed a smile, a smile that changed his whole countenance. His lips parted, revealing perfect white teeth, and his hooded eyes opened wide. He even seemed to straighten a little. The vulture had vanished. Esther thought he ought to smile more often.

"Detective Sergeant Penman," he intoned in a deep, rich voice. "I've read your statements and case notes. Very impressive. I was hoping to have a go at the conspiracy charges—I think we might have had a shot with a favourable jury—but alas, those are not my instructions."

"Thank you, Mister Robinson, I appreciate that."

"Unfortunately, as I've been telling Detective Inspector Wilcox, the directing prosecutor actually wants to throw out the murder charges as part of a plea deal for the rest. I think those charges are strong enough to run with, but he doesn't agree. Apparently that initial ruling of suicide is a bit of a sticking point for him."

Esther looked at Jared. "That was… a colleague's

assertion. One that neither of us shared from the outset." Jared would know she was talking about their recent head of department, Detective Chief Inspector Warren Porter. He'd been banished to the Records Department, and it had a lot to do with that mistaken ruling of suicide in the Jack Barry case.

George Robinson sighed and gave her a sympathetic smile. "I understand. It's a problem, though. If the defendant's legal team are willing to do a deal and plead to all the finance offences, the CPS will drop the murder charges. We can ask for the drug-trafficking to be left on the books. I'm not sure if we'll manage to do the same with the Barry murder."

Esther bristled. Fucking CPS. She hated all this cattle-trading and backroom dealing. Stats. It was all about stats. Better to secure half a dozen convictions than gamble on an extra two, regardless of how serious they were. She knew she was scowling and made an effort to soften her features.

"I understand, Mister Robinson."

"Well, I must get inside before Judge Reynolds takes her seat," the giant barrister told them in an apologetic voice. "She is notoriously grumpy on Fridays."

He nodded to both of them and disappeared through the courtroom doors, carting his little wheeled travel bag full of files behind him.

Jared turned to Esther. "You're supposed to be taking some time off. DCI's orders. You buried your mother yesterday!"

"And I took the whole day off to do it," Esther replied. "I can't just kick about the house all day. Wouldn't be good for me. Trust me. I want to be here. I need to keep busy."

He regarded her levelly. "Everyone needs a bit of time

off now and again, Esther. Christ knows you've earned it these past few months. If the DCI is giving you a free pass to get your head cleared, I'd take it."

"I'll let you know when I need some time, Jared. Thank you for your concern."

Jared grunted and muttered something inaudible.

"Come on, Detective Inspector Grouchy," Esther said, as she slipped her arm through his and steered him towards the courtroom doors. "Let's get inside and get some front row seats. I want to see Peter Darren in prison manacles."

"That does it for you, does it?"

"Like you wouldn't believe."

He chuckled quietly as they stepped through the doors to the gallery, where a scattering of people sat in ones or twos or threes. Most of them were police officers, judging by the bad shoes and the paper file folders clutched on their laps. There were hearings for at least half a dozen other cases this morning.

Jared and Esther took seats near the front, behind the prosecuting counsel's bench, in case Mr Robinson had to ask them anything during the arraignment. To their right was the dock, a waist-high woodwork enclosure topped by reinforced glass to a height of eight feet or so, with narrow gaps in the glass panels so that the defendant could hear the proceedings clearly while being kept safely segregated from everyone else in the court. On the other side of the chamber were the jury benches. Empty now, they'd remain that way for the day; according to the docket, there had been no trials scheduled for Courtroom Sixteen today.

The central area of the courtroom was lined with desks facing the lofty judge's bench, which presided over everything. There were a few bewigged barristers there, going over notes as they waited for Her Honour to appear. Esther recognised one or two, including Francis Unwin, a notoriously good defence barrister, known for defending big corporations against civil litigation as well as larger criminal cases. This area—where the barristers postured and expounded, appealed and grandstanded—was the arena, the theatre where cases were lost or won. Sometimes Esther thought it was the acting that mattered. The lawyerly soliloquies. The facts were just props, and the jury were just a bunch of regular punters who'd been hauled in off the street for the performance, more used to detective shows on TV, shows that provided closure and certainty. That wasn't real life. Real life didn't have flashbacks at the end of the trial, or defendants who threw up their hands and confessed to everything. In real life, jurors had to draw their own conclusions, and sometimes the persuasive abilities of a good barrister could undermine even the strongest evidence.

Esther and Jared had hardly taken their seats when the tipstaff appeared from the chambers behind the judge's bench.

"All rise," he commanded, before announcing Judge Reynolds, a portly battle-axe of a woman whose wig and gown only made her look more menacing. She lowered herself into the throne-like chair overlooking them all before Jared, Esther, and the rest of the courtroom took their seats again.

As the clerk began going through the morning's business, Judge Reynolds slid into her routine of barking commands and haranguing the barristers with questions. Esther found it hard to imagine the woman ever *not* grumpy. She had that air about her. Which, if they secured a conviction against Peter Darren, might actually be a good thing. Grumpy judges gave longer sentences.

Esther's mind began to wander as the court discussed a serious assault case that was going to trial early in the new year. She thought about what Jared had said about the DCI wanting her to take time off. She still wasn't sure what to make of their new detective chief inspector. Brian Small had been parachuted in as a caretaker after Warren Porter was bundled off to his backroom post in Records. It was obvious to everyone that he was just another career man, but there weren't too many senior officers in the police who weren't in it for themselves; Esther was learning that lesson more and more as the years went by. What mattered, though, was whether he was an interfering boss or a boss that recognised the importance of letting frontline detectives like her get on with the job; the jury was still out on that one. She didn't like his greasy gaze, but then, lots of men gave her greasy gazes.

She found herself fiddling with the cuff of her coat again, staring at the phone number scribbled on her cast. With a tug of her sleeve, she covered it up and forced herself to concentrate on the proceedings.

Her Honour was now in the process of chewing out a diminutive man with a scraggly beard and a wig so old it looked on the verge of falling apart. His gown had slipped from his shoulders, revealing a cheap suit and a shirt that was grey around the collar. Head bowed, he responded to the angry diatribe with murmured acceptances and assurances. Esther had made a mental note long ago that if she ever found herself in need of a barrister, she would disregard the trite saying that appearances could be deceptive. Not in this arena. It was the well-fed barristers—the ones who wore designer suits and Rolexes—who fared best here, the ones with confidence and the ability to manipulate a jury's feelings. Barristers like Francis Unwin.

Unwin was still there, sitting at a desk a few spaces over, watching the bollocking with barely concealed amusement as he waited for his own case to come up. Esther had seen him in action on a few occasions. The man had a gift for turning wavering jurors. He could take apart solid-seeming cases by making the most minor technical issue seem like grounds to suspect corruption of the highest order, or by making a shaky witness look like a twisted and vindictive liar. After a good closing argument, Francis Unwin could have some jurors doubting their own names, let alone the evidence.

And then the tongue-lashing was over, and the clerk was calling out Peter Darren's name.

"Bring him up," Judge Reynolds commanded.

There was a rattle of keys as the gaoler in the dock opened the heavy door that led directly into the custody wing. He disappeared into the network of tunnels beyond. A protracted hush followed, filled with subdued coughs and quiet shuffling. Then came the clinking of chains. The heavy door was pulled open again and Peter Darren appeared, secured by shackles to two burly guards.

As the gaolers removed his manacles, Darren scanned the gallery. His eyes fell on Esther, and he stared at her. She stared right back, doing her best to keep her features impassive. It was Darren who looked away first, and Esther felt a little swell of triumph.

But then Francis Unwin rose to address the court and her heart sank. Of course he'd be representing Darren!

They clearly hadn't found all of Darren's cash. That, or someone higher up the food chain was bankrolling him.

The beefy barrister asked Judge Reynolds's permission to speak quickly with his client, and the request was granted. Unwin strode to the dock, and he and Darren held a brief, whispered conversation through a gap in the glass plates. The barrister then moved to the prosecuting counsel's bench, where he exchanged a few words with George Robinson, who nodded. More words, and Robinson shook his head this time. Judge Reynolds cleared her throat noisily and Unwin quickly took his place back at the defence bench.

"Is your client ready to enter his pleas to the list of charges?" the judge asked, one eyebrow cocked. Clearly, she had a little more time for Unwin than she'd had for the other poor sod, but she was still bristly.

Unwin nodded. "He is, Your Honour."

The judge looked at Robinson. "Are there any changes to the charges being brought?" she asked.

Robinson half-stood as he responded. "Not at this stage, Your Honour." He sat back down.

Judge Reynolds nodded. "Very well. Let's get on with it."

The court clerk called out Peter Darren's name again, and Darren stood.

The charges were read out.

To every charge, from dangerous driving to concern in the supply of controlled substances, from money laundering to conspiracy to murder, Peter Darren replied "Not guilty."

The plea deal had been turned down. They were going to trial.

Esther realised she'd been holding her breath. She exhaled quietly.

Once the formal declarations were made, there was some haggling over dates for the next hearing, to iron out some of the legal issues before trial. Darren was sent back to the cells. As the shackles went back on his wrists, he glanced at Esther again. She thought she saw the ghost of a smile touch his lips, before the gaolers urged him back through the door and out of sight, and the court began moving on with its other business.

Jared gave her a nudge, startling her. She had been staring fixedly at the door to the cells. She followed the DI's lead and headed for the exit.

Once they were back out in the lobby, Jared let out a loud harrumph.

"Well, we're going to trial then," he said. "With the next hearing in January, I'm guessing it'll be scheduled for the spring or early summer."

"He'll make a High Court bail application before then," Esther said, feeling a touch of fear at the idea he might be successful. She crushed her foolish concerns; the fucker would get out eventually no matter what.

Jared shook his head.

"He'll probably make several," he replied, "but they'll never be granted. No chance."

Maybe he sensed her darkening mood.

"You want to go for a coffee before I head back to the station?" he asked. "We can call it a line management welfare meeting."

Esther nodded. "Sure. If you promise that your conclusions at the end of said meeting will be that I am fit to return to work and don't require any further period of bereavement leave."

Jared thought about it for a moment. "As long as you

take the rest of the day off. That way I can tell the DCI you took a couple of days and not be lying."

Esther smiled. "Throw in a bun with the coffee and you have a deal."

"Sold!"

In the stairwell, Jared's phone began to buzz.

"Detective Inspector Wilcox," he intoned mechanically by way of greeting.

He stopped short as they reached a landing, frowning at whatever the person on the other end was saying.

"Where exactly?" he asked, his frown and serious tone piquing Esther's interest. "Who's on scene now?" He listened to the answer, then replied: "Okay, I'm at the courthouse. I'll be there shortly."

As he hung up and put his phone away, he looked at Esther, who raised her eyebrows questioningly.

"You sure about not wanting to take a bit more time off?" he asked.

Esther gave him an exasperated look. "What is it, Jared?"

"There's been a body found in a dumpster off Gable Street."

Esther didn't hesitate. "Let's go," she said, and set off down the stairs.

She heard him grumble something about buns as he followed.

3

A SMALL MEDIA scrum had already formed at one end of the street, with local and national TV reporters vying to get the best angle of the police activity in the background of their shots.

Jared pulled up as far from the press as he could. He and Esther showed their warrant cards to the uniform officer standing guard at the cordon. They signed the crime scene log he held out for them, then ducked under the police tape and waited for the sergeant on duty to come and brief them. When he finally appeared, Esther recognised him straight away. She'd worked with Sergeant Terry Waide when she was temporarily stripped of her detective status and sent back to uniform duties at Yorkgate Police Station two months ago; it had been DCI Warren Porter's way of punishing her for not dropping the Peter Darren case when she'd been told to.

"Alright, Esther?" Waide greeted her in his Cockney twang. "You here from CID?"

Esther hadn't warmed to Terry Waide during her short time at Yorkgate. He'd come across as cocksure and arrogant. He didn't look so arrogant now, though. Despite his attempts to appear relaxed, there was an uneasiness in his expression that told her he had never managed a murder scene before, and wasn't entirely confident he'd covered all the bases.

Esther gave him a toothy smile. "I am, Terry. You've met DI Wilcox." She indicated to Jared. Waide gave him a quick nod, but didn't appear to recognise the older man. In spite of herself, Esther suddenly felt a touch of sympathy for Waide, as she watched him rake a hand through his hair. The guy had a lot on his plate this morning. "Have you transferred to Central now?" she asked.

"No, still at Yorkgate. Just covering a shift for someone today." Uniform officers loved their overtime, but Sergeant Waide looked like he was regretting having taken this turn of duty.

"So," she said, "what have you got for us?"

He indicated a garbage truck that was parked up nearby. There were two garbage men sitting on the kerb next to it. They wore grubby hi-viz outfits with the Belfield City Council logo emblazoned on their backs. Both of them were smoking, and looked a little shaken. "Bin men over there rang it in about an hour ago. They were emptying the dumpsters in the alley"—he tilted his chin towards a small entry between an off-street parking lot and an office building—"and they found him half-buried among the rubbish bags. One of the officers first on scene found blood in the carpark as well, and there's a car with a smashed driver's window. Blood on the ground beside it. I've had the lot cordoned off. FMO is on his way; ten minutes out, last I heard. I've had CSI and mapping and photography tasked, too. Thought it might be better to get things moving? Duty officer is apprised, and the press office are aware."

Esther nodded, grudgingly conceding that Waide had covered the bases after all. "You manage to identify the deceased?"

"We think so," he replied. "Carlton Riddell. Wife phoned in to report him missing late last night. It's Riddell's car that's got the smashed window and the blood around it."

"Has she been spoken to yet?"

He shook his head. "No. Wanted to get it confirmed first. Let you guys take the lead on that."

Jared nodded his approval. "Good work, Sergeant. You got any forensic suits we can use to take a quick look before the doc arrives?"

Waide grinned, looking relieved to hear he hadn't fucked up. He told them he'd go find some suits and be right back.

While he was gone, Esther studied the area. The neighbourhood was all office blocks and boutique stores, the kind of posh shops where nothing bore a price tag and everything looked expensive. Waide had sealed off most of the street. Curious onlookers and people who had been prevented from getting to work by the police cordon hovered near the news reporters, watching with that morbid fascination people have for crime scenes.

Esther glanced across at the council workers. They appeared to be chain-smoking while they waited.

"They shouldn't be smoking," she muttered. "The cigarette butts will contaminate the scene."

"They're far enough away," Jared replied. "They've just

found a dead body. I think we can give them a pass."

Esther shrugged. He was the DI.

Waide returned with three sets of white forensic suits, as well as overshoes, masks, and a couple of boxes of nitrile gloves. Esther had to use an XXL glove for her cast-encased left hand, but once they were all suited up, they approached the inner scenes. The carpark was the nearest of the two, so Esther suggested they check that one out first. Jared agreed, and Waide followed along behind them.

The parking lot was half-empty. Some of the cars were coated in ice, obviously having sat there overnight.

"Did we get a note of all the licence plates here?" Esther asked.

"I'll get that done," Waide replied quickly.

"And a note beside each to say if it's iced over or not, please," she added.

Jared went and stood next to a blue BMW convertible with a cracked driver-side window.

"Good work, whoever spotted this," he mumbled.

Esther could see what he meant. A high wall at the back of the lot cast a shadow across the whole carpark. Not only was the BMW's window coated in ice, but the pool of blood on the ground was frozen over, just like the rest of the tarmac. It was hard to make out the blood under the sparkling white frost even when you were staring right at it.

"They were looking for the car," Waide conceded. "The officers who got here first, I mean. We had the vehicle alerted as part of the earlier misper report, so they looked about, put two and two together..."

The BMW was still locked and secure. Esther got down on her hands and knees and checked underneath the car itself and those adjacent to it. Nothing. After a quick walk-through of the carpark, scanning the ground but seeing nothing strange or obvious, they headed for the alleyway where the body had been found.

She spotted the dumpster in question straight away. It looked like the council workers had been in the process of hauling it to the street for emptying when they made their grim discovery; it stood apart from several others with its lid thrown back. Some of the bags from inside had been removed and were lying next to it.

"Who removed those bags?" Esther asked. "The binmen or the officers?"

"The binmen," Waide replied.

She studied the street. There were no CCTV cameras covering the mouth of the alley, or the alleyway itself. No windows on the gable wall of the five-storey office building that overlooked it either. She ran her gaze slowly down the walls to the ground at her feet, then began to proceed slowly and carefully towards the dumpster, scanning the ground along the way. Jared followed a pace behind and to her right. Waide hung back.

The alley floor was covered in frozen refuse. Even the ice that coated the scattered puddles was brown and filthy. But nothing presented itself as obviously out of place as Esther made her way forward. When she reached the dumpster, she had to lift herself on her toes to get a good look inside.

The dead man lay on his back, his rifled wallet and open briefcase tossed on top of him. The letters and documents from the briefcase were scattered across his deathbed of garbage bags. She studied his face. There was a fan of blood across his cheeks and jaw from a cut on his temple, but she could still make out his features. He was in his late twenties or early thirties, with dark hair that was dishevelled and coated in frost. His overcoat had fallen open to reveal the label—Armani—and his suit and tie looked expensive too. He might have been good-looking when he was alive, but it was hard to tell with his eyes bulging and his mouth frozen open, a permanent expression of surprise affixed to his lifeless features. The bruising around his neck was obvious even in the dim light of the alleyway. She pointed it out to Jared.

"Strangled," the DI grunted. "You thinking robbery?"

Esther frowned. "Bit heavy-handed for a robbery, isn't it? Robberies usually involve a few punches, or a knife in the gut." She looked at the scattered contents of the briefcase, the files and papers flung haphazardly about. "Unless there was something particularly important or valuable in the briefcase." She reached out with her right hand and plucked a business card from amongst the jumbled papers.

CARLTON RIDDELL
Global Marketing
Belfield BioTech (UK) Ltd.

She handed the card to Jared. "Belfield BioTech. Does that name ring any bells with you? Have we dealt with them before?"

He frowned at the card. "Don't think so. Why?"

"Sounds familiar."

There was a staticky transmission on Waide's radio.

"That's the doc and CSI arrived," he told them. "There's a couple of your detectives with them too."

"Tell them to suit up and come join us," Jared called

back, and Waide relayed the instructions over the radio.

A few minutes later, a small crew in masks and white suits approached. Jared briefed them all on what they had so far. The FMO—the Force Medical Officer, or police doctor—completed his assessment quickly, and it was no surprise to Esther that he came to the same conclusion they had: it looked like Carlton Riddell had been strangled to death. They'd have to wait for the autopsy to confirm it, but it was a safe bet for the moment as far as working theories went.

The CSI officers took swabs and photographs of the body in situ, while the two detectives helped Esther check the far end of the alleyway for any indications that it formed part of the scene. Derek Grant and Liz Fellowes were two of the most competent detectives on the team, and Esther trusted them to see anything she might miss. But they found nothing of interest, and once they were satisfied there was nothing to examine beyond the dumpsters, she tasked them to take statements from the council binmen and canvass the local area for witnesses and CCTV.

Meanwhile, the CSIs had recovered two mobile phones from the dead man's pockets. Unfortunately, both phone batteries were flat, so Esther directed they be boxed up for proper analysis at the station.

As the detectives and the CSIs went about their tasks, Waide asked again about the dead man's wife. He had a crew assigned and seemed anxious to get the death message delivered in good time.

"Tell the officers assigned to lie up near the house and wait for us," Esther said, as they headed for the scene's perimeter, peeling off their forensic gear. "DI Wilcox and I will take the lead."

A twitch of Jared's eyebrows told her he hadn't been expecting that. But he didn't say anything until they were out of the scene and it was just the two of them again.

"You want to deliver the death message?" he asked her quietly, as they crossed the street to his car.

"I want to speak to the widow Riddell." She glanced down at the note Waide had given her. "Eva Riddell."

Jared shook his head slightly. "I know the spouse is usually the first recourse," he said, "but I'm not seeing an obvious domestic here. You don't agree?"

"Well, I'm not thinking she strangled him herself, if that's what you mean." Even sprawled in a dumpster, it was clear Carlton Riddell had been a well-built man, about five foot ten or eleven, and at least a hundred and ninety pounds. "Unless she's a wrestler and as big as he is. But there's something odd about it. If this was a robbery, it wasn't opportunistic."

"Something in that briefcase, maybe?" Jared mused.

Esther pulled out her phone and tapped Belfield BioTech into the search app. The first result that popped up was a headline Esther recognised immediately.

BELFIELD BIOTECH ANNOUNCES BREAKTHROUGH CANCER TREATMENT DRUG: LOCAL FIRM SET TO PUT BELFIELD ON THE INTERNATIONAL MAP

Now she understood why the name had sounded familiar. She'd read this article in *The Belfield Chronicle* a few weeks back. The story had even made the national news.

She showed it to Jared. His eyebrows rose.

"You think it might have something to do with that?" he asked.

She frowned as she studied the article again.

"I don't know," she conceded. "But there's gotta be a hell of a lot of money in revolutionary medical breakthroughs like this one."

"I should say so," Jared replied, as he started the car.

"But let's take things one step at a time," she said, putting her phone away. "Let's go see the widow first."

4

JARED DROVE THEM north into the Norwick Hills. It wasn't long before they found themselves wending their way along oak-lined avenues, where massive, architecturally bespoke houses sat beyond tall walls and manicured gardens.

Twenty minutes from the crime scene, they rolled to a stop behind a patrol car. It was parked just shy of an open set of wrought-iron gates, out of view of the house, a sprawling, redbrick affair with a colonnaded front porch. When Jared pulled in behind the squad car, the doors opened and two uniform officers got out. They introduced themselves as PCs Jason Dalton and Molly Rhys. Dalton was stocky and had the face of a failed boxer. Rhys was short, with pale blonde curls done up in a French Twist. They fell in behind Esther and Jared as the two detectives set off up the cobbled driveway.

Esther noticed that the lawn was mown in a checked pattern, even this late in winter, and the hedgerows looked like they'd been trimmed using a ruler. Christmas lights adorned the trees lining the drive and two plastic snowmen stood guard at the house's white-pillared front entrance. Another BMW—a white SUV—was parked in a sheltered yard to one side of the house. Beyond it, in the back garden, Esther could see a little girl in a puffy pink parka bouncing on a trampoline. A pang of sympathy struck her as she watched the girl, who appeared no older than seven or eight; Esther had wanted to observe Eva Riddell's reaction, to gauge whether there had been anything going on on the domestic side of things, something which might have led to the murder, but seeing the little girl on the trampoline made her suddenly regret volunteering for this task.

The child didn't notice them approach. She was attempting to do a handstand or a flip of some sort, and not doing very well in her bulky winter clothes.

As the four police officers reached the front porch, Esther stepped forward and pressed the doorbell. She heard it chime inside—a familiar classical piece—and a woman's voice echoing within, growing louder.

"Tracy, honey, be careful! No backflips! I've told you before!"

The door opened to reveal the owner of the voice. Eva Riddell was in her mid-twenties. Short and slim, she was more than pretty, with high cheekbones and flowing blonde locks. Her big blue eyes rested on the uniform officers at first, before shifting to Esther, who had positioned herself in front of the others. Dark shadows under the woman's eyes were evidence of her sleepless night.

Whatever greeting she'd been about to give them died on her lips. It might have been their expressions, or perhaps it was PC Dalton removing his hat that telegrammed what was to come, but whatever it was, Eva Riddell's tiredness vanished in an instant.

"Eva Riddell?" Esther asked.

The woman nodded, her face fearful now. "What's happened?" she asked. "Have you found Carlton?"

"May we come in and speak with you, ma'am?" Esther asked.

"What is it?" She sounded panicked. "Is he alright?"

Jared interjected, his voice firm but not unkind. "It would be better if we could speak with you inside, madam."

Reluctantly—as if keeping the police out of her house might hold back the bad news she sensed was coming—Eva Riddell held open the door for them. They trooped in, one after another, and she led them through a broad, marbled entryway to a spacious slate-and-oak kitchen beyond. Esther could see flashes of pink parka through the tall windows that overlooked the garden. She tried to focus on Eva.

"What is it?" the woman demanded, her voice hardening. "Tell me."

"Please sit down, Missus Riddell," Jared advised.

But Eva Riddell was growing angry as well as anxious now. "Just tell me! What's happened to him? Where is he?"

"I'm afraid your husband is dead, ma'am," Esther said, making an effort not to glance out the window at the little girl again. "I'm very sorry."

There was a long pause, a moment where Eva Riddell stood frozen like a statue, before her knees buckled and she fell heavily into a chair. One trembling hand went to her mouth. Her face contorted, and a high-pitched keening escaped her lips. Tears began to flow. She shook her head, as if trying to deny what she'd heard.

"Is there anyone we can call for you?" Esther asked.

But the woman seemed not to hear. PC Rhys, God bless her, was straight over. She knelt down next to the grieving widow, took her by the hand, and murmured soothing condolences. PC Dalton went to the sink and fetched her a glass of water.

Esther watched Eva Riddell while the two officers fussed over her. The woman was clearly in shock, and there was no hint of foreknowledge or nervous pretence. She shared a glance with Jared. His grim expression told her he had come to the same conclusion.

She couldn't help looking out the window at the small girl bouncing on the trampoline then, oblivious to the police officers in her kitchen who'd just told her mother that her father was dead. Esther would have liked to have left right that instant. She'd have liked a stiff shot of vodka. Or a bottle of it. But there was more to be done before they could leave the uniform officers to the basic task of filling out the coroner's forms with the poor woman.

After a few minutes, the two PCs managed to get Mrs Riddell talking again. They repeated Esther's query about anyone who might be able to come over, any family or friends nearby, and eventually succeeded in getting the sister's name and phone number out of her. PC Dalton stepped into the hallway to make the difficult call.

"Wh-what happened to him?" Eva asked, her breath catching between stifled sobs. PC Rhys, still crouched next to her, passed her another tissue.

Esther pulled out a chair, setting it so that she was sitting directly in front of Eva Riddell and could look her in the eye.

"It appears your husband may have been killed."

Eva seemed stunned. "*Killed?* Why? Wha-who?"

"We don't know the who yet, ma'am," Esther replied. "Or the why. But it looks like he was attacked late last night, or in the early hours of this morning, while he was out in the city centre."

Eva Riddell suddenly regarded her sharply. A ray of hope had appeared in her eyes, as if she was thinking that maybe the police had got it wrong…

"No," she countered, "he said he had a late meeting at work. At the office. Why would he be in the city centre? Are you sure it's Carlton you've found?"

"Did he work at Belfield BioTech?" Esther asked.

The woman nodded, and the glimmer in her eyes dulled slightly.

"We'll need you to come down to the mortuary to identify him formally, of course," Esther explained, "so that we can be sure, but we do believe it's Carlton."

Eva winced. All the same, Esther could tell she was clinging to that sliver of hope now, the tiny possibility that when she got to the mortuary, she might find a stranger lying there. It seemed to steady her nerve as Esther pressed on.

"Can you think of any reason why your husband might have been in town last night?" she asked.

Eva shook her head again.

"When did you last speak to him?"

The woman took a deep breath and dabbed at her eyes with the crumpled tissue.

"Yesterday afternoon, on the phone," she replied. "About four or five o'clock. He said he had a meeting—a meeting at work, that's what he said—and that he was going to be late getting home. That's why I didn't ring you people until"—her voice caught on a half-stifled sob—"until I woke just before midnight and he still wasn't back and he wasn't answering his phone."

"Did he say who he was meeting?" Esther asked.

"No," she replied. "No, Carlton doesn't really talk much about work." She squeezed her eyes shut and brought the tissue to her mouth.

Esther gave her a moment. She needed information, but getting it out of people in this fragile state was a delicate task.

PC Dalton came back into the kitchen to tell Eva that her sister Penny was on her way over. This seemed to steel her a little. She nodded, blew her nose and sipped some water at PC Rhys's urging. Esther took this as her cue to continue.

"Did your husband have any enemies? Were there any recent conflicts with anyone at work? Or outside of work?"

Eva frowned at the tissue in her hand as though thinking hard about the question.

"No," she replied finally, "but he's definitely been more stressed about work recently. Quieter than usual. There was this breakthrough drug, you see. A cancer treatment drug. It was big news. But there were issues with licensing and testing, and things haven't been moving as quickly as they wanted. I don't really know much beyond that. They're very secretive about these kinds of things at that company."

Esther noticed Jared jotting hasty notes. He stood off to one side, out of Eva Riddell's view.

"What did Carlton do at Belfield BioTech?" she asked.

"He works in sales," Eva replied. "He does contracts,

for the NHS and export markets."

"What about his clients?" Esther pressed. "Was he concerned about security after the drug breakthrough was made public? Personal security or security at work? Anything like that?"

Eva Riddell stared down at her hands, frowning again.

"He had a phone call recently." She said it haltingly, as if the memory was only just coming back to her. "He was at home, and I remember being annoyed that it was his personal phone—because he was spending so much time at work, you see, and it was clear how stressed he was, so I remember thinking 'why are they bothering him on his personal phone now too?' I had started getting him to switch off his work phone at home, just so he could wind down, you know? I could tell the pressure was getting to him. But this call… it wasn't work."

"Who was it?" Esther asked.

"An old friend, he said. Some guy called Mark Sterling. I'd never heard the name before."

"When was this?"

"About a week ago. Maybe two?"

"What was the phone call about? Did Carlton say?"

"An old schoolmate of theirs had gone missing in London. This fellow Sterling had phoned to tell him about it."

"Do you remember the name? Of the missing person?"

"Gary Henderson? Something like Henderson, anyway. Gary was his first name, I'm sure of that."

"Were they close? Carlton and Gary?"

Eva shook her head. "He's never mentioned either of them before. But it seemed to shake him. He didn't say much on that phone call. He went into a different room but—I wasn't eavesdropping, I was just concerned, you understand—but I listened and, to be honest, Carlton didn't really say very much. This man Mark Sterling seemed to be doing all the talking. I asked him about it afterwards. Asked if they had been close, but he just said they'd been at school together. He and Gary—the one who's missing—played on the rugby team. He wouldn't say any more than that. He got a bit testy when I asked him again, so I left it. But that phone call bothered him, definitely. Do you know anything about him? This missing person?"

"If he's gone missing in London, then the police there should be able to assist us with that," Esther replied. "And this man Mark Sterling… you say your husband hadn't mentioned his name before? Did Carlton speak much about his friends, or socialise without you often?"

"No, he hardly ever went out. And I really don't think he'd heard from this man in a long time, just from the way he answered the phone, you know? He seemed surprised. *Not* happy-surprised."

"Was there some issue between them?"

"I don't know. He just… I don't know. It was just the way he answered the phone."

"And did he hear from Mark Sterling again after that? Was there any more news about Gary Henderson?"

Another headshake.

"We recovered two phones from his coat," Esther said. "Can you confirm which of them was Carlton's personal phone and which was for work?"

"The iPhone was his own phone," she replied. "His work used Google or Samsung or something, I'm not sure."

Esther saw Jared jot the information down. Examination of the devices would probably have made it obvious, but this would make things quicker for the analysts. If Riddell had been up to some kind of subterfuge involving his work, it was more likely the communications would be on his personal phone, but knowing which one was which from the off would speed up the cross-referencing process.

"Anything else that sticks out as unusual?" she asked. "Like that phone call?"

"He was at work so much," she said, her voice cracking. "But when he was at home he was a good husband, and a good father." Her face crumpled. "He was so good with Tracy!"

She began sobbing again.

Even the uniformed officers gave her a bit of space this time.

It took several minutes, but Eva Riddell managed to compose herself once more. A sudden change came over her. She grew serious, and met Esther's gaze steadily, as though determined not to flinch.

"How did he die?" she asked. "Was it… was it bad?"

Esther glanced at Jared, who half-nodded, half-shrugged.

"Nothing is conclusive until after the post-mortem examination," Esther told her gently, "but from our initial observations at the scene… we think he may have been strangled."

The composure disintegrated, and Eva began crying again. PC Rhys reached out to comfort her once more.

They all turned when they heard the front door slam and a woman's voice calling Eva's name. Without waiting for a response, the new arrival came clip-clopping on heels towards the kitchen.

The woman who appeared in the doorway was a slightly older, slightly heavier version of Eva Riddell. The sister Penny, Esther guessed. She was done up as if getting done up was the norm for her, in an expensive-looking three-quarter-length beige coat and knee-high leather boots with big heels. Her hair spilled in gleaming waves over her shoulders as though she had just come from a salon, and there were diamonds at her neck and on her fingers. She surveyed the scene quickly, and when her eyes fell on her weeping sister, she hurried over, glaring at the police officers as if they were to blame for the state she was in, which in a way, Esther supposed, they were. Penny took the place of PC Rhys—all but barging the officer out of the way—before wrapping her arms around her sister and murmuring soothing commiserations. Eva buried her face in Penny's shoulder and they both cried.

The police officers and detectives all gave them a few moments, standing in awkward silence until Esther felt it was finally time to interrupt.

"We'll need you to formally identify your husband, Missus Riddell," she broached again. "Is that something you think you would be up to doing? Not right away, but possibly tomorrow morning, before the autopsy."

"Does she have to?" the sister asked. "Can someone else not do it?"

Eva gave an emphatic headshake. "No. I'll do it."

"Are you sure, Evie?" Penny asked.

Eva Riddell wiped her eyes and met her sister's gaze. "It should be me. I'll do it," she said, her tone firm. She pulled another tissue from the box on the table and blew her nose.

"Why is mummy crying?"

Everyone turned to look at the little girl in the pink parka who was standing at the back door. Esther wasn't much good with children's ages, but now that she saw her at close hand, she guessed Tracy was closer to five or six. The child looked frightened and confused, whatever age she was.

There was a long moment when no one quite knew what to do or say. Then Eva gave her sister an imploring look, and Penny quickly wiped her own eyes and whirled into action.

"Oh, honey," she cooed, as she hurried over to Tracy. "Come with me and we'll put on the television and then mummy will be in, just as soon as the police are finished talking to her. Come on with me." She held out her hand.

Tracy—suspicious and uncertain, but not quite ready to argue—took her aunt's hand and allowed herself to be led from the kitchen, with a glance over her shoulder at her mother, who made a strained attempt at a reassuring smile despite the tears in her eyes.

"I'll be there in a minute, darling," she told her daughter.

Esther felt it was time to leave the questioning for now. She indicated to PCs Rhys and Dalton and explained to Eva that her uniform colleagues had a few forms to go through, just some technical and medical questions about Carlton for the coroner and the pathologist, but that it shouldn't take too long. She gave the woman her card and told her to ring if she had any questions, assuring her that she or one of her detectives would be in touch about organising the identification later.

With that, Esther left Eva Riddell with the uniform officers, and she and Jared took their leave. She glanced through the door to the living room as they made their way out. Penny was sitting with Tracy, using a remote control to flick through a selection of cartoons on the television.

Tracy was clearly quizzing her aunt as they browsed, and Penny was doing her best to dodge the questions until she and Eva were ready to break the news together.

Once they were out and walking down the driveway again, Jared spoke.

"I think we can rule Eva Riddell out as a suspect," he said.

Esther nodded. "We have to track down this Mark Sterling chap," she replied. "And that misper from London."

Jared consulted his notes. "Gary Henderson, or something similar."

"We can do a scan of PNC for anyone missing in the London area with a similar name and age profile when we get back to the station."

"And then there's Belfield BioTech," Jared mused. "We'll need to investigate that corporate espionage angle. Wife seemed surprised he was in the city. Maybe Carlton Riddell was doing some double-dealing."

"Or having an affair," Esther added, as Jared unlocked the car.

"Or that," he conceded.

They sat in, but Jared hesitated before starting the engine. He checked his watch.

"We could try and narrow down those angles now," he said, taking out his phone. He tapped on it for a bit. "It'll take an hour to get to the industrial estates from here on a Friday afternoon, but maybe there's someone still in the office we can talk to."

He put the phone to his ear.

"Hello, my name's Jared Wilcox, I'm a detective inspector with Belfield police. I'm looking to speak with

Carlton Riddell's manager if that's possible." He paused and listened. "Hmm. I see. Well, would it be possible to meet him over the weekend? It's quite urgent." Another pause. "All of the management team? Okay. No, I'd rather speak to someone in person. Is there anyone available this evening or tomorrow morning?"

Jared pulled out his notebook and pen and began jotting something with his free hand.

"That's great, thank you. One more question. Do you have access to Carlton Riddell's meetings and schedules? I'm looking for a list of his meetings yesterday." The DI frowned. "I see. No, no, we'll speak with Mister Lightbody in the morning and clarify everything then. Thank you very much for your help." He hung up.

"Well?" Esther asked.

"Most of Belfield BioTech's senior management team are away in the Netherlands. Been there for the last two nights. Something about regulation negotiations with the EU. They'll be flying back tonight. Receptionist's going to have someone arrange to meet us at the offices tomorrow morning. A man called"—he checked his note—"Robert Lightbody, Executive Director in charge of Sales. Apparently, he's the senior man in Carlton Riddell's department."

"We can head there after the post-mortem and see if he can shed any light on the contents of that briefcase," Esther said, as Jared put away his phone and notebook. "What about Riddell's meetings yesterday?"

"No meetings yesterday," he said as he started the car. "At least, none that are on the company's planner."

"Could be an affair after all."

Jared nodded. "I'll put a rush on his phone triage, see

what recent numbers it throws up. We can get the nearby hotels checked as part of the door-to-door. Let's get back to base and start doing some digging on the system."

He pulled out and headed for Belfield Central.

5

MOST OF THE desks in the CID office were empty when Esther and Jared got back to the station. All of their own team were still out on enquiries, helping Grant and Fellowes knock doors and check CCTV footage within a square mile of the crime scene. Other teams were slipping away as early as they dared on a Friday afternoon.

Esther and Jared had already decided to split the police systems checks: Esther would dig up whatever she could on Mark Sterling, while Jared would look into missing person cases in London.

First, though, she had another call to make.

She and Jared had separate offices; Jared had one to himself, while Esther shared with two other detective sergeants. She wasn't surprised to find the sergeants' office empty, as she hung her winter coat on one of the empty pegs behind the door. Caroline and Spencer bunked off early at any given opportunity. She sometimes wondered how they'd survived Uniform, let alone made it into CID.

But whenever she looked at the framed photos of kids and spouses on both their desks—the 'Best Dad' mug that Spencer always used, and the drawings and finger-paintings all over the wall behind Caroline's workspace—and then at her own workstation, which had none of those things, she would remember that other people had lives outside of work. Being a police officer was Esther's *whole* life. For some reason, the thought made her glance at her cast again, and at the name and number scribbled in blue marker on it. *Triona.* She stared at the name for a moment before giving herself a shake. That wasn't the phone call she needed to make.

She fired up her computer and logged into her police account. A couple of clicks threw up the number she was looking for. She picked up the phone and dialled.

"Hello, Traffic Cameras and Automated Speed Detection."

"Wow, that's a mouthful," Esther said to the voice on the other end of the phone.

"Tell me about it," he sighed. "What can I do for you?"

"My name's Esther Penman. I'm a DS in Belfield Central CID. I need to run a check for vehicles linked to organised crime, drugs in particular, and possibly a specific individual. I need it to cover four square miles around Belfield City Cemetery between nine and ten this morning. What do you need from me?"

The officer gave her the name of the form she was required to submit, and added that she would need her inspector's authority. That wouldn't be a problem. She knew Jared would sign anything she put in front of him. The guy also told her she'd need to add the details of any particular persons she was interested in on the form itself.

Esther brought up Peter Darren's profile on PNC. She knew it was a long shot, but she couldn't take any chances. If that man watching her this morning had been one of Darren's gang, she needed to know. He might track her back to her aunt's house in Sarsbury, and Esther wanted to avoid a repeat of what had happened the last time Darren had sent someone after her. The memory of that attack, a stranger coming at her in her own apartment with a syringe full of powerful sedative, still made her shiver. God only knew what Darren had had planned for her. She was just lucky Jared had been there to knock the guy out. No, she definitely didn't want a repeat of that. And she especially didn't want to put Jean in any danger.

When the officer had given her all the instructions she needed, she thanked him and hung up. She would have to remain watchful on her way home from work until she got the results back from the traffic camera department. She could still picture the man from the cemetery. Despite the distance between them, she was sure she would recognise him again if she saw him, but she couldn't rule out the possibility that there were others.

Once she'd completed the form, she closed Peter Darren's profile and turned to more pressing matters. She tapped *Mark Sterling* into the PNC search engine.

The results page contained hundreds of hits. Thankfully, when she added filters to the search criteria—addresses in the Belfield area only, age range of twenty-five to thirty-five—the results fell to only three, one of which was deceased. She checked the remaining two nominals, and quickly surmised that the one she wanted was the one who was born the same year as Carlton Riddell.

She read through the file. Sterling had received two

juvenile cautions in his teens, one for cannabis possession and another for shoplifting. He'd been in a spot of trouble since then too, with a couple of suspended sentences for possession with intent to supply. Just cannabis, according to the case files, no hard stuff. Not on his record, anyway.

Esther jotted down the last known address linked to him on the system. It was a flat in a seedy neighbourhood near the docks; it seemed Sterling's fortunes had not kept pace with his friend Carlton's.

There was a tap at the door, followed by a chirpy "Hey-ho!"

Esther looked up from her computer screen. DCI Brian Small's florid face hovered in the doorway.

"Just fulfilling my managerial responsibilities, Esther," he said, as he stepped into the office. "Need to check you're okay. Sure you don't need a bit more time off?"

Brian Small was short and plump, but seemed to think an awful lot of himself nonetheless. His mane of blonde hair was fastidiously coiffed, and its sheen spoke of careful tending. His suit was an expensive, tailored pinstripe affair, and both his shirt and tie looked to be silk. Even from across the room, she could smell his cologne; Esther suspected that this too was something expensive, and it might even have smelled good had it not been so copiously applied.

Esther forced a brittle smile. "Yes, sir, thank you. I'm fine."

The DCI made a concerned face as he crossed the room and planted himself on the edge of her desk. Esther pushed her chair back an inch or two reflexively. Small didn't seem to notice; he let out a sympathetic sigh.

"I'm sorry again about your mother," he said. "The

death of a parent can be difficult. I just want you to know that I'm here for you. And I want to be sure you're not pushing yourself too hard. Your welfare is my responsibility, after all."

Esther couldn't discern a question in the remarks, but Small was looking at her as if he expected some kind of response. She cleared her throat.

"I'm okay, sir, really," she replied awkwardly. "We… weren't that close, actually."

"You sure you don't want a little more time?" he asked, placing a hand gently on her good arm. "It won't be a problem. I can get it arranged. Whatever you need. I'm here for you, Esther, to help you through this."

Esther extracted her arm carefully and tried for a grateful smile. "Thank you, sir, I appreciate it. But I'm fine. Really."

"Because it's no good you pushing yourself to be back at work if you're not ready," he went on. "All that will do is nudge the problem on down the road. So, if you want me to have a chat with HR and get you a week or two, just say the word. One phone call and I can get it sorted."

Esther thought about being stuck at home for two weeks. Well, at Jean's house, which was home for the moment. Two weeks with Jean's cats to keep her company. Two weeks with nothing to do.

Two weeks with that niggling desire.

It was always there. Sometimes in the background. Sometimes so strong it overwhelmed everything else and took over her thoughts completely. She'd managed fifty-one days so far. Fifty-one days without a drop. But if she was sent home for a fortnight with nothing to do, she didn't think she'd manage to get to sixty. No. Time off was absolutely the last thing she needed right now. The prospect of it terrified her.

She took a deep breath. "To be honest, sir, what I need is to keep busy," she said. "To keep my mind occupied, to focus on something. Staying at work is right for me. If that changes, I'll let you know, straight away. I promise."

DCI Small nodded, his brow pursed in a thoughtful frown. He patted her arm again, letting his hand linger for a moment.

"If that's what you need, Esther," he said, "and if you're sure. But don't be putting yourself under any pressure. Take a back seat for a bit. I understand you're something of a go-getter, but there's no shame in taking a breather now and again."

"Yes, sir," Esther replied, and was relieved to see Jared appear in the doorway. "Inspector," she said, to divert Small's beady little eyes from her as much as anything else, "I've found a Mark Sterling on the system that seems a likely match for Riddell's associate." She lifted the Post-it note she'd jotted the address on, extracting her arm from the DCI's sweaty palm in the process. "We should go knock his door this afternoon."

Brian Small slipped casually from Esther's desk as Jared stepped into the room.

"Jared," he said, the dripping concern he'd directed at Esther a moment ago replaced suddenly by a brusque and professional tone. "I was just telling DS Penman that she is not to exert herself, with all that she's had going on recently. I've offered her some more time off, but she seems determined to stay at work. I trust you'll keep an eye on her? Make sure she doesn't push herself too hard?"

Like she was a fucking child and wasn't sitting right there! He sounded so condescending that Esther half-opened her mouth to object, but Jared must have caught sight of her expression, because he quickly cut in.

"Yes, sir," he said. "Esther's more than capable, sir. Best I have. But I'll keep tabs on her workload."

The DCI gave him a curt nod. "Good man," he said. He turned and gave Esther a sympathetic smile. "My door's always open, Esther, if you need anything." And then he winked—*winked!*—before turning and stepping past Jared and out of the office.

Esther rolled her eyes, shaking her head as she logged out of her computer and grabbed her coat.

"What was all that about?" Jared asked. "Everything okay?"

"Nothing's changed," Esther replied, determined not to mention the DCI's direction that she take a back seat in casework. "He's just 'fulfilling his managerial responsibilities'. I've told him I don't need any more time off. I'm fine." She changed the subject. "What about our misper in London?" she asked, as they left the office and headed for the stairs.

"Found a likely match," the DI replied. "Guy called Gary Hetherington. Same age. Closest I could come to the name Eva Riddell gave. He's been missing just over a month. There was no one at the missing persons desk when I phoned, but the Met are going to have someone ring back."

"This guy Hetherington have any links to the pharmaceutical industry?"

"Nothing obvious. But he does work at a finance firm in the City."

"Some insider trading perhaps?" Esther mused. "Maybe his old buddy Carlton was passing him some sensitive information and they got found out by the wrong crowd."

Jared shrugged. "Maybe. Or Hetherington's disappearance is just a coincidence."

Esther frowned. "I don't like coincidences."

"Coincidences *do* happen," Jared replied, although there wasn't a whole lot of conviction in his voice. She could tell the idea was growing on him.

"We'll wait and see what the Met say when they get back," she said, as they crossed the yard to the car. "For now, let's go find out what Mister Sterling has to say."

6

ESTHER GLANCED DOWN at the address on the Post-it note in her hand, then back up at the squat apartment building in front of her.

"Not quite managed to get into the same income bracket as his mate Riddell, by the looks of things," Jared muttered.

It was true. Riverview House was pretty grim-looking. It might not have been quite as bad as the tower blocks on the Drakehill Estate, but it was not somewhere anyone would be proud to call home, either. The ground-floor windows of the building were protected by rusted grills, the brickwork walls covered in a montage of tags and obscene graffiti. It looked as if some aspirational city planner had envisioned a tree-lined walkway around the perimeter, but the saplings had never stood a chance, not in this neighbourhood; the local kids had stripped them of their branches, where they hadn't ripped them out of the ground altogether, leaving behind only the stakes that had supported their thin little trunks. The grass all around was churned to mud by endless scramblers and bikes and plodding feet.

"No," Esther replied, turning up the collar of her coat. It was late afternoon and already growing dark. "Or his friend Hetherington, by the sounds of it. I wonder what went wrong for poor Mark. And whether he's got some kind of gripe about it."

"Fishing for motives already, DS Penman?" Jared asked.

"Just limbering up," she replied.

It didn't look like the front door's buzzer panel worked anymore, but the main door itself had been put in so many times that a firm push unclicked the lock and let them inside.

Esther wrinkled her nose. The entry hall smelled of piss and boiled cabbage. More graffiti covered the walls and the doors of the elevator, which bore a notice declaring it to be 'Out of Order'. She was grateful to take the stairs. Even without the sign, she wasn't sure she would have trusted the lift.

There were seven storeys in all. Sterling's apartment was on the third.

The corridors grew cleaner and less odorous the higher they climbed. There was even a stretch of freshly laid carpet on the third floor, where one of the apartments had a potted plant and a welcome mat out front. Not Mark Sterling's though. The door to Sterling's flat was cheap and plain, apart from a cartoon cock that someone had drawn in magic marker right at eye level. Esther knocked on the cock. She was answered by a muffled shout from within.

"Just a minute!"

A moment later, the door was snatched open.

Given the change in his expression, it was clear that the man standing in the cloud of dissipating vape smoke had been expecting someone else. He was short for a bloke, a shade shorter than Esther herself, and his floral shirt hung open to reveal a string vest and a surprising amount of body hair. There was a paunch to go with the vest, and the thinning, greasy hair on his head had been swept forward to hide some significant receding. *Christ!* Esther thought, though she did her best to keep her face professionally blank.

"Help you?" he asked curtly, his expression now stony and suspicious.

"Are you Mark Sterling?" she asked.

"Who's asking?"

They both took out their wallets and flashed their warrant cards.

"Police," she replied. "May we come in? We need to speak to you, and I'd rather not do it out here."

Sterling leaned forward slightly and squinted at one ID and then the next, sucking on his vape pipe as he did so.

"Do I need a lawyer?" he asked.

"That depends on whether you've done something wrong, Mister Sterling," Esther told him as she put away her warrant card. "Do *you* think you need a lawyer?"

Sterling exhaled another cloud, enveloping them all in fruity-smelling vapour. He glanced from Esther to Jared and back again.

"Make it quick," he said finally, leaving the door open as he turned and walked back into his apartment.

Esther and Jared shared a glance before following.

The flat was cluttered and untidy, and there was a sour smell that the fog of cloying vape smoke didn't quite mask, but it was far from the worst she'd seen in her time on the job. As they passed the grubby kitchen, she noticed a big black Labrador lying in a tatty, fleece-lined basket under the table. It was going grey, and its only acknowledgement of their presence was a momentary lifting of its eyebrows. Esther suspected the poor thing didn't get out much.

"What's the pooch's name?" Jared asked, as they followed Sterling into the living room.

Sterling didn't answer. Just planted himself on his couch and started sucking on his vape again.

"What do you want to talk to me about?"

"You *are* Mark Sterling, I take it?" Esther asked.

He nodded.

"And you know Carlton Riddell?"

Sterling's disinterested gaze changed subtly at the mention of Riddell's name. "Sure. Went to school with Carlton. Belfield Grammar."

"Have you seen him recently?"

"Nope."

"Been in touch with him at all? Phoned him? Messaged him? Anything like that?"

Sterling's eyes narrowed. It was a calculating, weighing look. He finally nodded. "Yeah, I spoke to him. Couple of weeks ago. Phoned him. Why?"

"What did you phone him about?" she asked, ignoring his question.

Again, the man paused to study her. Took a long draw on his pipe. "A friend of ours is missing," he replied, exhaling a cloud of smoke with his words. "Gary Hetherington. You know about it?"

Esther glanced at Jared, who took out his notebook.

"Where did Gary go missing from?" the DI asked.

"He's been living in London last few years," Sterling replied. "Thought you guys might be involved, since he's from here. He's been missing for over a month." The tone was accusatory, but Esther didn't buy it. Sterling was hiding something and trying to deflect.

Jared wasn't ruffled either. "I'm sure our colleagues in uniform have been helping the London Met with their enquiries," he replied levelly. "We deal mostly with homicides, Mister Sterling."

"Homicides?" Sterling asked. "You mean, like, murders?"

Esther decided to drop the bombshell, try to knock the guy off-balance.

"Carlton Riddell was found murdered this morning," she said.

Sterling froze, vape halfway to his mouth. He stared at her.

"Where were you last night?" she asked.

He looked at her as if she was mad, and then his face darkened.

"I was down in the Arms," he replied, trying to keep his voice even, but she could see he was surprised and shaken by the news.

"The 'Arms'?" Jared asked, pen poised.

"The Kennington Arms," Sterling replied. "Pub just down the street. Watching the match."

Jared jotted a note while Sterling ran his fingers through his greasy hair.

"Were there many there?" Jared asked. His tone was innocent enough, but Sterling wasn't slow. He knew what the DI was getting at.

He scowled. "You think I killed Carlton? *Jesus!*" He muttered something to himself. Esther thought she caught the word 'clueless'. Then, more loudly, he said, "There were about thirty other people. The barman, Craig, he'll confirm it for you."

Sterling took another draw on his vape and seemed to compose himself a little.

"Where did it happen?" he asked. "Here? In Belfield?"

Esther nodded.

"Can you think of any reason why someone might want to kill Carlton Riddell?" she asked.

Sterling shook his head without saying anything.

"What about Gary Hetherington?" Jared put in. "Are you close with him?"

"No," he replied reluctantly. "No, I haven't spoken to Gary in about eight years."

"How did you find out he was missing?"

Sterling was getting agitated now, fidgety. He lifted his vape pipe but then lowered it again, as though he wasn't quite sure what to do with his hands. "Social media," he mumbled. "Facebook and shit."

"And Carlton?" Jared asked. "When you spoke with him, had he been in touch with Gary? Were they close?"

Sterling shook his head again. He began rocking back and forth slightly. When he realised what he was doing, he made himself stop.

"No," he answered. "Said he last spoke to Gary when they were in Uni. Years ago."

"What does Gary do for a living?" Esther asked. "Do you know?"

"Hedge funds or stockbroking or some shit. Not sure. Something with money."

"Is there any reason to believe Carlton's murder might be linked to Gary's disappearance?"

Sterling snapped. "What the fuck are you asking me for?

Shouldn't *you* know that?"

It was Jared who replied, his voice calm and level. "It's our job to find that out, Mister Sterling, which is why we're here. We weren't acquainted with either of these men. But you were. We're here to establish whether there's anything you can tell us about them that might help us find some answers."

Sterling scowled, chastened a little by the DI's firm and reasonable response to his outburst.

"I haven't seen either of them in almost a decade," he muttered.

"And you say they hadn't seen each other either?" Esther asked.

Sterling shrugged. "That's what Carlton said. Said he hadn't spoken to Gary in years. I just assumed he was telling the truth. Didn't sound like he was lying." He was avoiding their eyes now, staring at the floor.

"And what about Gary's disappearance?" Jared asked. "What can you tell us about that?"

"No more than what you fuckers are putting out to the press," he replied sullenly. "Which is fuck all, I have to say. Clearly not doing a good job there."

Esther ignored the remark. He was trying to deflect again. There was something he wasn't telling them. "Were you guys close in school?" she asked.

"We hung out," he replied. "Yeah, we were friends. But we drifted after graduation. Didn't really stay in touch."

"Why?" She was thinking again about the stark difference between the crumby flat she was standing in and the luxury of the Riddell house.

Sterling stared at her for a long moment. "It's just what happens, isn't it? It's just fucking *life*."

Esther had to give him that one. She hadn't spoken to any of her old classmates since leaving school either. And she could probably count on one hand the number of girls from any of the numerous schools she'd been dragged through who'd even remember her name.

"So, you're saying you had no contact with Carlton for years except to suddenly call him up, out of the blue, and tell him about Gary?" she asked. "Why?"

He shrugged again. "Old mate goes missing… it's weird, innit?"

"Did you talk about anything else?"

Sterling watched her, a touch of defiance creeping back into his expression. "Like what?" he asked.

"Like the good old times at Belfield Grammar?" she fired back.

"No," he replied, jaw clenched.

"Just rang him up after ten years and said, 'Hey, Carlton, did you know Gary is missing?'"

The defiance didn't last. Sterling was growing uncomfortable again.

"It wasn't like that," he said slowly.

"How was it?" she asked.

"I just… I just said it was me and said it's been a while, shit like that, and asked if he'd heard about Gary."

"And he hadn't?"

"No."

"Did you ring anyone else about Gary?" Jared put in. "Any other old classmates or friends or anyone?"

Sterling opened his mouth to reply, then hesitated. "Didn't really have many other friends at that school," he told them. "So there wasn't really anyone else to ring."

His reaction to the news of Carlton Riddell's death was

enough to convince Esther that Sterling wasn't a suspect himself, but he was definitely lying about something. They weren't getting anywhere with him at the moment, though, and not likely to until they knew a bit more.

She pulled a contact card from her pocket and dropped it on his cluttered coffee table. "If you think of anything else that might help us," she said, "please get in touch."

His withering look as he rose from the sofa told her she probably shouldn't hold her breath on that count, but when Jared asked him for his own contact number, he offered it up reluctantly. The DI jotted it in his notebook and told him that they would let him know if the Met had any further updates on Gary Hetherington's case.

As Sterling led them from the room, Jared threw in a final question about whether he was acquainted with Gary's parents, or Carlton's, but Sterling claimed that he wasn't, not anymore. The man seemed relieved to be walking them to the door.

"We'll be in touch, Mister Sterling," Jared said, as he and Esther stepped out of the flat.

In the corridor outside, a skinny blonde woman with dark bags under her eyes was shuffling towards them. She wore pyjamas and fluffy slippers and was smoking a cigarette, despite the *No Smoking* signs that were posted all along the corridors. She slowed when she saw them and glanced at Sterling in his doorway. Out of the corner of her eye, Esther saw Sterling give a slight shake of his head. The woman dropped her eyes and hurried past.

Esther turned, but Sterling was already closing the door in her face. She regarded the retreating form of the woman for a moment, then shared a look with Jared. He shrugged. They headed for the stairs.

Esther didn't speak until they were a couple of flights down and she was sure they were alone.

"What do you think that was about?" she asked. "He dealing, you think?"

"Probably."

"He's lying about something. And I'm not talking a couple of bags of weed. He knows something about Riddell and Hetherington that he's not telling us."

The DI nodded. "I'd be inclined to agree. But we're groping in the dark at the moment."

Esther stopped suddenly on the second-floor landing, making Jared pull up short.

"What is it?" he asked.

"I want to work this case," she told him.

Jared raised his eyebrows. "The DCI wanted your workload lightened, not added to. Remember?"

She shook her head. "I don't care. I know what I need and what I need right now is to get stuck into something. Something like this. Let me work the Riddell case."

Jared puffed out his cheeks, cast his eyes about the grimy walls, and sighed. Looking back at her, he finally nodded. "Okay. But it's the usual deal. I'm still SIO. And I'm going to pass some of your smaller files to one of the others. Agreed?"

Esther nodded. "You're the boss."

She turned and continued down the steps, smiling to herself as Jared mumbled something about not really feeling like it half the time.

* * *

Mark Sterling waited until he heard the two coppers go through the door to the stairwell before he returned to his living room. Crossing to the window, he held the curtain aside and watched them make their way down the litter-strewn path to the street. The old man didn't look up, but the woman—the hot one—she glanced back at the building as she reached their unmarked sedan.

Instinctively, he pulled back and let go of the curtain. Then he felt foolish. She wouldn't be able to see him from down there, not with all the streetlights around.

When he looked again, the sedan was pulling away from the kerb. He watched it disappear in the direction of town, then hurried over to the couch and snatched up his phone.

He typed out a quick message and pressed send. Went to the fridge and grabbed a beer, knocking back half the contents in one gulp. Betsy shifted in her basket under the table, watching him disinterestedly.

His phone pinged.

He read the message, then re-read it, trying to decide what to do while he finished the rest of his lager. He was tempted to grab another one, but he knew that wasn't a good idea right now.

Not before he did a little investigating of his own…

7

Hello, everyone. Most of you know me. For those of you who don't: Hi, I'm Esther and I'm an alcoholic.

A murmured "Hello, Esther" rises from the group. This end of the half-lit community hall is lined with rows of chairs, although most of the seats are empty. It is cold in here—Reverend Thomas didn't turn the heating on early enough—and the congregated vulnerable are still wrapped in their scarves and coats, steaming teas or coffees in mismatched cups clutched in frigid fingers, wisps of breath lingering in front of their faces. Although he might be lax with the heating, Reverend Thomas is never to be found wanting when it comes to snacks and hot beverages. The plates of biscuits on the side-tables have already been reduced to a scattering of crumbs.

It's been fifty-one days since I last had a drink and I'm still just taking it one day at a time. My mother—I spoke about her before—she was sick. Very sick. Cancer. Well, I wasn't here last week because… because she died.

Noises of commiseration from the group. Reverend Thomas, whom she'd spoken to earlier, gives her a look that is a mix of sympathy and encouragement.

I thought that her death and the funeral and everything would make me want a drink more. But it hasn't.

No, sorry, that's not really right. I do want a drink—all the time. All the time.

Murmurs of understanding.

But I thought it would be harder to avoid it, harder to ignore that… that need, *at a time like this, with her death and all. But it actually hasn't been. I'm managing okay. The grief hasn't made me run to the nearest bar, like I was afraid it might. I suppose there was so much to do, arranging the funeral and everything. And I guess her death reminded me of what drink did to her. She was an alcoholic too, but it took her a lot longer to… to deal with it. She didn't come to meetings like this until much later. I think I'm lucky to have got a grip on it quicker and admitted*—she sighs—*admitted that I have this addiction.*

So now I try to stay focused on things, stay occupied. Stay busy with work. That sort of thing.

I think keeping busy helps. Keeping busy, and taking it one day at a time.

* * *

Esther hopped off the bus in Sarsbury's village square, her breath fogging as she pulled her coat more tightly about herself and made her way across the flagstone plaza. As she passed the giant Christmas tree dwarfing the World War One monument in the square's centre—the bronze soldier atop forever frozen in the act of thrusting his bayonet at an unseen enemy—she reflected on how she'd come to be living with her aunt in this little chocolate-box village three miles from Belfield. It had all fallen into place so seamlessly. Forced to move from her apartment shortly after the attack, this had seemed the obvious choice, with Jean working so many hours and the NHS only able to provide a nurse to check in on Hannah a couple of times a week. It had been meant as a temporary arrangement—at least in Esther's mind—but no one wanted to talk about the transient nature of it, and no one had expected Hannah to die so soon.

Now here they were, just Jean and Esther, living together in a village that had a population with an average age of about eighty-five. Not that it wasn't pleasant to walk down the old-fashioned cobbled streets in front of old-fashioned craft shops and tea rooms. No hooded teens loitering about, no litter on the pavements. And yet despite its proximity to the city, it seemed somehow detached from life. Quaint and peaceful as Sarsbury was, living here felt like having one foot in the grave.

Unfortunately, Jean seemed to have really taken to having Esther about the place. She had already waved away her niece's talk about moving back to the city, telling Esther she ought to take her time, that there was no rush, and how nice it was to have family close again after living alone all those years before Hannah moved back.

As she reached Jean's street and made her way up the winding lane of terraced houses, windows twinkling with festive lights, Esther realised she wasn't really looking forward to coming back here anymore. It wasn't Jean. Jean was a sweetheart. Esther had lost count of the times her aunt had stepped in to rescue her when she was young, whenever Hannah had gone off the rails. No, it wasn't Jean. And it wasn't just sleepy Sarsbury either. It was the other occupants of the house that would drive her out, sooner rather than later.

Esther hadn't paid much attention to Jean's cats while Hannah had been around, but now that she was often alone in the house, she couldn't ignore them. Esther didn't like cats. She wasn't allergic, not to their fur anyway; their personalities on the other hand… Selfish, arrogant creatures, slinking about the place like the little hoods they were. And Jean had *five* of them! Only the other day, Esther had glanced up from some chore or other to find two of the things staring at her with haughty, judgemental eyes. Even if there wasn't one in the room with you—which was rare—there were pictures of the damn things everywhere, along with cat-shaped trinkets and ornaments in every nook and cranny. Jean had always liked cats, but Esther didn't remember her being this obsessive.

No, she wouldn't be able to stick living with the cats much longer. She was going to have to find a way to broach the subject of moving back to the city, and do it without hurting her aunt's feelings…

Fishing her key from her pocket, Esther opened the door to find Jean—still in her yoga gear—bustling out of the kitchen to greet her, wiping her hands on a tea-towel.

"Hi, Esther, love, I've made a veggie lasagne, if you're hungry?"

The mouth-watering smell of freshly baked lasagne already filled the hall, and Esther realised she was famished. She smiled gratefully and nodded, shrugging out of her coat and kicking off her shoes as she followed her aunt to the kitchen. All of a sudden, she felt terribly guilty about her ungenerous thoughts of a moment before. She reminded herself that her aunt was coming to her rescue once again, just like she had when Esther was a girl.

She saw that Jean had already set the table for two. Ignoring the tabby that was purring and rubbing itself against her legs, Esther sat down.

"So, how did the meeting go?" her aunt asked, as she used a set of oven gloves shaped like giant kitten paws to set a big dish of lasagne onto a wicker placemat at the centre of the table.

"Fine, yeah. Usual."

"They help though, right? Hannah said they helped. Towards the end, when she really gave them a chance, I mean."

Esther nodded. "Sure. They help."

Jean finished dishing out the lasagne and sat down across from her, setting her giant kitten paws to one side.

"How was work?" she asked, as they both tucked in. "I heard on the news they found a body in Belfield today. The reporter said the police were investigating."

"Yeah, I'm working that case," Esther replied. "It's early stages, though." She changed the subject, hoping to put an end to the conversation without seeming rude. "Was Delilah's busy?"

Jean nodded. Her aunt worked part-time at a local coffee-shop called Delilah's and spent her days off and most weekends giving yoga lessons to seniors at a nearby care home. She was not a woman who liked to be idle.

"Really busy," she replied. "There was a book signing at Ali's Bookstore this morning. Some crime author, I think. I'm not sure, not being a big reader, but she must be popular because half the village was in at lunchtime, all chattering about it, and carrying their signed editions about. We had to ring Maisie Talbot when she left her book behind. The barista girls found it and were going to just send it back to Ali's. None of them had bothered to open it up and see who it was dedicated to! After all, it was a book signing! So I opened up the title page and showed the oldest girl, Ethel, and of course, there, in black and white, it said 'To Maisie, thanks for all your support', and then a wild squiggle—why do famous people always have such crazy signatures? I just write my name. That's my signature. Anyway, Ethel made some remark about me being a detective, and I thought of you, but then I thought, it was pretty obvious, wasn't it? It's just the youth of today. They're just completely zoned-out, or self-absorbed, or stuck with their noses in phones and tablets and whatnot…"

Jean had a habit of rabbiting on when she started talking, but Esther didn't mind. In fact, she found it soothing to just stay quiet and let her aunt's words roll over her. Apparently, Maisie Talbot had been so happy to get Jean's phone call that when Jean dropped it off after work, she'd hugged her; Jean said she was a bit taken aback because Mrs Talbot was normally such a conservative woman, prim and proper and almost nineteenth century in her mannerisms. But she was ecstatic to have it returned, having been frantic about losing the thing, so naturally Jean felt obliged to hug her back and share in her relief. It meant she was about half an hour late getting home, since Mrs Talbot had insisted on treating her to a cup of tea and a custard cream. That worked out well, timewise, as Esther was coming home late, and she could make dinner for the two of them.

Finally, Jean stopped to take a breath. Esther couldn't quite understand how she managed to talk so much and still get through her meal. She took the pause as an opportunity to compliment her on the lasagne.

"It's Missus Fenton's recipe," her aunt replied. "I have to confess this is my second attempt. First one didn't work out so well, but she set me right. You know Missus Fenton? She called by after the funeral. Maybe you don't remember her, but I've always said she should've been a chef. Thought she was, to be honest, the first time she brought over a pie to welcome me when I moved in. But no, thirty years in the civil service, minus a few years to rear the children, as she says. They're both in Australia now, if you can credit that. Her husband Blake died five years ago, but she still won't move out there, even though they keep inviting her."

"Maybe she likes the peace and quiet here. It's a pretty quiet place," Esther offered, hoping to steer the conversation to a way-in on the topic of moving out.

"But she's all alone here," Jean replied. "And she won't be a spritely seventy forever. She'll need someone to look after her. Not that I can't look in on her, and I will of course, but she doesn't have any family nearby anymore." She smiled at Esther then and tapped her on the hand. "Which is why I'm so happy to have you about, love. Good to have family about, I think, don't you?"

Esther smiled weakly and stuffed another forkful of lasagne into her mouth. So much for a way-in on that front. The time would present itself. Eventually.

She glanced across the kitchen at a white longhair that was watching her from the doorway. Jean began chatting about the weather forecast for the next day, and what the predicted storm might do to footfall at the café. Esther couldn't remember most of the cats' names. Tobey? One of them was called Tobey, she was pretty sure. The cat watched her, as if it knew what she was thinking. She glared at it until it squinted and looked away. Esther smirked, then her smile soured. She stabbed at her lasagne, feeling a bit pathetic for taking satisfaction in staring down a cat. Jean kept yammering on, and Esther let her mind drift and bob on the tide of her chatter.

8

DOCTOR VENTNER INDICATED to the body that was laid out on the stainless-steel table in front of him, keeping his mask on as he spoke. Carlton Riddell had already been cut open and sewn back up; the post-mortem was complete, but the pathologist seemed to prefer carrying out his debrief to the investigating officers by pointing to the evidence in the flesh, literally.

Esther was finding it hard to focus. It had nothing to do with the pallor of the corpse, or the smell of antiseptic and death that permeated the mortuary. She'd been here many times in the past; it was never pleasant, but not something that really fazed her anymore. No, this morning she was distracted by watching Ventner's perfectly hairless pate catch the light whenever he leaned over to point at something on the corpse. She was wondering if he waxed it.

"And although there is an injury to the temple, here," Ventner explained, pointing to the side of the dead man's head, oblivious to the examination of his own gleaming crown, "from which we have extracted small elements of glass fragment, the laceration is only superficial, and there is no fracture to the bone of the skull below the injury."

Ventner was taking a long time to tell them something they already knew: the bruising around the neck indicated strangulation was the likely cause of death. When Esther said as much straight out, he looked at her, clearly irritated at having his briefing interrupted. But he did nod—a quick, impatient motion—before returning to the subject on the slab.

"Asphyxiation would certainly appear to be the cause. The hyoid bone, here"—he touched the cadaver's neck—"is broken. This suggests significant force was applied. Somebody strong did this. Not conclusive, but probably a man. Severe petechiae on the eyes, as well as cyanosis on the lips and fingers, are all indicators of acute asphyxiation."

He shuffled half a pace down the table and lifted Riddell's right hand.

"We've also managed to retrieve scrapings of skin and blood from beneath two fingernails," he announced. "There is a strong possibility that these scrapings will belong to the perpetrator."

"I'll have our forensics team put a rush on the DNA analysis," Jared declared. "See if it comes back to anyone on the database. With any luck, we'll get a result back before the end of the day."

"So, our suspect should have scratches," Esther mused. "Most likely to his face or arms."

Jared nodded. "Most likely. Sterling didn't have any scratches that I could see."

Esther shook her head. "No. He didn't."

Ventner cleared his throat noisily. When he was satisfied that he had their attention again, he continued to expound his findings. But apart from the fingernail scrapings, there were no major revelations.

At length, he concluded his briefing, unceremoniously dismissing the two detectives as he snapped off his gloves and went to retrieve some fresh ones. There were three more bodies lying under sheets on nearby slabs. Those unfortunates might not be dead in suspicious circumstances like Carlton Riddell, but the pathologist clearly had a busy morning lined up, and he wasn't wasting any time before moving on to his next subject…

A mortuary assistant escorted Esther and Jared from the examination theatre. They headed back down the corridor to the police waiting room, where a pale-looking officer in uniform was pacing up and down nervously. He was young; a rookie at his first autopsy, Esther guessed. Cops got used to dead bodies, but the first post-mortem could be something of a milestone for those who weren't used to it, no matter how strong a stomach you had. She couldn't think of anything to say to the kid—his wait would be over soon, and he'd see it was no big deal—so she left him to his worried beat of the room.

She followed Jared out through the doors and up a flight of stairs that led from the basement to the main floor of the hospital. The DI had his phone out and was listening to a voice message. He must have had it on silent during the autopsy; Ventner was notorious for throwing tantrums when interrupted by mobile phones, no matter what the rank of the officer in attendance.

After a moment, he lowered the phone and glanced at his watch.

"That was Robert Lightbody," he told her, "Carlton's boss."

"Has he agreed to meet us?"

"He's waiting for us at their offices now."

They quickened their pace. Esther knew from experience that the smell of death would haunt her for the rest of the day, but it didn't stop her hurrying to get clear of it.

When they reached the hospital foyer, she saw that the storm the weather forecasters had been predicting had finally hit. The rain fell sideways in thick grey sheets, the trees between the parking bays whipping back and forth wildly in the wind.

"I'll get the car," Jared offered. "You sit tight."

Esther wasn't about to argue. She watched Jared hunch his shoulders, pulling his trench coat tightly around himself, before rushing clumsily out and away between the cars. It was almost midday, but dark enough for dusk.

A few minutes later, he pulled up right outside the front doors. Esther stuffed the autopsy papers under her jacket to protect them from the rain and then, bracing herself, darted across the plaza to the waiting car. It only took seconds, but she was dripping wet when she sat in. She could see Jared had fared even worse, his trench coat dark and slick from his run through the carpark.

"What a shitty day," he growled. "It's just storm after bloody storm these days. I remember when it used to snow in winter."

"Yeah, well… climate change," Esther replied. "We're all fucked. What did you make of Ventner's report?"

"The fingernail scrapings are a bit of good news," he said, as he rolled away from the kerb and followed the one-way system towards the exit. "Might have a suspect sooner than we thought."

They pulled out into a river of taillights, merging with the slow-moving city traffic as they set out in the direction of Belfield's industrial estates.

"Let's hope the parking lot at Belfield BioTech is empty," Esther muttered, as she watched the wipers whip the sheets of rain from the windscreen, "so that we can park ten inches from the door."

The parking lot at Belfield BioTech *was* empty, but traffic on that wet and windy Saturday morning was turgid and it took them the better part of an hour to get there. Jared pulled up to the kerb right outside the main entrance, where they saw a man in a suit waiting for them. He held the doors open while they dashed through the rain and ducked inside.

"Robert Lightbody?" Jared asked, extending his hand as Esther shook the rain off herself.

"Detective Inspector Wilcox?" Lightbody asked in turn, shaking the proffered hand. Lightbody had either aged remarkably well or he was far too young to be the executive director of anything. This guy would get ID'd at the door to any nightclub in town. Esther looked at his smooth cheeks and wondered if he even had to shave every day.

"That's me," Jared confirmed with a nod, "and this is my colleague, Detective Sergeant Esther Penman."

Esther took Lightbody's hand and gave it a quick, firm pump. It wasn't just his face: his hands, too, were soft as a child's.

"Come," Lightbody said, "we'll go to my office. It's warmer there, and I have a pot of coffee brewing."

It was only as they followed him to the elevators that Esther was able to appreciate the enormity of the place. The lobby was a cavernous space. Four storeys tall, it was all polished grey concrete, apart from one wall of glass that looked out onto the storm-swept parking lot. The scattering of fashionable settees and coffee tables was dwarfed by the size of the room.

The elevators were at the other end, a bank of copper-coated doors next to a long marble reception desk. There were no receptionists here today, and the place had a feeling of abandonment; this was a place designed for the bustle of the working weekday. In clear weather it must have been warm and bright, but on a day like today, with the rain running in rivulets down the massive panes of glass, it was dark and foreboding, the buffeting wind echoing off the stony walls.

A single silvery-white Christmas tree stood at the far end of the reception desk, its red fairy lights blinking on and off, even with no one around to appreciate them.

"We run a reduced staff on weekends," Lightbody explained, sounding apologetic, as they stepped into one of the elevators and he pressed a button for the fourth floor. "The only people in today are those who work on the production lines and the offices overlooking the factory floors. We rotate the work, obviously. Try to give our people weekends off as much as possible. We consider ourselves something of a family here at Belfield BioTech and I'm afraid news spreads fast. As you can imagine, Carlton's death was a shock to us all. Everyone's very upset. We've made arrangements for his department colleagues to take a couple of days off if they feel the need. That's the kind of company we are. We are very welfare-focused here."

Esther studied the young executive out of the corner of

her eye as they rode the elevator upwards. He held himself straight-backed, with his nose in the air, like he was trying hard to give an impression of confidence at all times. But he was anxious. Anxious, and doing his best to hide it.

The elevator pinged. The doors slid open to reveal a plush corridor with tall, narrow windows on one side and a row of bright pinewood doors on the other. Standing plants provided a splash of greenery at intervals. A janitor was vacuuming the thick-pile carpet halfway down the corridor. Lightbody led them in the other direction, where he ushered them through a set of double doors at the end of the hall.

It was a corner office, with the same floor-to-ceiling windows looking out over the industrial estate, the city skyline in the distance, and the forested slopes of the Norwick Hills beyond. The interior walls were panelled in more brightly lacquered pinewood. Matching shelves contained binders and books, but there was plenty of wall-space left for a host of framed diplomas and certificates, as well as a few pieces of Cubist art. Décor aside, the room was big enough to contain Lightbody's massive desk, a conference table with eight chairs, and still leave plenty of carpet space to pace about. Or to practise putting, Esther thought, as she spotted a putter and a handful of golf balls in one corner.

"Coffee? Tea?" Lightbody asked, unbuttoning his jacket and striding to the conference table, where a percolator and a teapot sat over an artfully crafted iron grill with tealights beneath to keep both pots warm. They were all part of a matching set, Esther noticed. "We have a variety of herbal teas as well, if either of you would prefer something else?"

"Wouldn't say no to a cuppa coffee, thanks," Jared announced, his eyes scanning the luxuriant office. Esther could almost read his thoughts. You could have fit both their offices into this space and still have room left over. And she shared *her* office with two other sergeants.

"I'm okay, thank you," Esther said, as Lightbody poured a cup for Jared and indicated to the cream and sugar nearby.

"So, Carlton was killed in a… a mugging?" he asked, finally betraying a touch of the earnestness he was trying so hard to hide. "A street robbery?"

"We're exploring several lines of enquiry," Jared replied as he took his coffee. "It's early doors yet."

"It's just that… that's what we'd heard," Lightbody said. "That he was killed in a mugging. Is it the most likely explanation, do you think? Is it a bad… a bad *area* for that sort of thing? Where he was found?"

It was Esther who answered.

"Not particularly," she said, watching him for his reaction. "It's relatively safe at night in that part of Belfield."

Lightbody licked his lips, brow knit, as he took a sip of his coffee. "So, it's unusual? What happened to him?"

She pulled out copies of the documents they'd retrieved from the dumpster—items they presumed had come from Carlton's briefcase—and set them on the conference table.

"These were found at the scene," she told him. "Do you know what they are?"

Lightbody practically darted towards the papers. He began leafing through them, growing visibly paler as he scanned one page after another.

"Mister Lightbody?" Esther pressed. "Do you know what these are?"

He finally nodded. "I do."

Esther shared a look with Jared.

"Would you care to enlighten us?" she asked.

"These are highly sensitive documents relating to the development of our new drug Fluraxonyl—" He looked up from his study of the pages. "You're aware of our new cancer treatment product?"

Esther and Jared nodded in unison.

"This is material that… well, to be frank, it is material that Carlton should not have had at all."

"He stole it?" Esther asked.

Lightbody opened his mouth, but didn't reply straight away. Esther could see the little cogs spinning madly behind his eyes. The young executive was thinking fast, and he didn't like where his thoughts were leading him…

Before he could answer, someone knocked on the door.

9

LOOKING RELIEVED TO be interrupted, Lightbody straightened and gathered up the pages.

"Come!" he called.

The door was pushed open and a squat man in his late fifties stepped into the room. He wore old-fashioned, square-framed glasses and a brown suit. His steel-coloured hair was thick but impeccably tidy, with a rigorous parting on one side. Although he was closely shaven, an early five o'clock shadow gave his face a dark grey pallor. He carried a thin file-folder in one hand.

"This is Mister Donald Preston," Lightbody announced, "head of our legal department."

The young executive was still on edge, but it seemed he was once again making an effort to hide his unease.

"Donald, this is Detective Inspector Wilcox and Detective Sergeant Penman from Belfield CID."

Preston offered them both a polite "Good afternoon".

In a few quick steps, Lightbody intercepted the lawyer

and said something quietly in his ear. He handed over the pages Esther had brought. Preston murmured something back as he took them, then Lightbody bobbed his head and the two men parted.

"I've taken the liberty of preparing a few things for you, Inspector," Preston announced, as he offered Jared the file-folder.

Jared set down his coffee and opened the folder, leafing through the sheets inside while Preston circled the conference table.

The lawyer settled himself on the other side of the table and began a quick perusal of the documents Esther had given Lightbody.

"What's this?" Jared asked.

"Forgive me for being presumptuous, Inspector," Preston replied, without looking up from his own study, "but I thought it might save time. I anticipated your requests and I've gone through the last couple of weeks of Carlton Riddell's schedule and made copies of all the entries for you, as well as any recent correspondence. It's all on an internal server, you see, so that other managers and administrators can access it as needed."

Jared lifted one of the pages from the file. Even from where Esther stood, she could see that most of the text was blacked out.

"It's all redacted," he said, looking from Lightbody to Preston. "Content, names, contact details: it's all blacked out."

Lightbody licked his lips and glanced at Preston.

The lawyer gave Jared a level look and replied, "I have removed the contact details of business colleagues, as well as the detail of private business matters. The content you cannot see is not relevant."

"With respect, Mister Preston," Esther said, "I think *we* should be the judges of what is relevant and what is not."

Donald Preston was unmoved. "Nevertheless, you will require a warrant, signed by a judge, to disclose further details. In the meantime, and before you go to all that effort, I hope you will see from what you *do* have that there is nothing of relevance to be gleaned, and therefore no grounds for a warrant."

"You understand that this is a *murder* investigation?" Jared said, more than a touch of exasperation in his voice.

"Please, Inspector, of *course* we understand that," Lightbody interjected. "We're on the same side here. If Carlton was killed because of these documents"—he indicated the pages Preston was studying— "then we are just as keen to have the perpetrators apprehended as you are, believe me! But please try to see this from our point of view for a moment. Belfield BioTech is on the brink of something incredible, something game-changing. We have a product coming to the end of trials that will revolutionize cancer treatment. We are at a very sensitive stage, and we are entrusted with maintaining the privacy and security of all the parties involved in the endeavour. We *do* have legal obligations of our own to respect, to our partners and to our shareholders."

Jared opened his mouth, but Esther forestalled him.

"Carlton's wife said he was working late the night of his death because he had a meeting at work. That's what he told her."

Jared looked down at the file in his hands. "There's nothing in his schedule for Thursday," he said. "Last meeting, according to these pages, is a video conference at three p.m. Wednesday with… a black rectangle," he finished dryly.

A long look passed between Lightbody and Preston. It was the lawyer who replied. Esther got the impression that the older man was taking a messy situation in hand, while the younger man was quietly panicking.

"We'll check all of our security footage for the past month," he told the two detectives. "That's as long as it's stored for. And we'll go through the internal servers as far back as necessary—I'll have our IT department sift the codes line by line, if needs be—and we'll have more answers for you when you return on Monday." Esther sensed the lawyer was speaking to Lightbody as much as to them. She also noted that there was no hint of a question in the suggestion that she and Jared would return on Monday.

"So, as far as you're concerned," Jared said, waving his useless, blacked-out pages about, "if corporate espionage is a line of enquiry, this correspondence isn't relevant? I find that hard to accept."

Again, another look passed between the two corporate men.

"Give us a day to do some further internal investigation," Preston said, "and if it appears there's more information that needs to be revealed, you will have it. You can be quite assured of that."

"We should have access to everything," the DI replied. "We'll need to interview your staff as well."

"Surely not everyone is—" Lightbody began, but Preston raised a hand to cut him off.

"It is just as Mister Lightbody has said, Inspector," he replied. "We are on the same side here. It is *very much* in our interest that you succeed in locating and apprehending

Carlton Riddell's killers. However, we do have *legal* responsibilities in respect of data protection and shareholder assets, which means that—despite the fact that any delay caused by judicial hearings is as unacceptable to us as it is to you—we will still be obliged to challenge your warrant applications in court. This will prove a terrible waste of time because, and let me be quite clear about this, *no* judge is going to grant you free access to all of our data.

"So, let us help you to avoid these unnecessary delays. We will carry out our internal investigation, and we will do it expeditiously. You may, of course, interview whomsoever you wish, but if we can assist in narrowing the focus of your investigation to the relevant people, it will save time in the short term. For all of us."

If Jared looked a little disgruntled by the lecturing tone, Esther could see that the benefits of Preston's suggested approach weren't lost on him. She didn't like it all that much either, but she suspected Preston was right: if they butted heads with this company, they would find themselves tied up in the courts for weeks.

Lightbody spoke into the growing silence.

"Again, can I just implore you to see this from where we stand," he said, attempting to play the role of mediator. "We want the culprits caught as much as you do, not only because they killed a friend and valued colleague of ours, but because they may have stolen our property in the process. Property we are legally obliged to do our best to protect. Property that represents *significant* sums of money. If this product is replicated by one of our competitors this early, it will mean severe losses for our investors and our shareholders. I'm sure you can appreciate that there is no point in us working hard to protect our investment, working hard to retrieve whatever's been stolen, simply to divulge it to every officer in your constabulary. From our point of view, we would be in an even worse position than we are at the moment."

Esther raised an eyebrow at him, and he had the decency to blush. So much for a caring workplace. All they were worried about was their new drug, and their profits.

At length, Jared nodded. "Very well. We'll try it your way, Mister Preston, but if we don't have real and tangible cooperation, we may end up seeking warrants in the end."

The lawyer acknowledged the concession with a gracious nod.

Esther decided to change tack.

"What about Carlton's state of mind?" she asked Lightbody. "His wife told us he was very stressed at work recently."

Lightbody frowned, half-shrugging before he could stop himself.

"Carlton was struggling with his figures, if the truth be told," he said. "He wasn't getting the level of pre-orders, the number of bigger contracts, we might have expected with Fluraxonyl. It wasn't that he was being put under any pressure by management, I want to assure you of that. But the sales team… well, they are a bit competitive, internally. It's a culture in sales teams. There's always been a bit of jostling to be the alpha salesman. Or woman." He gave Esther a sheepish grin.

"And not reaching the top spot," she said, "is it something that would have bothered Carlton Riddell?"

"Probably, yes," he conceded. "Carlton was once our top sales executive. But we've had some fresh blood into the firm recently. Real go-getters."

"Was his job at risk?" she asked.

"Lord, no!" Lightbody did his best to seem aghast at the suggestion. "Not at all! Carlton had a good track record. He would have known his position here with us was secure in the long run. No question of that."

"But the sales results," Jared pressed. "Would the better performers have attracted financial rewards?"

"Well, yes, naturally," Lightbody exclaimed. "There is an end-of-year bonus for good sales figures. It's an incentive most companies use."

"Did Carlton Riddell receive these bonus payments in the past?"

"He did."

"But not recently?"

Lightbody shook his head. "Not last year, or the year before."

"And his… *competition* in the sales team," Esther put in, choosing her words carefully. "Did it come in the form of any particular person?"

Lightbody regarded her for a moment.

"Gavin Smythe," he replied at last. "Joined us straight out of Cambridge two years ago. Has a real good way with people. Born to the job. He's been our top salesman these last two years."

"I imagine a rivalry like that can cause a bit of tension," she remarked.

Lightbody looked thoughtful. He was the one choosing his words carefully now. Preston watched the exchange over the dark rims of his glasses, but didn't intercede.

"They got on fine, from what I could see," Lightbody told her. "I've never seen either of them behave with anything other than cordial professionalism towards one another. I don't believe they were very close, but they got on well at work." He paused. "Rewarding good work is how companies operate in the private sector," he said pointedly to the two public sector police officers. "It's nothing new or unusual. Carlton would have been used to it."

"But it sounds to me like he was used to being top dog," Esther replied. "Before Mister Smythe arrived."

Lightbody made no reply to that.

"What about other people in the team, or the firm generally?" she asked. "You say these two men got on well. 'From what you could see.' Did anyone else mention any spats or arguments? Was there anyone else Carlton might have had issues with?"

Lightbody shook his head. "I've not heard anything of the sort. Carlton Riddell got on well with everyone, as far as I'm aware."

"Where is Mister Smythe now?" Jared asked. "We'll want to speak with him. Does he live locally?"

"He's out of the country, I'm afraid."

"Out of the country?" Esther asked.

"He's been on company business in Canada for the past five days," Lightbody told them. "He's due back tomorrow night."

"We'll need the details of his flights and accommodation," Jared said.

Preston, perhaps sensing his boss's fraying patience, answered. "Of course. If you leave a card, I can have that information emailed to you later today."

As Jared fished in his pocket for a business card to hand to the lawyer, Esther addressed Lightbody.

"Did Carlton Riddell have his own office, or did he share

a workspace?"

"He had his own office. All our senior salespeople have their own offices."

"May we take a look?"

Lightbody glanced at Preston. There was a protracted silence, before the lawyer seemed to reach a conclusion.

"Very well," the older man said. "But we'll accompany you."

She and Jared followed Lightbody and Preston out of the office and down the corridor to a much smaller office, although it was still bigger than either hers or Jared's, and it too had a wall of floor-to-ceiling windows on one side. It was also immaculately clean. The shelves held giant glossy ring-binders, manuals about sales and marketing, and sets of pharmaceutical periodicals lined up neatly in chronological order. Many of the shelves were left unfilled, but Esther was quite certain she could run her finger over any one of them and not pick up a trace of dust. Some offices at the police station had cobwebs in the corners.

The desk itself contained very little, apart from an in-tray with a couple of pieces of correspondence, a computer keyboard, mouse, and leather desk pad. Jared pulled open the drawers one by one; none of them were locked. Memoranda and sales charts, which he flicked through quickly and dropped back into the drawers. Nothing of interest. Preston and Lightbody remained at the door, watching them, but neither made any move to stop them from perusing the papers.

Esther scanned the walls. A couple of graduation certificates. Some pictures of Eva and Tracy. One picture showed all three of them, faces close to the lens, beaming for the camera. Staring at that picture, seeing Carlton alive and smiling with his wife and young daughter, made the loss for the family strike Esther more keenly than it had until now. In that moment, with Jared fumbling through the desk drawers, turning over pages half-heartedly, and with the two corporate men looking on, she felt the personal side of her job crash over her; this was not a routine task, not a puzzle to get stuck into. These were people's lives. She suddenly needed to be outside, rain or no rain. The room felt claustrophobic.

She was saved by the trilling of Jared's phone, and it looked like he too was happy to be diverted from his fruitless rummaging.

"Detective Inspector Wilcox," he said, straightening as he listened to whoever was on the other end. When he spoke again, he gave Esther a meaningful glance. "We'll come straight there."

He hung up.

"We'll have to leave it at that for the moment," he told Lightbody. "We'll be in touch to discuss the results of your internal enquiries."

"Of course, Inspector," Lightbody said, although he looked like he almost wanted to ask the DI about the phone call. Instead, he handed Jared a business card. "Please, contact me personally as soon as you discover anything."

Jared took Lightbody's card with a promise that he would, and the meeting ended more amicably than Esther had expected. Lightbody offered to arrange a sit-down with Gavin Smythe as soon as he returned to England. Preston bid them both good day and disappeared down the corridor, while Lightbody escorted them back to the lobby. Esther thought the young executive walked a touch more quickly than he had on the way up, no doubt eager to rejoin Preston and discuss their war-plan.

Down at the main entrance, he unlocked the front doors for them, and Esther and Jared made a dash for the car through the driving rain. Only when they were inside it, shaking off the water, did Jared explain the phone call.

"That was Derek Grant," he told her. "They've tracked Riddell to a hotel near the crime scene. Seems he met with someone and went up to one of the rooms shortly before he was killed."

"A woman?" Esther asked.

"A man."

Jared started the engine, hit the wipers and spun out of the carpark, back towards the centre of town.

10

THE CCTV ROOM at the Marriott Hotel was about the size of a large wardrobe, crammed with open-backed metal shelves full of hard drives and old monitors. Jared and Esther were squashed in alongside Derek Grant. All three detectives crowded around a small desk at the back of the room, where the hotel manager sat at the main computer, running the footage for them. She was flicking through settings and camera angles, and loading them onto the USB drive Grant had given her.

The detective was quietly pleased, Esther could tell, even though he was normally a very impassive character. A veteran of the force, Esther had a lot of time for Detective Constable Derek Grant. He was the best type of officer: he caused no issues, did his work well, kept himself to himself, and didn't dump any of his personal shit at her door. And he'd always been respectful towards her, right from her first day as a DS in CID, when some of the older hands had made no effort to hide their scepticism about her youth, or her gender. Grant had been the one who'd set the standard, and most of the team had followed his example. He'd given Esther her place right from the start, and taken instruction without quibble. With most people following his lead, it had saved her a whole pile of work in the long run, leaving her only a handful of grumpy old gits to set straight, and those few had quickly fallen into line or transferred out. She'd always been grateful to DC Grant for the support he'd given her back then. Not that they'd ever spoken about it directly; she'd just done her best to make it up to him over the years by giving him latitude to do his own work without smothering him. You could do that with some detectives, just let them run their own investigations. Others, not so much.

"Here we go," the manager murmured. A small, gold-coloured badge pinned to her ample bosom declared her to be 'Mandy'. She was a tall woman in her thirties. Heavily overweight, her grey suit jacket was riding up her back to reveal a strip of pale, fatty flesh spilling out over the top of her matching grey trousers. Esther tried to avoid looking at it and concentrate on the screen instead.

What the monitor was showing now was an angle from one of the CCTV cameras on the ceiling of the hotel lobby. It covered the main doors to the hotel. As they watched, the doors slid open and a couple came in, arm-in-arm. The quality of the footage was good, with no pixelation or jerky time-lapse motion. The couple disappeared offscreen in the direction of the bar, and then Carlton Riddell entered. Esther recognised him more from his clothing than his face. In life, he looked taller, his face fuller and more handsome than the one on the body she'd seen in the mortuary that morning. He carried his briefcase in one hand. As he walked out of frame, the camera angle switched, showing the bar and an area of the lobby given to chairs and sofas and low coffee tables, again from ceiling height. The artfully lit Christmas tree they'd passed on the way in blocked some of the view, taking up a lot of the foreground and casting the rest of the lobby into relative darkness, but Esther could just about make out Riddell approaching a man at the bar. They shook hands. The second man's features were obscured by the gloom of the background, and as Jared frowned and leaned in, Grant spoke up.

"Don't worry, Inspector," he said. "We've tracked them to a room upstairs and we get better facial captures from the footage in the corridor."

Sure enough, a moment later, Riddell and the other man left the bar together, heading towards the elevators. The footage cut to an angle above the elevator doors, and at a direction from Grant, the manager paused the footage.

Now that she had a better view of him, Esther could see that the second man was a touch shorter than Riddell, with swarthy skin, jet-black hair and a beard that was trimmed square and narrow.

"See that we get printed stills of that man's face for the investigation team," Esther murmured, as she studied the darker man's features, committing them to memory.

"Already on it, Skipper," Grant replied. "I've spoken with the digital imagery department. They said they can have it done for us by this evening if I bring them the footage today."

Esther nodded. "Good work. Play it on."

Mandy hit the playback button and the two men came to life again. They were exchanging words as they waited for the lift, but it seemed to Esther that they were avoiding each other's eyes. They held themselves stiffly. Strangers, or near-strangers. Or involved in something that made them nervous in each other's company.

A set of elevator doors opened, and both men stepped in together. The camera cut to an upstairs corridor, where they emerged and headed towards a room at the very end of the hallway, almost out of view. The bearded man used a keycard to unlock the room and then stepped inside. Carlton Riddell followed, and the door swung closed.

"What are we looking at here?" Esther murmured. "A conspiracy, or a gay tryst?"

Grant shook his head. "Doubt it's the latter, Skip. They don't spend too long in there. Five and a half minutes, to be exact."

"More than enough time for some men," Esther muttered, and the hotel manager chortled.

Derek stifled a smile. "Forward it on to when he leaves, Mandy, if you don't mind."

Mandy fast-forwarded the footage five minutes, hit playback again, and a moment later Carlton Riddell reappeared and hurried back towards the elevators. He still had his coat on and his briefcase in one hand. He didn't press the button for the elevators this time but went straight through a door just below the camera.

"The staircase," Mandy explained.

They were watching the ground floor once more; the same angle that covered the lifts also took in the door to the stairwell. Riddell emerged, moving briskly. A cut to the main doors as he headed back out onto the street, and then the final shot was from a camera outside the building, angled along the pavement in front of the hotel. Riddell was striding away down the footpath. Esther could tell that he was headed in the direction of the carpark where his car had been found. He glanced over his shoulder twice before he disappeared from frame, and the footage froze.

"That's it as far as Carlton Riddell's concerned," Grant said, straightening and turning to face Esther and Jared. "We've scanned forwards quite a bit and no one follows him. The other man stays in his room and checks out early the next morning."

"Have we managed to confirm the room number?" Jared asked. "Have we a name for this guy?"

Grant nodded. "Room Five One Three. Booked under the name Gerhard Steiner. Mandy's already printed out all the details they have on him. It's not much. The booking was made using a third-party booking website, so it's basically just his name and a credit card number at the moment."

"Do we have anything on this Steiner fellow?" Jared asked.

He meant on PNC, the Police National Computer, but Grant shook his head. "Mandy spoke to the staff member who booked him in. She says he had an accent. From the name, I'm going to guess German, Swiss or Austrian. We have no record of him in the UK."

"How long until we can get some more details?" Esther asked.

Grant shrugged. "We'll have to go to the booking firm or credit card company ourselves with an application, maybe even a warrant."

"Put it together, Derek," Jared said, "and I'll sign whatever you need."

Grant nodded. "Will do, Inspector. Should have something for you after lunch."

Esther was frowning at the screen. Mandy had wound it forward to where Mr Steiner was checking out. He appeared cool and casual, and not the least bit concerned. No glances over his shoulder. Smiles for the receptionist. Esther studied his face. Without the Germanic name, she would have guessed he was of Middle Eastern extraction, based on his features.

"So, Mister Steiner remained in the room all night, after Carlton Riddell left?" she asked.

"Appears that way from the footage," Grant replied.

"Doesn't mean he wasn't involved, of course," Jared murmured, looking at the screen. "Given the shady nature of that meeting, I'd say we have reason to speak to him at the very least. And a refusal to cooperate would probably tip it into reasonable grounds to bring him in."

Esther nodded. It was true. Just because Steiner hadn't dealt the fatal blow didn't mean he wasn't involved in the murder. If he *was* a conspirator, though, he was looking pretty calm about it. On the screen, Steiner hefted his bags and moved to the windows of the lobby, thumbing a message into his phone and glancing into the street every now and again.

"Waiting on a taxi?" Esther asked.

"He ordered a cab to the airport," Grant told her. "Liz is back at base putting together a manifest production application. Taxi company said he was brought all the way to East Midlands Airport. If Steiner is his real name, then with any luck we'll have his airline and passport details by the end of the day."

Esther smiled. "Good work, Derek." She turned to the hotel manager. "Thank you for your help, Mandy."

"No problem. I'll have a copy downloaded for you folks

in a jiffy."

The detectives moved out into the corridor. Esther turned to Grant.

"If you confirm that Gerhard Steiner *is* his real name," she said, "see if you can find any links to pharmaceutical firms, here or internationally."

"You think the murder might be linked to Riddell's job?" he asked.

"Not sure yet," Esther replied. "But it's starting to look like a pretty strong lead. Let's chase it."

Grant nodded. "Will do, Skipper."

* * *

Esther glanced at the screen above reception, waiting for her number to appear. She adjusted her position in the narrow plastic seat in a vain attempt to get more comfortable. Doctors and nurses in blue scrubs hustled up and down the corridor next to the waiting area, and she found herself constantly watching for Triona.

She'd been sitting here for forty minutes already. The Emergency Department was busy today. She had thought that having a scheduled appointment for a routine procedure might have made things quicker, but no; apparently they'd merged Minor Injuries with A&E recently as part of a budget cut, so she had to sit here and wait with everyone else.

As the minutes ticked by, she found herself searching the faces of the staff, hoping for a glimpse of the nurse who'd scribbled a phone number on her cast six weeks ago. She looked down at the digits scrawled in blue felt-tip. That number was the only mark on the plaster. She had a sudden urge to jot it down before she lost it, but then she chastised herself. She wasn't gay. She couldn't imagine kissing a woman in public. It would be totally unfair to call Triona out of curiosity and lead her on.

Or *was* it just curiosity? Esther found herself searching the faces of the nurses scooting around behind reception again.

And that was when she realised she was being watched.

She glanced across at the row of seats opposite. A little boy was staring at her. About four or five years old, he wore a bloody bandage over one eye. The other was red from having done a lot of crying recently.

"What happened to your arm?" he asked her.

The woman next to him—his grandmother, Esther guessed; she looked too old to be his mother—glanced up from her phone.

"Don't be so nosey, Billy," she scolded gently, and offered Esther an apologetic smile.

"It's okay," Esther said with a smile of her own. "I had an accident," she told little Billy. "I fell and someone landed on it."

"Who?"

"A bad man," she replied. "But he's in jail now. What happened to your head?"

"I fell out of my treehouse."

"Bit cold for climbing trees, isn't it?"

"That's what I told him," his granny chimed in. "But he loves that treehouse. Spends whole days up there sometimes."

"I was putting up my Christmas tree," the boy protested.

"A Christmas tree?" Esther asked, eyebrows rising. "In your tree house?"

The granny used her hands to indicate that it was only about a foot high. "A cut-off. Grandad had to cut the top off the big tree so it would fit in our living room, isn't that right, Billy?" Billy nodded. "He wanted the offcut for his tree house. And his grandad rarely says no to this little boy." That was delivered in an askance tone to show what granny thought about grandad's approach. Abruptly, she leaned toward Esther and lowered her voice. "Would you mind awfully if I asked you to keep an eye on Billy for two minutes? I really need the loo, and I have no idea how much longer we're going to be."

Esther smiled. "That's fine." She turned to Billy. "My name's Esther. Will you be okay to sit with me for a few minutes?"

"Thank you so much," the woman said. She told Billy she would be back in a tick and then scurried away toward the restrooms.

Esther looked again at the screen above reception.

"Was he a very bad man?"

Esther turned back to Billy, who was watching her owlishly now.

"I'm sorry?" she asked.

Billy pointed at her cast. "The man who's in jail. Was he a very bad man?"

"He was. But he's all locked up now."

"Did the police catch him?"

"We did."

Billy's one good eye went wide. "Are you a police?"

She chuckled. "I *am* a police."

"Is it scary being a police?" he asked.

Esther thought for a moment and then shook her head. "Not really. You go to police school where they teach you how to be a police officer and that makes it less scary. You want to be a police officer when you grow up?"

The boy smiled and nodded, nerves overcome by sudden enthusiasm. "My brother and me play cops and robbers. He's bigger than me and sometimes is the robber but mostly he's the cop. I like being the cop. You get the badge and the good gun."

"The badge is the main thing," Esther told him with a wink.

Billy frowned. "I like the gun better."

"Hmm, I'm not so sure," Esther replied. "Does your brother have a gun too, when he's the robber?"

Billy nodded. "The robber gets the water pistol. It's green and doesn't look as good but it's the robber's gun."

"So, the robber has a gun and the cop has a gun?"

Billy nodded emphatically. "We both do."

"And the only different thing the cop has is the badge," Esther said.

Billy looked at her thoughtfully, considering this. His grandmother reappeared and murmured her thanks to Esther.

"I hope he didn't bother you too much," she said.

"On the contrary, we were having a very good conversation about cops and robbers."

The woman chuckled. "Is that right?"

"Granny, Esther is a police offerser!" the little boy exclaimed, stumbling over the unfamiliar word.

The grandmother looked at Esther, taking in her broken arm again. "Is she now? I hope you were behaving yourself then."

"She says there's a police school!"

Just then Esther's number appeared on the screen. A small Filipino man in scrubs called her name. She stood and excused herself, with a last comment to little Billy to work hard in school if he wanted to go to police school when he grew up. Billy replied that he would, sore head and bandaged eye momentarily forgotten.

Esther followed the nurse down the corridor, studying every face along the way for signs of the woman with the pixie smile who'd written her number on her cast six weeks ago. The little Filipino chattered away as he led her to a treatment room and sat her into a seat, commenting on the weather and asking about holiday plans as he carefully went about cutting the cast from her arm. After a month and a half locked away in plaster, it was an ugly sight, paler and skinnier than its counterpart. Esther replied in monosyllables for the most part, as he slipped from nattering about the storms to asking her questions about any pain or discomfort while he gently tested her fingers and elbow movements. The whole time, Esther just stared out the open door, checking the faces of every person in scrubs who passed…

And then the nurse was dropping the broken pieces of plaster into a bin and announcing happily that Esther was good to go.

Esther stood and went to the door. There were still a couple of blue digits visible on the broken plaster in the bin. She should have copied it out, she thought. Too late now.

With one last, lingering look at the remains of her cast, she thanked the nurse and left, doing her best to ignore the nagging regret that formed in the pit of her stomach as she walked from the hospital and back out into the howling wind and rain.

11

THE SUN HUNG low in a pale blue sky. The storm had cleared overnight, leaving Belfield's streets glistening in the wintry sunshine. It was so cold that some of the roadside puddles were still frozen, even as noon approached.

Esther, free of her cast after six weeks, had decided to take a drive. She had not been sure whether her battered little Fiat would actually start; both her first and second attempts at getting the engine to turn over had produced only gasping rattles. Third time lucky though, and it had sputtered to life.

Now, out of Sarsbury and coasting along the main streets of Belfield, she began to feel a sense of liberation. The Sunday morning traffic was light, but it was less than two weeks to Christmas and it would be busy soon, once the stores opened. There were already a few keen shoppers looking for parking spots before the rush, couples and small knots of tourists walking about and admiring the festive décor.

Esther drifted towards the suburbs. She didn't bother stopping at the station. The CID floor would be empty on a Sunday morning, and she'd already made a note of Carlton Riddell's parents' address and looked it up on Google maps. She had her notebook and pen with her, as always, so there was no need to go to the office first.

As she made her way up Woodland Road, she veered off and headed east, taking the long way rather than crossing the Valley Bridge. It had only been a couple of months since she'd tried and failed to stop a man from jumping to his death from that place, and she knew driving past the spot would darken her mood. She wanted a clear head when she met the Riddells. The drive was helping, and she didn't want to spoil it. So she took a long, winding route that moved intermittently between the forested slopes of the Norwick Hills and Belfield's rich northern suburbs.

By the time midday arrived, she'd had enough of driving. She decided it was sufficiently late for a house call, and she was eager to get some work done under her own steam without the need to be ferried everywhere. Jared wouldn't mind, not on a Sunday.

She headed for the Riddell residence.

When she arrived at the house, she found half a dozen cars parked along the huge front driveway, with several more on the verges of the road near the gate. It seemed the Riddells already had visitors.

She pulled in behind a dark, sporty-looking Mercedes and killed the engine. All the cars were high-end brands—Jags and Bentleys, Maseratis and Mercedes—and her little old Fiat looked conspicuous in their company. Grabbing her grungy leather handbag, she got out and set off through the open gates.

It was clear that Carlton's parents, like their son, were not short of a few bob. The brickwork driveway rose gently between rows of bare cherry blossom trees, evenly spaced to either side all the way to a courtyard, where an empty stone fountain served as centrepiece. The visitors' cars were parked somewhat haphazardly here, and among the Porsches and Ferraris were two Range Rovers coated in frost. The Riddells' cars. Counting the unfrozen cars, Esther estimated that there were between a dozen and two dozen guests in attendance.

She was standing in front of the massive oak doors, beginning to wonder whether she should, perhaps, have called ahead, when the door was opened by a woman in her sixties. She wore her age well; her silver hair was held back in a tight bun, and she looked trim and fit under her slim plaid dress, a designer affair complete with a diamond brooch that would probably have cost Esther a couple of months' salary. But even carefully applied make-up couldn't hide the signs that this woman had cried recently, and had been crying a great deal of late.

"Can I help you?" she asked.

"Agatha Riddell?" Esther ventured.

"Yes?"

Esther fished out her warrant card. "My name is Esther Penman. I'm a detective with Belfield CID. I'm investigating your son's death. I know that my colleagues have been out with you already, about the procedures and everything, but I wanted to speak to you in person." She indicated to the cars parked all around the courtyard. "Is this a bad time?"

Agatha Riddell shook her head and stepped back, gesturing for Esther to come in.

"No, it's fine. We've had people coming by every day since…" She trailed off and heaved a sigh. Esther could see she was fighting back more tears. "We've had a lot of support from family and friends," she finished.

The entrance hall to the Riddell house was as big as the entire ground floor of Jean's little terrace. A sweeping staircase led to a balcony that ringed the first floor. The lightwell high above was made from stained glass, some kind of maritime scene.

Esther followed Agatha to the kitchen, where people stood in small clusters chatting, or sat at the tables, one of which was covered in film-wrapped cookware and bunches of flowers. There were about twenty people in all, but Esther spotted Carlton's father straight away. He sat at the head of the main kitchen table, talking solemnly to two men who looked to be of an age with him. He had his son's features, but he was stockier, his hair a mane of grey. He looked the way Esther imagined Carlton would have, had he been given the chance to grow old.

"Harold, this is the detective investigating Carlton's death," Agatha announced, trying to keep her voice even, but Esther heard the tremor.

The whole room fell silent and every eye turned to Esther. She resisted the urge to smile nervously under all the attention. Schooling her features to a professional impassivity, she addressed Harold Riddell.

"I wonder if I might have a few words with you and your wife in private, Mister Riddell?" she broached. "Unless this is a bad time?"

Harold was motionless for a moment. Then he shook himself visibly, as if waking from a daydream. "Not at all. Of course." He rose from his seat. "Can I offer you a drink,

Detective…?"

"Penman. Esther Penman. And no, thank you, I'll try not to take up too much of your time."

She was painfully conscious of the dozen pairs of eyes focused on her. It was not a hostile attention, but the curiosity and the intensity of all those stares made her break out in a sweat, and she was glad to be following Agatha and her husband out of the kitchen.

They led Esther down a corridor and into a study, where she took a moment to survey the room. This was no pokey little home office with DIY-made shelves overflowing with ring-binders and cheap paperbacks. This room was fashioned in the vein of a nineteenth century library. Glass cabinets lining one wall housed sporting trophies, and the shelves held sets of uniformly designed leatherbound volumes, all intact and well-tended. She recalled from the file notes she'd read that Harold Riddell had been a barrister. A glance at the nearest shelf told her most of the books were legal tomes. The mahogany desk at one end of the room was bare, save for an Apple laptop, and a sepia-toned globe in the corner stood as tall as Esther's shoulder, the mountain ranges rising up from its surface in miniature.

As much as she wanted to launch straight into her questions, the circumstances wouldn't allow it. The atmosphere was taut. Agatha Riddell's eyes were red from all her recent tears, and her husband's efforts to steel himself against the emotions of the tragedy made him seem tense and weary. He indicated to the leather seats ranged around an elegant stone fireplace, where a stack of logs sat neatly, waiting to be lit.

Once they were settled, Esther asked whether they had heard from the forensic mortuary yet.

"We've been in touch with the funeral parlour," Harold Riddell replied. "They'll be collecting Carlton tomorrow. The funeral will be Tuesday morning at St Christopher's."

"I know you'll be keen for answers," Esther continued, gently moving on to her agenda as she slipped her notebook and pen from her handbag, which she set at her feet, "but I need to be straight with you and tell you that the investigation is at an early stage. There are no suspects yet, and we're exploring a number of lines of enquiry. I want you to know, as the officer in charge of investigating your son's murder, that this case has my full attention. And I have a good track record. I will do my very best to catch whoever did this and bring them to justice."

Harold's mouth firmed as he dropped his eyes and nodded in gratitude. Agatha made a small noise, possibly a stifled sob. Esther pressed on.

"When was the last time either of you saw or spoke to Carlton?"

"Only last week," Agatha replied. "He always phoned, once or twice a week."

"So, it was a phone call?"

"Yes."

"And he came over to the house with Eva and Tracy earlier this month," Harold added. "A Sunday dinner that Agatha organised."

"I invite them over every few weeks for a Sunday get-together."

"What was the phone call about?" Esther asked. "Did he phone you, or did you phone him?"

"He phoned." Agatha shook her head. "It wasn't about anything in particular, just a check-in, you know?"

"How did he sound on the phone? Was there anything

unusual about the call?"

"No. He sounded fine."

"What about Carlton's recent behaviour? Any change in his habits or demeanour? Anything odd that sticks out, thinking back?"

Harold Riddell interjected. "I'm sorry, Detective, but what is it you're getting at? We were given to believe Carlton was targeted in some kind of street robbery. Is that not the case?"

Esther hesitated, taking a moment to frame her statement carefully. "We don't yet know *why* Carlton was killed. It does *look* like a robbery, but I think we owe it to Carlton to explore every possibility. We are working on several lines of enquiry, from street robbery right through to his work. Exhausting every line of enquiry *thoroughly* gives us the best chance of catching his killer, or killers."

Agatha made another faint noise, and Harold seemed to sag a little in his seat. Esther got the impression that here was a man used to being in charge, a commanding personality. Pulled apart by the death of his only son, it seemed Harold Riddell had lost the confidence to command. She gave him a sympathetic look.

"I understand how difficult this is," she said. "I'll try to make it as quick as I can. If my questions become too much, just say the word and we can do this another time."

Agatha smiled gratefully and gestured for her to go on.

"So, no strange behaviour at all?" Esther asked them. "Nothing odd recently that either of you recall?"

"He might have been a bit overworked these last few months," Agatha offered. "His firm made a big breakthrough with a cancer medicine. But he didn't talk much about work. It was Eva who told us he was stressed.

That he was working too hard. He seemed… He seemed alright to us, didn't he, Harold?"

Harold nodded.

Esther scribbled some notes. "Did your son have any enemies that you know of?"

They both exchanged slightly alarmed looks, then shook their heads.

"Not at all," Harold replied. "Carlton was a people-person. Been that way since he was a boy. Always seemed to get on well with everyone."

"He was such a charmer," Agatha added. "He was so very well-mannered as a boy. So popular in school, with all the teachers as well as the other students."

Her husband nodded. "Yes. Popular with his coaches too. He was the fly-half on the school's rugby team right up to senior year." He tilted his chin towards a cabinet full of trophies and medals. "Thought he might make it professionally, but he picked up a bad ankle injury in the regional semi-finals and, well, that was that. I still think if it hadn't been for that break, we'd have seen him in an England shirt. Didn't I say that, Agatha?"

"You did," Agatha agreed as if by rote.

"So, he had a lot of friends when he was younger?" Esther asked. "But less so recently?" She made a show of consulting her notes. "His wife said he didn't socialise much.

Harold let out a heavy breath. "He became very work-focused after college," he told her. "Not a bad thing, being industrious and ambitious. He was doing well for himself."

"What about friends from his childhood? Did he have any close ones he kept in touch with?"

Agatha frowned thoughtfully, but it was Harold who

replied.

"He used to be friendly with most of the rugby team," he said. "I remember Don Hawkins's boy Charlie, and Gary Hetherington. You remember Gary, Agatha?"

Agatha nodded, and her face became pinched with sympathy. "Oh yes, poor boy!" She turned to Esther. "Gary's parents were killed in an accident when he was in college. A car crash in… Was it France, Harold?"

"I think so," he replied. "Somewhere down the south of the country."

"And Gary an only child too. Very sad," Agatha said, distracted from her loss for a brief moment, although Esther watched her face as her own tragedy stole over her again.

"You think he might have kept in touch with them? Charlie Hawkins and Gary Hetherington?"

Harold shook his head. "Haven't heard him talk about any of the old team in quite a while. Not sure what the Hawkins boy did after school. Not rugby, though he was a pretty talented young fellow. And it was from one of Agatha's friends that we heard about the Hetheringtons' car accident. At the funeral, I got the impression Carlton and Gary hadn't been in touch for a while."

"Was there tension between them?"

"No, not tension, just… they weren't as natural with each other as they had been. Carlton went to Cambridge and Gary attended some business school in London, King's College, or maybe it was UCL, can't be sure. You know how it is with friends from school… you just drift apart."

Esther quashed thoughts of her own childhood, dragged from school to school. She hadn't had anyone close enough to drift away from.

"What about Mark Sterling?" she asked.

Harold's face seemed to darken when he heard the name, and Agatha's mouth tightened into a firm line.

"Was he a friend of Carlton's too?" Esther asked.

Agatha gave her husband a sideways glance before she spoke. "Yes," she said. "In their final year at Belfield Grammar, Gary, Mark and Carlton became a bit of a trio. Thick as thieves."

"Bad influence, that boy," Harold growled.

"Were they in any bother together?"

"A few minor things," Harold said dismissively. "That Sterling kid was behind it all. Gary was a good lad, and he and Carlton were never in any trouble before they fell in with that brat."

"What kind of minor things do you mean?"

"Silly pranks," Harold replied, a touch exasperated.

"There was some vandalism at the school," Agatha explained, sensing her husband's mood but realising Esther needed a bit more detail. "Spray paint. The boys were implicated, although they never confirmed who actually did it. That, and the police caught the three of them smoking some pot once. Just foolish things. Kid stuff."

"Carlton was grounded for a month after the drugs incident," Harold muttered.

"We tried to get Gary and Carlton to stay away from Mark," Agatha said. "But you know what teenagers are like. They were very close in their final year."

"And they all just drifted apart after school?"

Agatha nodded. "I'm not sure what happened to the Sterling boy, but we haven't heard Carlton mention his name for a long time either."

"Can't say I'm sorry about it," Harold remarked.

"Were either of you aware that Gary Hetherington has gone missing in London?" Esther asked.

From their surprised expressions, it was clear that they weren't.

"When did this happen?" Harold asked, a deep frown furrowing his brow.

"He's been missing for over a month now," Esther replied. "The London Metropolitan Police are working to try and find him."

"Has that got something to do with what happened to Carlton?" Agatha asked. Esther could see she was getting upset again.

"I can't say that it has," she replied. "It's quite possible that his disappearance is completely unrelated. Especially if they haven't had any real contact with one another for a long time. I'm just trying to get as much background as I can on Carlton, his associates, his past relationships."

Agatha had pulled a tissue from her sleeve and was blowing her nose as discreetly as she could. Esther sensed it was time to leave. She retrieved a card from her bag and handed it to Harold.

"I'll let you get back to your guests," she said. "If you think of anything else, or you have any questions, just give me a call."

She shook their hands and allowed herself to be escorted to the front door. The hum of conversation still emanated from the kitchen. More refreshments had been laid out in the hall. There was a table with plates of biscuits and teacups and, off to one side, bottles of whiskey and brandy. And vodka. Esther averted her eyes quickly as Harold Riddell opened the front door for her. Murmuring her condolences once again, she reminded him that she was only a phone call away, and hurried out.

12

BELFIELD BIOTECH WAS a different beast on a Monday morning. The parking lot that had appeared so huge on Saturday seemed inadequately small now that it was packed full of cars, and Esther and Jared were fortunate to find an empty space in the visitors' section.

Once again, Lightbody was waiting for them at reception. The young executive was different today too, brisker and more business-like. The trace of anxiety remained, but he seemed more focused than he had on Saturday.

After hurried greetings, he led Esther and Jared straight to the elevators.

"We've made something of a discovery," he told them, keeping his voice low. "I'll explain after you've met Gavin. He knows you're coming and he's waiting in his office for you."

Esther had already made enquiries with Border Force. They had confirmed that Gavin Smythe was indeed in

Canada when Carlton Riddell was killed, but Esther felt he was worth a quick shakedown all the same, given what they knew about his relationship with the victim.

"Does this discovery pertain to Mister Smythe?" she asked, as they stepped into the lift and Lightbody pressed the button. "Because if it does, I'd rather we knew before we met him."

Lightbody shook his head. "Not at all. If anything, I think it might rather rule him out. We made extensive enquiries into all the recent activity at the plant. I had our security team go through the CCTV in our restricted areas hour-by-hour for the past month."

"And what was it you found, Mister Lightbody?" Jared asked.

Lightbody took a deep breath. "It seems Carlton Riddell was accessing information that he shouldn't have been accessing, shortly before his death."

The elevator pinged and the doors slid open. They were on the same floor as last time, although on this occasion they struck out in the opposite direction. The place was alive this time round, the sounds of people talking on phones or taking part in video conferences drifting from open office doors, along with the clattering of keyboards and the whirr of printers and copiers. The odd passer-by glanced at them curiously, stepping to one side to let them pass.

Lightbody stopped at an open door a few down from Carlton Riddell's office. Gavin Smythe stood at his window with his hands in his pockets, staring out across a rather bleak vista of parking lots and factory roofs. He turned when Lightbody tapped at his door and led the police officers into the room.

Smythe was tall, and handsome in a roguish kind of way. He had a mop of brown hair and the kind of tan that doesn't come naturally if you spend most of your year under Belfield's grey skies. His square jaw sported a stylish stubble.

Lightbody made swift introductions. Smythe, unsmiling, indicated to a set of leather settees and an armchair, which were arranged around a coffee table at the back of the room. As Esther, Jared and Lightbody took seats, he lifted a large manila envelope from his desk and dropped it on the coffee table.

"That's for you, detectives," he said, a touch of surliness in his voice.

Esther lifted the envelope. It wasn't sealed. "What's this?" she asked, as she pulled it open and sifted through the contents.

"Receipts, ticket stubs, credit card payments," Smythe replied, taking the armchair across from them. "That's what you want, isn't it? Proof I wasn't here? That I didn't kill Carlton?"

Esther glanced sideways at Lightbody, who had the decency to look embarrassed. She turned back to Smythe.

"You are not a suspect in the killing of Carlton Riddell, Mister Smythe," she told him. "Not at present. If you were, we would not be having this conversation in your office. We would be down at the police station."

Smythe coloured a bit at that, then cleared his throat and fixed her with his sharp blue eyes. He really was quite good looking, even with the pout.

"What do you want to know?" he asked.

Esther pulled out her notebook. "Let's start with what you can tell us about your relationship with Carlton

Riddell."

Smythe shrugged. "We weren't close. I didn't know the guy all that well, outside of work. Sure, we're both senior sales executives, but that means we work different contracts. He works—he *worked*—the Asian and Pacific market, I work the American. There wasn't much overlap."

"What about the last time you saw him?" she asked. "When was that?"

"It was the monthly sales review meeting. About two weeks ago?"

He glanced questioningly at Lightbody, who smoothed out his tie and said, "We can confirm the date, but that's about right. Start of the month."

Smythe went on. "He gave a short presentation about a contract with an Australian pharmacy chain. I met him in the corridor afterwards. Told him it was a good presentation. He said thanks. That was it."

"How did he seem?" Jared asked.

Smythe grimaced. "Same as usual. Tense. Truth is, Carlton never seemed anything *but* wound up, as far as I could tell. Maybe he wasn't always like that, but I've only been here a couple of years. He didn't seem any different to his usual self that day."

Esther studied Smythe as he spoke. It was a pretty routine method that she and Jared used, the other person asking a question here and there to let the lead interviewer study the subject. Smythe seemed credible. A bit disgruntled at having thought himself a suspect, perhaps, but he didn't appear to be trying to hide anything. She told herself that his handsome square-jawed face and beautiful blue eyes had nothing to do with her wanting to cross him off her list of potential suspects.

"There must have been a little bit of rivalry between you two, though," Jared said. "Both top sales executives, competing for a bonus every year."

Smythe fixed him with a level look. "That bonus is generous, but certainly not a reason to commit murder, Detective," he said flatly.

"No big blow-outs, then?" Esther asked. "No arguments or disputes?"

Smythe turned his gaze on her. "No. Nothing like that. If you need convincing of it, then I suggest you talk to the other staff here."

Jared asked a few more questions about the structures of their teams, how the other staff interacted, and whether there was any tension or unusual behaviour within the department. But he was grasping at straws now, and Esther had already decided there was nothing more to be gained from questioning Gavin Smythe.

When she finally caught Jared's eye, she gave him a quick nod—time to wrap it up—and they both stood and thanked Smythe for his time. Esther passed him her card, with a suggestion that he call her if he thought of anything else that might be useful to the investigation. He seemed to relax a little now the interview was over. He finally cracked a smile as he studied her card and said he would be sure to do that. She had to suppress the urge to smile back. She saw a flash of the charm this guy could deploy. He probably made a very good salesman.

They left Smythe and followed Lightbody back to his large corner office to see what it was he had discovered.

Esther was not surprised to find Donald Preston seated at the long conference table as they stepped into the room. On the table in front of him were three sets of documents.

The first, Esther recognised as the copies of the papers they'd found in Carlton's briefcase. The second was a page that looked like some kind of log or account, with a USB stick sitting on top of it. The third was a sheet of paper containing what appeared to be a list of addresses.

"Detectives, you know Donald Preston from last time?" Lightbody said, as he circled the table.

Instead of sitting, however, he moved behind the top chair and leaned forward with his hands gripping the back of it. Preston had risen as they'd entered, and so now all four of them were standing around the table.

"As you know," Lightbody continued, "the documents you brought us consisted of developmental research. Information Carlton shouldn't have had access to, and certainly not something he should have been carrying around the streets in his briefcase."

More focused or not, Lightbody still sounded on edge. He glanced at Preston, and the lawyer seemed to take this as a cue.

"Our security team and I have reviewed CCTV from the last month in all the restricted areas of our plant and offices," Preston said. "This is your copy of our findings." He slid the log sheet and USB stick across the table towards them. "It shows Carlton Riddell using a stolen swipe card to access laboratory offices on the eighteenth and twenty-first of November. Since our footage is only kept in memory for a month, we have nothing covering him taking the swipe card, or any previous trespasses into the secure areas… but I think we can safely assume this was the last in a series of such breaches."

"What did he do in the lab?" Jared asked.

"The lab offices," Lightbody corrected. "These are the

offices of our scientists and technical supervisors. It's where the test results, formulae and technical information about our products are kept on secure servers. Although Carlton got into the laboratory wing, he didn't have any way of logging in. Unfortunately, there appears to have been a certain amount of hardcopy data available there. One of our laboratory supervisors' desks was insecure and Carlton managed to get his hands on… well, we're still confirming exactly *what* Miss Anderson had on hardcopy in there, but part of it forms what you retrieved from Mister Riddell's briefcase. It contains detailed information about an early stage of the development of Fluraxonyl. I'm sure I don't need to explain to either of you how damaging it would be to our company and the confidence of our shareholders if this information was leaked. We can only assume that Carlton was planning to sell it, if he hadn't done so already. Fluraxonyl is worth billions."

Esther decided to play devil's advocate.

"If Carlton's killers were after the formula for your new drug, why would they leave these documents behind?" she asked.

The conversation was making Lightbody tense again. His knuckles were white on the back of the chair.

"Perhaps there were more copies?" he offered. "Or they got spooked?"

"And these documents," Jared put in, "the ones we've found… they'd be worth a pretty penny, I take it?"

Preston and Lightbody exchanged glances. It was the lawyer who answered.

"At the moment we don't know *how much* information has been compromised," he said. "The material found in Mister Riddell's briefcase"—this with a nod towards the first pile, the copies of the documents Esther had shared—"are not enough on their own to give a competitor all they need to start their own manufacturing. But it's a healthy boost to anyone trying to develop something similar."

He leaned forward again and slid the third pile, the pages with a list of addresses, across the table.

"This is a list of pharmaceutical companies, both British and international. Firms we would class as prime suspects for this type of activity." He paused and fixed Jared with a firm look. "Make no mistake, we are reporting the theft, or attempted theft, of this material, and we would like you to look into this criminal behaviour, given how intrinsically linked it appears to be to your murder investigation."

It was Esther and Jared's turn to share a look.

"Okay, Mister Preston," Jared said, "we'll arrange to have formal statements taken from you and Mister Lightbody and begin making some enquiries." He hesitated, then pulled the list of suspect companies closer, brow furrowed. "I see a lot of German-based companies listed here."

It was Lightbody who answered this time. "Germany is home to the biggest pharmaceutical sector in the EU. If Carlton was selling the secrets of Fluraxonyl, he would have had more potential buyers in Germany than any other country. Carlton spoke German fluently, and had used it to his advantage when he worked the EU market."

Jared glanced at Esther again, and she immediately knew what he was thinking. *Steiner.*

"What about Riddell's contacts in Britain and the EU?" she asked. "Do you have a record of people he corresponded with?"

"We've supplied the entirety of Mister Riddell's contact

list," Preston replied, nodding towards the set of numbers and addresses. "We trust you won't abuse the information, and will apply your professionalism and discretion."

Sure enough, as Jared leafed through the pages of the third pile, Esther could see it was an alphabetized contact list full of phone numbers as well as addresses. Jared flicked from G to S quickly, but there was no Gerhard Steiner.

"And these are all of Carlton's contacts?" Esther asked. "No other names he might have listed somewhere?"

"That's all we could find," Preston told her emphatically. "If Mister Riddell had other contacts, he didn't keep them here."

Esther frowned. They'd already had a search team go through Riddell's home office—a sensitive task in the circumstances, but one that Eva Riddell had not raised any objections to—and they'd found very little there. Suspiciously little. It seemed Carlton Riddell had been careful to avoid keeping too much evidence of his dealings on record. Unfortunately, that cautious approach was now hampering their investigation into his murder…

"Can we trust you'll keep us updated as victims in this matter?" Preston asked. "Now that we are filing a formal complaint of theft?"

Jared nodded. "Of course. We'll keep you apprised of anything that concerns your company. I'll have someone call in this afternoon to record the details."

Once the DI had made arrangements with Lightbody and Preston, they took their new exhibits, bid Donald Preston good day, and followed Lightbody back down to reception. He escorted them all the way to the front doors once more. Their ten minutes of conversation had eroded his mask; Esther thought he looked every inch the man under pressure again, as he said to Jared, "I trust you'll keep us fully updated, Inspector? With any breakthroughs?"

Jared nodded. "Of course, Mister Lightbody."

Lightbody's smile was limp, his brow a touch damp as he said his goodbyes.

Back in the car, Esther sat for a moment, hands on the steering wheel, staring up at the impressive glass edifice that served as Belfield BioTech's corporate façade.

"You're not convinced?" Jared asked.

"I've been thinking about it," Esther replied. "Thinking about it a lot, actually. If you wanted to steal the details of a medicine potentially worth *billions* of pounds, you'd be doing your best to keep it on the down-low, don't you think? Try to avoid letting anyone know they'd been stolen *at all.* Killing your source is a big fail from a clandestine point of view."

"Maybe there was a last-minute hitch, a fall-out over terms? After all, it is *big* money. When people fall out over big money the consequences can be… well, fatal."

"Then why leave all the documents behind?" she mused. "They must have known or suspected it would raise alarm bells here."

"Maybe it's like Lightbody said, they got spooked. Or they had what they needed, and leaving the paperwork behind was a bid to throw us off."

"You heard what Derek said. Gerhard Steiner never left the hotel room after his meeting with Riddell. He stayed in there until he checked out the next day."

"But we know that Steiner might not have been working alone."

"One thing's for sure," Esther said, as she stuck the car into reverse and finally pulled out, "we need to get our hands on this Steiner guy."

13

IT WAS LATE. The CID offices were in darkness apart from the sergeants' office, where Esther sat alone in the silence. She was staring at an email from the Traffic Camera Department, advising her there'd been no noteworthy vehicles picked up by any of their cameras within four square miles of the cemetery on Friday morning. Nothing linked to Peter Darren or local drugs gangs. Reading the email again didn't really bring her any relief; she was still sure the man standing among the gravestones had been watching her. Just because there hadn't been any suspect vehicles nearby at the time didn't mean he hadn't been one of Darren's goons.

She clicked the email closed and turned her attention to the task at hand.

She and Jared had come straight back to the station after their visit to Belfield BioTech that morning. During a sit-down with Derek Grant, they had worked their way through their new lines of enquiry. But an enthusiastic start was quickly dampened by the inherent bureaucracy of getting information from other agencies. Grant had come back to her after a few hours with very little in the way of solid feedback about Steiner or his movements. Most applications had either been returned for clarification, or answered with a generic line to advise them their request was being processed. It was frustrating, but Esther was getting all too used to it. As technology advanced to make policing quicker and more efficient, some wanker at a desk on the top floor invented a way to slow everything down again with more paperwork. The truth was, they might be days waiting for anything to come back from the European forces, the German Bundespolizei chief among them. And even though the nature of Riddell's murder, the brutality of it, had been leading Esther away from the idea that it was linked to the trade in industrial secrets, the CCTV clearly showed Steiner and Riddell had been up to *something*, and that something was starting to look very much like corporate espionage. She hoped Grant discovered something soon; she wanted to know who this Steiner guy really was, and what he'd been up to with Carlton Riddell in that hotel room.

She looked at the collection of pages spread out next to her computer keyboard. Late in the afternoon she'd managed to get in contact with the London Met detective working the Gary Hetherington case, a guy called Pierce Goddard. He'd emailed the documents to her and talked her through most of them over the phone.

Just as Agatha Riddell had said, Hetherington's parents had been killed in a car crash on a motorway north of Nice eight years ago. The accident had happened in the early summer, so the timing didn't coincide with his recent disappearance, and there was no indication he'd vanished on the anniversary of any other tragedy either. Goddard had interviewed both Hetherington's ex-girlfriend and his boss several times—these two being the closest contacts Hetherington had in his life these days—but both had dismissed the idea that he was depressed or suicidal. The ex-girlfriend insisted their split had been amicable and it was Hetherington who'd ended it. Too busy at work, apparently. And the hedge fund manager said Hetherington was on a long, successful run with his portfolio and really seemed to enjoy his work, always in good spirits.

Still, Goddard hadn't completely ruled out the possibility of suicide; Hetherington's ex and boss were the closest people the man had to friends. With no siblings and no close family, it seemed Gary Hetherington had become somewhat isolated during his time in London. Add in that he hadn't seen his ex in almost four months, that he wasn't all that close to any of his colleagues outside of work, and the personal circumstances factor led Goddard right back around to the idea he might be depressed and potentially suicidal.

In an effort to cover all bases, he had asked the manager at the firm to have their accountant double-check every one of his transactions, in case they were missing something—perhaps Hetherington had been embezzling, or covering a huge loss somehow, or perhaps he had straight-out stolen and done a bunk. But no, it all turned out clean and clear. The Met had run checks on Hetherington's personal accounts too. Everything looked normal—normal for a rich guy, anyway—and nothing had been withdrawn since he'd gone missing.

Goddard told Esther he'd taken several colleagues with

him early on in the investigation and done a thorough search of Hetherington's flat. Again, nothing of any relevance had turned up. No suicide notes, no letters from abroad. His passport was in a bedside drawer, and all the ports had been checked already in any event. If Gary Hetherington had left the country, he'd done so incognito. His car was still in the underground parking lot at his apartment block too. A Ferrari Portofino. Goddard had spoken of this as if it should mean something to Esther, and when she hadn't replied he'd gone on about how Gary Hetherington must have been pretty flush to have a car like that just sitting about.

The London detective had ended the call with an admission that he was stumped, and if Esther spotted anything he'd missed, he'd be very grateful for any help. She had perused the paperwork he'd sent her for an hour or so now, but she didn't see anything Goddard hadn't already considered and made enquiries about. Nothing, that was, apart from the fact that Gary Hetherington and Carlton Riddell—a missing person and a homicide victim—had both been childhood friends…

Somewhere out on the darkened CID floor she heard a jangle of keys. A moment later she sensed, more than heard, the presence of someone at her office door. She looked up to see DCI Brian Small standing in the doorway, his coat slung over one arm.

"Hey-ho," he said, in his nasally, high-pitched voice, "I heard you had a tendency to burn the midnight oil, DS Penman."

"Just running over some case notes, sir," Esther replied. "I find it easier to concentrate when there are no phones ringing."

The DCI chuckled. "I hear ya," he said, as he tossed his coat across the back of a nearby chair, sat into it and rolled it across the floor until he was sitting next to her at the desk. "What is it you've got here?"

Esther tried to sound casual, despite the unease she felt at his sudden proximity. "It's the misper case from London," she replied, a little stiffly despite her efforts. "He went to school with our murder victim. Went missing shortly before Riddell was killed. It might be nothing, but…"

Small leaned in closer as she spoke, so close that she could smell his cologne thick in her nostrils. Could feel his knee pressing against her thigh.

She cleared her throat, "Sir, I—"

But Small cut in before she could finish. He was looking at her intently now, his face way too close for comfort, his voice breathy as he spoke.

"You sure you can manage this case, Esther?" he asked. "It's a big one. If you need a little extra help, I can arrange it. I'm here for you. I'm here to take the load off." He placed his hand over hers. "Whatever you need, Esther."

Esther snatched her hand back and used her foot to push herself backwards, rolling her seat away from him so that there was another yard between them and she was facing him squarely. She glared at him.

"Thank you for your concern, sir," she snapped. "But I'm fine. And I think you should leave now."

Small studied her for a moment. He looked amused, but when he spoke there was more than a trace of malice in his voice.

"Well, Esther, that's for me to decide," he replied. He stood and picked up his coat. "And you needn't act so prim and proper. Not with your reputation."

With that, he turned and walked out the door.

Esther listened to his footsteps fade, too stunned to speak. All indignation had drained from her with that last comment, the disdain in his voice as he'd said it leaching the fight right out of her.

Not with your reputation.

After a while, she turned back to the papers on her desk, but she couldn't concentrate now. She switched off her computer and locked the pages of the misper case away in her desk. Then she grabbed her coat and headed for the door.

There was no one in the carpark as she made her way to her little Fiat, but that didn't stop her scanning the near-empty lot right up until she sat into the driver's seat and started the engine. Hard as she tried to put it out of her mind, the exchange replayed itself over and over in her head as she drove out of the station and east towards Sarsbury. The streets might have been bright with Christmas lighting, but the world felt suddenly dark to Esther now.

On the edge of Belfield city, she pulled in at the forecourt of a twenty-four-hour convenience store. Inside, she marched straight to the freezer section and grabbed the biggest tub of chocolate ice-cream she could find.

Then she noticed the liquor aisle at the back.

She wanted to believe that there was some small part of her that fought the instinct, some angel on her shoulder trying to pull her back while the demon inside drove her towards the booze. She wanted to believe it, but it didn't really feel that way. Before she had time to think, she was standing in front of a shelf full of vodka bottles. With only the briefest of hesitations, she reached out and selected a shoulder of her old brand and headed for the till.

Her fingers were trembling as she set the ice-cream and the vodka down on the counter in front of the clerk. He clearly noticed the shake in her hands because he gave her a double-take. Feeling her face flush, she kept her eyes down, willing the kid to hurry up and get on with it. When he asked her if there was anything else, she shook her head, paid, and left quickly, stuffing the bottle of vodka into her coat pocket as she went.

14

MARK STERLING WAS uncomfortably aware that his twenty-year-old Vauxhall looked well out of place in the neighbourhood of Belfield known as The Hills, a neighbourhood that was home to more than a few local millionaires. He was parked in the shadow of a bare-limbed oak, one of a host of old trees that lined the wide, arrow-straight boulevard. The houses here were gated, and guarded by high walls and fences, and Vicky's was no different. He stared across the road at the mansion she called home, all glass and balconies and expensive stonework. It squatted atop a small hill, overlooking the sandstone perimeter wall and positioned to capture an attractive vista of Belfield in the valley below. In the summer the house would be screened by the leaves of the street's oak trees, but now, in the heart of winter, Mark had a clear view of it through the branches, along with its paved driveway and elaborate fountains. Victoria Ellsmith—or Mansfield, as she was now—had done well for herself since high school.

He sank lower in his seat as the front door of the house opened and Vicky's husband emerged. Mark studied him. He wore a dark Mackintosh raincoat and carried a leather briefcase in one hand. The man was tall, but built like a stork, all knees and elbows. His face was gaunt and grey, and he wore spectacles perched on a beak of a nose. He was in his early fifties, with a cap of silver hair parted carefully on one side. Mark wondered what Vicky saw in the man, and then decided that what she saw was money. As he watched, Mansfield folded himself into a sporty black Porsche—one of three luxury cars that sat beneath a shelter extending from the side of the house—and the gate at the bottom of the drive began to open.

Mark stayed low in his seat as the Porsche emerged and disappeared in the direction of town.

When he straightened up again, Vicky was hustling from the house, bundled against the cold in a short fur coat that did little to hide her tight lycra work-out gear beneath. She was still the blonde bombshell with the cracking body she'd been in high school. With a pang, Mark suddenly felt an old flood of emotions surge through him, feelings Vicky used to elicit regularly in him during their time at school together. Feelings like desire, and obsession.

Feelings like jealousy.

He'd always envied Gary, who'd never seemed to appreciate just how gorgeous his girlfriend was. Mark had certainly appreciated it. And he wasn't the only one. Shit, half the boys at school had probably been picturing Vicky Ellsmith when they tugged themselves off at night. For Mark, seeing her now woke all those passions once more, like a wave crashing over him. He felt like he was sixteen years old all over again.

He tried to suppress the tide of emotion as he watched her scurry down the drive and cross the street towards him. She pulled open the passenger door and sat in. Her jaw was clenched and her tone was angry when she spoke.

"You shouldn't come by my house," she said. "How'd you know where I live?"

Mark feigned nonchalance. He shrugged, revealing no hint of the feelings she'd stirred, an art well-practiced during his teenage years.

"You don't keep up with old friends, Vicky?" he asked. "Not curious to see how everyone's doing these days?"

"We left school ten years ago, Mark," she replied acerbically.

"Was that old man Mansfield in the Porsche?" he said. "Shit, Vicky, he must be twice your age!"

She ignored the jibe. "From now on we meet in town, okay?"

Mark said nothing. He felt stung. He'd hoped their reunion might strike a different chord this time. Hoped vainly for some sign of a spark between them. A spark that had never been there when they were younger.

Vicky, perhaps sensing his darkening mood, softened her tone. "Well, what have you found out?"

"Alfie doesn't live at his old address. There's some old woman living there now. And I can't find him online."

She let out a long, shaky breath.

"Yeah," she replied. "Me neither." She hesitated. "Do you really think it's him?"

"I don't know," he told her, genuinely unsure. "But if it's a coincidence, it's a pretty fucking big one." He glanced at her. "Do you still have the video?"

She didn't answer straight away.

"Vicky, do you still have the video?"

"I'm not sure. It might be on an old laptop."

"You need to delete that video, Vicky! Search every device you have and get rid of it! Today!"

"Should we…" She looked at him, her brow knit in a worried frown. "Should we maybe tell the police—"

"Vicky, listen to me! You need to erase all trace of that fucking video. Every hint of it. Everything! Do you hear me?"

She looked irritated, but there was a touch of uncertainty in her eyes.

Mark forced himself to chill. Tried a different approach.

"We need to play this carefully," he said. "If it is him, then we don't want to go bringing up things we don't have to. I just need a few days to… to see what more I can find out. And come up with a plan." He was trying for a more confident, reassuring tone, but he wasn't sure how convincing he sounded. "We gotta make sure no one knows about that video, Vicky. You don't want cops linking you to that shit. You know what big, ugly, sex-starved prison chicks do to pretty things like you on the inside?"

He saw her shudder.

"You want to find out?" he pressed.

She shook her head.

"Then give me a day or two to come up with something."

The thing was, Vicky didn't know everything. She didn't know about the blackmail. What she *did* know, she considered bad enough, and Mark needed to keep the rest of it from her if he didn't want her blabbing to the Old Bill, because he knew that no matter how long ago a thing happened, the cops would come after him for it. And if he got convicted one more time, it'd be the slammer for sure.

"Besides, if he wanted to kill you, he'd probably have done it already," he muttered. "He always liked you."

That much was true. He'd always liked Vicky. But he had no reason to like Mark Sterling. Quite the opposite.

"Don't tell the cops anything about that video, understand?" he emphasised. "And keep your doors locked, just in case."

He heard her breath catch at that last comment, but it was clearly sensible advice in the circumstances. They didn't know what was happening yet. Didn't hurt to be cautious.

"Fuck!" she said. "Ten *years!* Why wait *ten fucking years?"*

Mark had no answer to that. "Keep your messages non-specific," he told her. "If we need to speak about this, we'll meet."

"Not here," she replied. "There's a coffee-shop half a mile towards town. Berta's. If we have to meet, we'll meet there."

"Okay. And if either one of us hears anything, we get in touch straight away."

Vicky nodded. Then, without another word, she got out of the car and slammed the door. He watched her hurry back across the street to the gates of her mansion, his eyes drifting down her body as she went. The sight of her perfectly sculpted ass in that tight pink spandex was making him grow hard.

With a frustrated grunt, he shoved his Vauxhall into gear and drove away.

15

THE FIRST THING Esther saw when she woke to the sound of her mobile phone ringing was the vodka bottle sitting on her beside cabinet, the label of her old favourite greeting her as it had so many times before. She sat up with a jolt, pushing herself away from it as though afraid it might attack her. But then she saw that the bottle was still full, the seal unbroken, and she felt a flood of relief.

She snatched up her ringing phone.

"Hello?"

"Esther?" It was Jared. Even half-asleep, she caught the edge in his voice.

"Yes, I'm here," she replied, swinging her legs out of the bed. "What's up?"

"We have Steiner!"

"We *have* him?"

"Well, we haven't actually *got hold* of him yet," he conceded, "but we've identified him, and we know where he's going to be in approximately… four hours. Derek tracked him down with the help of Border Force. Turns out Steiner is his real name after all. German national. He flew out of the country on Friday via East Midlands, but get this: he flew *back* into Stansted yesterday morning. He's due to fly out again this afternoon. Can you be ready if I stop by your place? I can be there in half an hour. We've already alerted the police at the airport, but if we hit the road straight away we can make it."

"Yeah," Esther replied quickly. "I'll be ready."

She hung up and dropped the phone onto the bed. Then she sat motionless for a moment, staring at the bottle of vodka. She didn't want Jean to see it, but she wouldn't be able to get rid of it right now without her aunt noticing; Esther could hear her pottering about in the kitchen below, the clink of crockery in the sink.

Quickly, as though it might bite her if she held it for too long, she snatched the bottle off the cabinet and stuffed it under her pillow. That would have to do for now.

She went to get changed.

* * *

This close to Christmas, Jared should have expected the heavy traffic, but it was frustrating him all the same. They were southbound on the motorway, sitting in the rightmost overtake lane where they'd spent most of the journey. Yet he'd hardly got over sixty miles an hour the entire trip, and there were strips of bypass which had been far more sluggish than that. Thankfully, the brief flurry of snow just outside Belfield had cleared and melted quickly, and the roads had stayed dry since.

He checked his watch again, even though the clock on the dash was right in front of him. A nervous habit.

He'd briefed Esther after he'd picked her up. Derek Grant seemed to have received feedback from every agency, foreign and domestic, all at once this morning, and he'd quickly pieced together a picture of Gerhard Steiner and his movements. The man was a freelance contractor who worked regularly with several European pharma giants. Forty-two years old. Registered addresses in Munich and Berlin. No convictions. Spent his life in an airplane, by the looks of his recent travel activities. He'd been in and out of the UK five times already in the last three months. He seemed to crisscross the skies of Europe regularly, travelling a couple of times a week, mostly within the EU, but not exclusively. Interpol had no intel, no alerts. On the face of it, Herr Gerhard Steiner was squeaky-clean. On the face of it. Some might see that as a strength, going into a criminal enterprise, but in Jared's experience it was the squeaky-clean ones who squealed first in an interview. It was the squeaky-clean ones who weren't used to being questioned by the police…

Derek and Liz had driven on ahead, and Jared hoped they'd arrived at London Stansted by now. If not, there would be officers from UK Border Force and Essex Police there anyway, standing by to detain Steiner whenever he showed up. Still, Jared wanted to be there. He pushed past another coach, closing in on the next set of taillights. A quick look at the speedometer. Fifty-five. He sighed and tapped the steering wheel irritably.

He glanced over at Esther, who was leaning with her arm against the car door, head propped on her hand, staring out at the traffic. She'd been unusually quiet ever since he'd collected her from her aunt's house. Now that he thought about it, she'd hardly asked him anything at all about Steiner, or any of Grant's other discoveries; she'd just let him talk away uninterrupted.

"You okay?" he asked.

She didn't respond.

"Esther?"

"Do I have a reputation at the station, Jared?"

Jared felt a sliver of unease creep through him. Shifting uncomfortably in his seat, he took advantage of an opening in the traffic to push past another couple of slower-moving cars.

"Jared?"

He cleared his throat. "You're the best detective on the force. You've got a reputation for that."

"That's not what I mean."

The silence stretched. Jared focused on the traffic in front of him.

"Jared? Do I?"

He was starting to sweat. "You might be known as a bit of a heartbreaker, I suppose," he said haltingly.

"A 'heartbreaker'?" Esther asked quietly.

He sneaked another sidelong glance at her. She wasn't looking at him. She was still staring into the distance.

"A 'heartbreaker'," she repeated, as if trying out an unfamiliar word. She turned to him. "What do you mean, a 'heartbreaker'?"

Jared fixed his eyes on the back of an articulated truck up ahead. His collar was too tight. The old Volvo that had seemed to take an age to heat up this morning now suddenly felt like a sauna.

"Jared?"

"Well," he said, as he reached down and adjusted the air-conditioner, searching for a breath of cooler air, "you remember James? And William? Both of those young fellas moved station under a cloud. You'd gone out with both of them briefly before they transferred out… and there were a few others too, I think. I guess you might have developed a reputation as a bit of a man-eater, maybe."

Esther snorted. "Man-eater. Heartbreaker. Why don't you just say it the way it is, Jared. People think I'm a slut."

Jared sucked in a breath. "Now, I never said that. I've never heard you called that."

"No," Esther replied quietly, eyes drifting to the distance again. "They wouldn't say that around you."

She lapsed into silence. Jared frowned. He'd never seen Esther like this before.

"Esther," he said softly, "where on earth is this coming from? Has something happened?"

When she didn't reply, he went on.

"Everyone in that office looks up to you. I know that for a fact. You're the best cop I've ever worked with, and the best sergeant they've ever had. You're a hands-on, get-the-job-done kind of skipper, and cops love that. I've had complaints about sergeants from teams over the years, but none of those detectives have ever complained about you."

He risked another sideways glance at her. She was still staring out the window, face expressionless.

"Esther, what's going on?" he asked. "What's happened?"

"Never mind. Doesn't matter."

"Esther—"

"No, Jared. Just leave it. Forget I said anything."

He couldn't think of anything else to say or how to change the subject without being clumsy and obvious about it, so he said nothing. The silence was like a suffocating blanket.

The truth was, even though he might not have heard that particular word used about Esther, she did have a reputation. Two very different reputations, really. She was the best detective in the constabulary, like he'd said, and she was known for being gutsy and clever, tenacious and thorough. But there was another side to her too. Her reputation for drinking and sleeping around was pretty well-established as well. These were things Jared had been happy to ignore. The drinking, because he came from a time when being a heavy drinker was synonymous with being a copper, and he had a fondness for the odd tipple himself. And the sleeping around… well, times were changing. She was a single young woman who wasn't ready to settle down yet—what business was it of his who she slept with?

He wondered what the hell had happened for her to be acting like this. But she was clearly not willing to talk about it, so they drove the remainder of the way in silence.

The first indication that they were growing close to the airport was the distant string of airplanes, rising and descending against the dull grey clouds. Then came the signposts. Jared flicked on his indicator. Pushing his way into the inside lane, he took the next exit, and almost immediately found himself stuck in a queue of traffic leading up to Bassingbourn Roundabout.

As he edged forward, he began tapping impatiently on the steering wheel again. Another glance at his watch. Steiner could be arriving any minute now, if he wasn't at the airport already. No word from Derek or Liz yet…

Over the course of the next five minutes, they made about twenty yards of progress, with Jared checking his watch a dozen times or more.

"Bugger this," he growled at last.

He flicked on the blue lights on the front grill, twisted a dial to make the sirens chirp a couple of times, and edged around the traffic as far as the roundabout. Once they were off the congested main thoroughfare and onto the emptier service road, he knocked them off again. A few minutes later, they pulled into a parking lot between the terminal and the big, glass-fronted building that was home to a variety of enterprises and agencies, including the airport police station.

He was relieved when Esther seemed to shake off some of her gloom as she fell in beside him. They both showed their warrant cards to the security guard at the door, who phoned upstairs to announce their arrival.

An officer in an Essex Constabulary uniform came down to meet them. She introduced herself as Amy and led them the rest of the way. Detectives Grant and Fellowes had already arrived, she confirmed, and were currently briefing the team.

When they got to the briefing room, they found Grant and Fellowes at a table with half a dozen uniformed officers, passing around printed stills of Gerhard Steiner. Grant was speaking.

"…is due to take the flight to Frankfurt, scheduled for departure at thirteen-forty hours, but since we know he hasn't passed through security yet, we'll try to intercept him once he gets to the scanners. DC Fellowes and I will approach him alone and ask him to step aside and take him to the security interview room. We hope he'll cooperate voluntarily at this stage, but, given the circumstances, any obstruction or evasiveness will give us probable cause for an arrest. If the rest of you could all spread out, we don't want the sight of too many uniforms spooking him in the queue."

Grant covered the basic grounds for the arrest, should it prove necessary, sketching a bit of background to the murder case they were investigating and highlighting the links between Steiner and the victim. But the plan was that he and Liz would carry out the approach and interception discreetly, along with a plain-clothes Essex officer. Everyone else was there as backup, and as extra pairs of eyes on the concourse to ensure they didn't miss their target. Grant concluded by asking if there were any questions, but no one had any.

He glanced at Esther, who nodded her approval.

"If you and Liz are going to the checkpoint lines," she said, "DI Wilcox and I will take up a position on the concourse-side of security." She turned to the uniform sergeant. "Is there anywhere that would give the best view of the crowds?"

The sergeant in charge of Essex's airport detachment was a wrinkled little man with a thick grey beard and bushy eyebrows. He nodded and stepped over to the giant maps tacked up all over one wall, displaying the airport grounds and a detailed plan of the terminal building.

"Best place for you and the good inspector would be here." He tapped at a point on the map next to a row of retail outlets, close to where people joined the queue to get through security. "Generally speaking, there's plenty of folks in and out of these shops here, but you also have a view of the security lines and the concourse itself. I'll pop a couple of foot patrols here and here, giving you some cover on both sides."

"Thank you," Esther said. "Now, let's run through callsigns and get out on point ASAP."

The uniform sergeant doled out radios with covert earpieces and gave each pair of officers a callsign. Jared and Esther were *Golf Tango Two.* Jared found himself struggling to get the fiddly bits of his earpiece to attach to the covert handset, and he had to let young Amy help him with it. He muttered an abashed "thank you" as she tucked the translucent cable under his collar. Slipping the radio into his pocket, he saw that Esther was already standing at the door, foot tapping.

"Coming, coming, DS Penman," he grumbled. "Don't get your knickers in a twist."

He immediately wanted to swallow back the comment. It wasn't a remark that would normally have fazed either of them, but after this morning's conversation in the car he decided he ought to avoid the mention of undergarments for a while. Luckily, it didn't seem to register with her. They fell in next to one another and made their way across to the terminal building on foot.

The concourse was bustling. Travellers of all sorts, from holidaymakers to businesspeople, filled the atrium with noise and movement. It was even busier than Jared had expected, and although that would help them blend in, it would also make it harder to spot Steiner. He scanned the faces of the crowds as they passed between rows of busy check-in desks and took up a position next to a newsagent, directly across from the security clearance area. A couple of the uniform officers from the briefing were nearby, strolling at a leisurely pace and chatting to one another. Nothing about their demeanour suggested they were looking for anyone, but now and again one of them would cast their eyes slowly over the crowd.

An overhead screen nearby told Jared the flight to Frankfurt was on time. Not boarding yet, but it had already been assigned a gate. A glance at the clock. Surely Steiner would be here soon.

They couldn't have been in position more than five minutes when, out of the corner of his eye, Jared saw Esther straighten and push herself from the wall she'd been lounging against. A moment later, without breaking stride, one of the uniform officers lifted his radio mic and spoke into it. Jared heard the transmission in his ear.

"Golf Tango One, have eyes on the subject. Approaching security desks from the south end. Grey suit, white shirt, brown overnight case."

Jared followed Esther's stare.

There he was, Gerhard Steiner, crossing the concourse towards the security lines, a small piece of carry-on luggage in his left hand. He appeared edgier than he had at the Marriott, searching the faces as he moved through the crowd.

And then, all of a sudden, he locked eyes with Jared, and registered the interest in his stare. A moment later, he noticed Esther watching him too. When he saw the two uniform PCs nearby, his wary expression turned to one of alarm, and he turned on his heel.

"He's turned around, heading back towards the doors," the male officer transmitted, instinctively moving after him.

Glancing over his shoulder, Steiner saw them following, and broke into a run.

* * *

Esther spotted him a split-second before the transmission came through her earpiece. He was wearing the same suit and carrying the same brown overnight bag he'd had when he checked out of the hotel in Belfield last week. Unlike at the hotel, however, this time he looked nervous.

As the uniform officer made his transmission, Esther realised that Jared was standing rigid, staring at Steiner. She was about to hiss at him to relax and look away when Steiner saw them. He noticed Jared first, but then he glanced at Esther and realised they were both watching him. When he saw that the two PCs had eyes on him too, he did a rapid about-turn and headed back the way he came.

As though governed by some kind of automatic reflex, the uniform officers followed him, the male officer talking into his radio mic again. Gerhard Steiner saw it, and immediately took to his heels.

Their cover blown, Esther took off.

Within seconds, she had overtaken Jared and the Essex police officers. A chorus of shrieks rose as Steiner barrelled into a group of Asian tourists coming through the doors. Several people lost their footing and fell to the ground in a tumble of suitcases and angry exclamations. Darting between knots of travellers—wide-eyed children as well as alarmed-looking adults—Esther skirted the melee and raced out into the cold winter air.

Outside, the place was just as busy. The road was choked with taxis and buses, the pavements thronged with pedestrians tugging bits of luggage on wheels this way and that.

As she emerged, Esther caught a glimpse of Steiner disappearing into the crowds on the far side of the road.

She bounded after him.

Slow-moving as the traffic was, a taxi still had to brake hard to avoid hitting her, the driver blasting his horn and shouting obscenities Esther chose to ignore as she hurried on.

She shoved her way between the crowded bus stands, trying to look in every direction at once, but suddenly there was no sign of her quarry. *Shit.*

She caught the eye of a young man lounging against a bus shelter with earbuds in his ears. He was in his late teens, trying to smother his upper-class background in grungy clothing. He nodded towards a taxi rank across the road.

"You looking for that guy?" he asked.

Esther followed his gaze back the way she'd come… and there was Steiner, climbing into the rear seat of a blue taxi just outside the terminal! Fucker must have doubled back as she reached this side of the road, cutting through the buses and coaches to hide his U-turn.

"Thanks, kid!" Esther said, as she turned and darted back through the traffic. She waved at Jared and the other two cops, who were just about to cross the road, and shouted: "The blue taxi! He's getting in the taxi!"

The others turned to look where she was pointing, but it was too late. Steiner's taxi pulled out, already moving away from the terminal building.

Esther was far enough ahead to be able to cut in front of it, and she didn't hesitate. She ran between the cars—attracting another couple of angry horn blasts as she went—and leapt a concrete barrier that separated the exit lanes. She landed about ten yards in front of the blue taxi, just as it was accelerating past a bus. Thrusting her hand out with all the authority she could muster from her traffic duty days, she winced as the blue cab skidded to a halt inches from her shins. The cabbie's eyes were wide, and he was even more startled when two uniformed police officers snatched open the back door of his car and hauled his passenger from the seat.

Esther finally let her hand drop as Jared arrived, puffing hard. He might have intended to say something, but all he could manage, red-faced and breathless, was a thumbs-up.

The two uniform officers put Steiner in handcuffs and led him quickly away. As crowds began to gather around the scene, and phones came out to video the spectacle, Esther grabbed Jared and hurried after them.

16

JARED STUDIED GERHARD Steiner as the German whispered into his solicitor's ear. The lawyer nodded and murmured something back.

He glanced sideways at Esther. She was brooding again. He'd hoped that whatever was eating at her on their trip to the airport had been banished by the excitement of chasing down their suspect and the task of interviewing him.

But things hadn't gone quite the way they'd expected.

They'd made it back to Belfield in less than three hours. The analyst from the Financial Crime Unit who'd been waiting for them when they finished booking Steiner into custody had sifted quickly through the documents seized from Steiner's overnight bag and confirmed that he was toting private accounts and memoranda from another pharma company based in London. Apparently, it was linked to some ongoing operation their unit was running—an operation Steiner had managed to step completely clear of until now.

While Jared was not really interested in the details of Steiner's data thefts, it hadn't stopped him indulging in a little gamesmanship with the lawyer, a small, sweaty man who kept mopping his brow with a monogrammed handkerchief. Jared withheld most of what they knew initially, carrying out a series of short interviews to gauge how much Steiner would disclose to them… and how much he'd disclosed to his solicitor.

Unfortunately, their sense of victory was short-lived. It quickly became obvious that Steiner was genuinely upset by the news of Carlton Riddell's death, and angry that he was suspected of being involved. Even when they'd sprung the prospect of further arrests for the corporate espionage, Steiner just shook his head and muttered angrily that he was not a killer. Only the lawyer seemed intimidated by the array of theft and fraud charges, charges he would have to plough through once Jared and Esther were finished here; the financial crime detectives were already somewhere in the custody suite, preparing to interview Steiner as soon as he was available.

As for the murder investigation, their prospects of a break in the case had diminished even further when the request for a rush on all the phone data from Riddell's and Steiner's devices came back to reveal very little in the way of clandestine communications. What limited contact there had been had come—as they'd both suspected—from Carlton Riddell's personal phone and not his work one. And everything they retrieved from the devices corroborated the version of events Steiner gave in his first interview.

According to Steiner, an initial contact had been arranged to discuss 'opportunities' for work on the continent, and to give Carlton Riddell a chance to show him some 'credentials' in person. The night at the Marriott was the first time the two men had met. There was no evidence that Steiner had been in touch with anyone else that evening; that, together with Steiner's persistent attempts to message and call Riddell in the days since, lent further credence to his story.

Of course, Steiner could be lying. Maybe he was an accomplished actor, and his indignant outrage at the suggestion he had something to do with Carlton Riddell's death was a show. Maybe there was another phone they hadn't recovered.

But Jared didn't think so. While he had no doubt that Financial Crime would glean plenty of damning evidence from Steiner's mobile when they analysed it further, Jared was fairly certain it wouldn't be evidence of a conspiracy to murder.

In fact, those guys had been dubious about that link from the start. The operation they were running involved plenty of theft and fraud and double-dealing, but nothing violent. Theirs was a world of white-collar crimes, offences that only became messy when the criminal stuff got tangled up with civil litigation. There was no blood spilled in the cases they were investigating.

It hadn't taken long for Jared to realise they were heading towards a dead end. Esther seemed to have come to the same conclusion, and she'd drifted away once more.

Jared sensed it was time to wrap things up. Steiner's twenty-four hours for the data theft matters had already begun. The financial crime boys wouldn't be too thrilled if Jared and Esther ate up much more of their custody clock, given the complexity of the stuff they needed to get through.

"Mister Steiner," Jared said, making a show of checking his watch, even though the interview room clock hung on the wall directly behind the suspect, "I shouldn't really have to explain to you how serious a matter this is. You are the last person to have seen the murder victim alive. Whatever dealings you are involved in, nothing could possibly carry as heavy a price as a murder conviction."

Finally, Steiner and his lawyer ceased their muttered conference and turned to face him. The German shifted uncomfortably in his seat and cleared his throat.

"I have already admitted to meeting Carlton Riddell," he answered in his accented English. "And I say again, we met only about potential recruitment. How many times must I say this? Mister Riddell was considering his position with Belfield BioTech and wanted to discuss a move to Stuttgart."

Esther spoke into his momentary pause. "Why don't you cut the crap, Herr Steiner," she snapped, startling all of them. "You weren't recruiting him. You were looking for information on Fluraxonyl. You need to be straight with us. This is a murder investigation. Do yourself a favour and pull your head out of the chopping block. Tell us what you know. All of it."

The solicitor opened his mouth to protest, but Steiner let out a heavy sigh and spoke before he had the chance to intercede.

"Yes," he said, "I have interest in the medicine. Fluraxonyl. Many companies do. All over the world. It is, how you say, a 'big deal' in the medical industry. But you are not correct, madam, about recruitment. We did discuss jobs. Carlton Riddell was interested in other jobs. Jobs in the EU." He frowned at the table. "I saw no details of the Fluraxonyl product at the hotel. You should know this. You know my moves already, I think. My checking in, my checking out. My flights. We met only for a short time, ten minutes maybe." He shrugged. "He showed me some manufacturing line audits. Nothing more. Was he showing me he had information? Yes. But that is all that was shown. No money, no… *exchanges*. Just an agreement to meet again. Do I have associates who are interested in the new medicine, Fluraxonyl? Yes. But there was no *trading* or anything like this. And my lawyer says I do not need to speak any more about it." He glanced sideways at the solicitor, who nodded.

Jared, hoping to avoid another outburst from Esther, spoke quickly. "So, there was nobody else involved in your meeting? No one else who knew about it?"

Steiner shook his head. "No, sir. Nobody. And I will say again, there were no exchanges. Nothing illegal. We discussed recruitment; this was the reason for meeting at the hotel, and not at his office. Mister Riddell was… nervous about his company finding out about the meeting. For obvious reasons."

"Did you see inside his briefcase?" Jared asked. "When he took out these… 'audits'?"

Steiner nodded. "Yes. But only for a short moment."

"Was Carlton Riddell carrying any money in it? Anything that looked valuable?"

"There were only papers," Steiner replied. "The audit papers I spoke about and some others. That is all. But I only saw this for a short moment, as I say."

"No exchange, just talk about possible… 'future opportunities'" Jared muttered. "And nobody else aware or involved."

"How did Carlton Riddell seem when you met him?" Esther asked, the heat gone from her voice now. "How was he behaving?"

Steiner paused for a moment, as if recollecting the encounter. "He was nervous," he replied. "Nervous, but trying to hide it. But I think he was nervous about securing a new job, and the possibility of moving to a different country." He shrugged. "This is natural."

"This is behaviour you've seen before in similar circumstances, you mean?" she pressed. "Because this is what you do, isn't it? Enable pharma companies to gain advantages by 'recruiting' rival employees?"

Steiner glanced at his lawyer, clearly unsure about the question. The lawyer gave a slight shake of his head.

"I do not wish to comment on that question, madam," Steiner replied stiffly.

The interview was pretty much over by that point, Jared knew. He wrapped up the session and escorted Steiner and his solicitor back to the consultation room, where he told them the detectives looking to interview him about the paperwork found in his case would be along shortly and he would be questioned separately about those matters.

When he got back to the gaolers' hub, he realised Esther had left instructions for the custody staff. The financial crime detectives had been wired off too; they were gathering their papers and getting ready to start their own interview. Of Esther herself, there was no sign. She'd already left the custody suite.

There was no putting it off, Jared realised. He was going to have to talk to her. Something was seriously wrong. He'd hoped it might pass by itself, but it wasn't passing.

He hit the buzzer to be released from the custody area and trudged to the lifts.

Somebody must have said something to her, or she'd read something on social media maybe, though Jared didn't think Esther really did social media… Whatever it was, he needed to get to the bottom of it. He wasn't a man much into heart-to-hearts, but Esther was more than a colleague, she was a friend. Although, come to think of it, that might actually make talking to her *more* difficult…

He stuck his head into the DS office, but Caroline Mulhern was the only one there, clacking away at her keyboard. She looked up.

"Hello, Inspector, what can I do for you?" she asked.

"Esther about?"

"Haven't seen her today. Somebody said she was interviewing. Have you tried custody?"

"I was just down there with her," he replied. "Thought she might have come back up here."

"Nope. Not seen her. You want me to send her around if she comes in?"

He hesitated, then shook his head. "No, that's okay. I'll try her on the mobile."

In his own office, he closed the door, pulled out his phone and dialled Esther's number. It went straight to voicemail. He left a short message, asking her to give him a call back when she got the chance. Then he set the phone down on his desk and frowned at it, mulling over her words in the car that morning.

Esther was a tough girl. It would take something significant to unsettle her. She'd had a difficult few months, there was no doubt, with the Peter Darren case and her mother dying. Not to mention getting attacked by a drug gang's henchman in her own apartment the month before last.

And kicking the booze. So far as he knew, she was still on the wagon.

But Jared was pretty sure it had nothing to do with any of that stuff.

He picked up the phone and tried her mobile again. Still switched off. Snatching up his keys, he decided he would try her aunt's house in Sarsbury, and then take a run by the cemetery. If he was lucky, he'd find her at one or the other. If he wasn't lucky… well, there were about a hundred bars and clubs in Belfield, and he couldn't check every one of them, but he might try the Crown and Lion down the street to start with. Just in case.

17

SHE HAD MISSED Jared by seconds. And Jean had come home early from Delilah's too. Luckily, her aunt had been waylaid at the door by a chatty neighbour, and Esther had taken the opportunity to grab her things and slip quietly out the back. The rear alley had brought her to the end of the street. It was from here that she'd sighted Jared's shabby old Volvo pulling up outside the house, watched as the DI hauled himself out of the driver's seat and trudged up Jean's flower-lined path to the front door. Esther had made sure she wasn't spotted as she'd hurried away towards Sarsbury's village square and the bus stand that would take her back into Belfield city. She hadn't risked going back for her car. She knew she was better off without it today.

Why was she feeling like this? Why had one stupid, fat little man's comments cut her so deeply? *Hey ho.* She was beginning to realise how precarious it was, the balancing act she had been performing. How thin the ice she'd been skating. She'd thought she was strong. She wasn't. Now every sideways glance in the office and every overheard comment was underscored by accusation and innuendo. Half of her wanted to curl up and cry, and the other half wanted to drown that weak and weepy Esther in vodka forever. She suddenly recognised that latter instinct for what it was. Cowardice. She was nothing but a coward and a weakling.

Having gone straight home from the Steiner interview, she'd rushed up the stairs and fished the shoulder of vodka out from under her pillow. After snapping open the lid, she'd sat and stared at it for what felt like the longest time, though truthfully, she wasn't sure it was really that long at all. The argument over whether to drink or not—whether to break her run of sobriety—had turned in circles through her head until finally she'd taken a swallow. And then another. Savoured that satisfying sting as the liquid hit her throat, the warm, fuzzy feeling that seeped through her like an old, familiar friend.

Less than twenty minutes later, she'd found herself sneaking out the back of her aunt's house like an errant teen, avoiding her aunt and her boss, with the bottle of vodka hidden under her coat like smuggled contraband.

That had been five or six hours ago. Now she was staggering through dancing crowds, the darkness cut by flashing lights, music pulsing so loudly it made her teeth rattle. She was at the club where she'd met Triona all those weeks ago. Why was she here, searching for a near-stranger, just because the woman had written her phone number on her cast? She wasn't a lesbian. And yet she couldn't stop thinking about her, or the way she'd looked at Esther in the hospital that day…

"Hey, watch it!"

Esther held up an apologetic hand to the goth girl she'd fallen against, a girl who couldn't have been out of her teens yet and might have actually been pretty if she didn't have so much metal in her face. Esther ended up backing into another group, and apologised again. And then she spotted the long red light of the bar—a haven in the flashing darkness—and staggered towards it.

She had finished off her vodka on the bus ride into Belfield. Spent the rest of the afternoon doing her bar-fly act at one pub after another, staying until the frowns of the bartenders told her she was close to being refused. No one had approached her. No sleazy guys looking to get laid. Not today.

Hey ho.

She kept trying to push away images of DCI Brian Small, with that contemptuous, sneery look on his face. *Not with your reputation.*

Hey ho.

Increasingly desperate to bury that memory, she found herself thinking about Triona more and more as the afternoon wore on. Not everybody regarded her the way Brian Small and people at the office did; Esther had clung desperately to that thought, clung to it throughout her drunken descent into oblivion…

"What'll it be?" the bartender asked. Nauseatingly skinny in his sleeveless T-shirt, the boy had a flop of brightly dyed red hair and a trace of dark liner around his eyes. He offered her a feminine pout when she answered too quietly and shook his head. "Louder, honey! I can't hear you!"

"Double-vodka, neat," she shouted back, and he sashayed away to get her order.

And suddenly there she was. Triona. Standing at the

end of the bar with two other women. She was even more beautiful than Esther remembered. Hooking a lock of her bobbed hair behind her ear, the nurse laughed at something one of the other women was saying.

As though sensing Esther's stare, Triona glanced over and spotted her. She hesitated, frowned, and it seemed to Esther that she mouthed her name.

Without waiting for her drink, Esther made her way down the bar towards her.

"Hey, Esther!" Triona called out loudly, smiling broadly when she realised it was really her. That look of delight, that enthusiasm, was like a balm. "Wow! Haven't seen you here in a while!"

Esther smiled. "I was hoping to see you," she replied. At least, that's what she tried to say, but she wasn't entirely sure her mouth was making the sounds she wanted it to. And with the pounding music, it looked like Triona hadn't quite caught her words. Esther leaned in to repeat herself, but she lost her balance and had to grab hold of one of Triona's friends. The woman let out a shriek as they both nearly toppled, her drink spilling everywhere. Esther only just managed to shift her balance at the last moment and prevent the two of them from landing on the floor.

"Sorry! I'm so sorry!" Esther cried. "I'll get you another drink!"

The look on Triona's face changed. No longer delight. A frown of concern.

"Esther, are you okay?" she asked, shouting to be heard over the din.

Esther needed air. She needed to splash some water on her face. She needed to get herself together.

"Where are the toilets?" Esther called out.

Triona, still looking worried, pointed towards a corridor lit by a blur of green and purple neon.

"You want me to come with you?" she asked.

Esther shook her head and moved away in the direction of the restrooms.

"I'll be back in a minute," she replied. Or tried to. The head shake had sent the room into a spin again and she wasn't sure what she said.

She did her best to walk as steadily as possible, but it felt like the floor was shifting. She stumbled more than once, falling into couples eating the faces off each other and drawing more than one angry rebuke as she righted herself and teetered on.

The toilets were unisex. Low-key lighting revealed large, gleaming black tiles everywhere, a variety of violet smudges highlighted by the blacklight. The sounds of a couple having sex further down the row of stalls was being ignored by everyone at the sinks.

Esther found an empty cubicle and closed the door behind her.

She had to pull herself together. She needed to get a grip. Triona was here! Her heart leapt at the thought, but then it sank a little again as she realised that she had drunk far too much. Never mind. A few minutes here to herself and she would be okay. She just needed a short break from the noise and the crowd.

Lowering the lid of the toilet seat, she sat down heavily. Five minutes to catch her breath and wait for the world to stop its queasy spinning, then a few handfuls of water on her face. She'd be good to go then. Good to go see Triona and see her look at her the way she'd looked at her in the hospital that day. Triona knew she wasn't just some trashy slut. *Hey ho.* Bastard. She had to block him out. Block out his stupid fat face.

Block him…

Esther opened her eyes. Where was she?

Oh yeah… Fuck…

Her vision was blurry. She blinked and wiped her eyes as she swayed precariously on the toilet seat. She must have dozed off for a minute or two. Or maybe even longer? Someone was banging on the stall door, shouting at her to hurry up. But Esther knew she wasn't quite ready to stand yet. The music thumped through the walls, a counterpoint to the angry knocking. She tried to reply that she would be out in a minute. Just one more minute. But the words didn't come out right. Her tongue refused to work properly.

As she sat there, her eyes found a bit of graffiti on the stall partition, set at eye-level for anyone on the toilet. Written in bold black marker, it stood clearly apart from the rest of the doodles and carvings, making it the only bit of graffiti Esther could make out in her current state…

Things I Hate:

1. *Vandalism*
2. *Irony*
3. *Lists…*

She found herself laughing as she read it.

Was it just her, or was there a slightly manic edge to her giggle? The thought made her laugh harder.

The pounding on the door ceased abruptly and there was an angry curse from outside. Whoever it was stomped off.

Then, with a sudden, violent hiccup, Esther's laughter stopped, and she threw up all over her shoes. The toilet stall tipped sideways, her head struck the floor tiles, and the world went black.

18

VICKY MANSFIELD SAT cross-legged on her giant sofa and turned up the volume of the celebrity quiz show in an effort to drown out the nagging from her husband at the top of the stairs. Where were his favourite platinum cufflinks? How the fuck should she know? And if the bedroom looked like a disaster zone, wasn't that why they had a fucking cleaner in the house four days a week? Christ, he could be such a bore! She sighed and drained the last of her chardonnay.

She couldn't concentrate on the TV. She kept thinking about her meeting with Mark Sterling, kept wishing she'd never heard from him. But then, if she'd never heard from him, she wouldn't have got his warning about what was happening. She shivered. Memories of that night kept bubbling up, no matter how hard she tried to keep them buried. All these years later, and still she was haunted by it. She should have left Belfield altogether. She should have turned down Tobias's marriage proposal and got the fuck out of Dodge. But she'd been hooked, not only by the money and the diamonds and the Porsches, but by his looks of adoration. He'd worshipped her at the start. And so she'd settled, for the sports cars and the jewellery and the declarations of love—thrived on them for a while—and now here she was. She stared at the fat diamonds on her wedding band and engagement ring while another barrage of angry remarks drifted down from the top of the staircase, breaking through the noise of the TV. She glanced at her empty wineglass. Time for a refill.

She stood up a little too quickly and had to take hold of the sofa to steady herself. Once the room had stopped spinning, she manoeuvred herself to the kitchen.

Without bothering to flick on the lights, she crossed the room to their giant fridge-freezer. The marble floor tiles were cool under her bare feet. Opening the fridge, she had to squint against the white light as she plucked another bottle of the same South African wine from the shelf.

She turned, scanning the island worktop for a corkscrew, when something caught her eye. A face—a pale visage—was peering in at her through the kitchen window.

She screamed and dropped the wine bottle. It smashed on the floor at her feet as she hopped backwards, hip striking the marble work surface behind her and making her scream a second time. She looked up at the window again.

The face was gone.

Vicky screamed a third time when all the lights suddenly came on. But it was just Tobias, standing in the doorway in his robe, looking irritable.

"What on earth is the matter with you?" he barked, but his expression softened as he stared at her, which meant she must have looked frightened indeed.

"Th-there was someone at the window," she stammered, "looking in at me."

Tobias Mansfield glanced uneasily at the big kitchen window. All they could see, now that the lights were on, were their own haunted expressions looking back at them.

It took Tobias a moment to realise there was only one thing for it, and no way of avoiding it. He heaved a nervous breath and stomped off into the utility, where he pulled a club from his golf bag, a flashlight from the cupboard, and headed for the patio door.

"Let's just call the police, Tobey," Vicky protested. She had reason enough to say it. She had *recognised* that face. He was different now. Different, and yet the same, with those deep-set black eyes of his.

But Tobias clearly felt his manhood was at stake. He grumbled something about checking it out first, then rolled open the sliding door and stepped outside into the inky darkness.

Vicky was shaking all over as she picked her way gingerly around the puddle of wine and shattered glass to the light switches. With trembling fingers, she knocked the kitchen lights off again and flicked on the patio lamps outside.

Tobias was standing at the edge of the decking, sweeping the beam of his torch over and back across the scrubby winter bushes at the bottom of the lawn. After a moment, he stomped off around the side of the house.

Vicky hunched there, trembling in the silence, waiting for her husband to reappear.

Mark had been right. He was back. Carlton dead, Gary missing in London… It couldn't be coincidence. She thought about poor Gary and felt herself welling up. It hadn't ended well between them, but she still had feelings.

They'd been childhood sweethearts all those years…

She stifled another scream when Tobias reappeared suddenly, then let out a long, shaky breath instead.

"No one there," her husband muttered, pulling the patio door shut again and making sure it was securely locked. "Everything seems in order. Garage and gates are all locked up. But I'll ring the police anyway, in case he's lurking in any of the neighbours' gardens. These burgling types are opportunists, you know—he'll probably be checking all the doors around about the area. Looking to steal a car, no doubt." He glanced at the broken wine bottle, and his face hardened. "You're sure?"

Vicky nodded.

"What did he look like?" Tobias asked.

She swallowed. Her mouth was suddenly bone dry.

"Pale face," she told him. "Dark eyes… late twenties, I think." She tried to sound uncertain, tried to deflect from any hint of the truth, that she *knew* who the man had been…

"Right then," Tobias said, appearing satisfied. "I'll ring the police. Clean up that mess, would you?"

She nodded mutely, another sure sign if Tobias had needed one that she was genuinely shaken; an acerbic remark like that would normally have been enough to spark a blazing row. He frowned at her and disappeared to fetch the phone.

Vicky retrieved the sweeping brush from the utility. She had to turn on the lights to see all the broken pieces of glass on the tiles, but she did so reluctantly, and it didn't stop her glancing at the windows from time to time, seeing only her own terrified face in the glass whenever she did.

Her mind was spinning, her heart thumping. Part of her wanted to tell the police, to confess everything she knew.

To tell them who it was. A ghost from the past, a ghost come for vengeance. But she knew she could not. Not yet. She needed to talk to Mark first.

She needed to warn him.

19

ESTHER WOKE TO the feel of silk sheets against her naked thighs. As she shifted slightly, a sharp throb of pain pulsed through her skull. Naked, in a stranger's bedroom, with the mother of all hangovers about to crush her… Christ, she hadn't just fallen off the wagon; she'd taken a running leap and nose-dived off of it! Already she could feel the headache that was preparing to launch an assault on her eyeballs from the back of her head. But she had to face the reality of what she'd done, and start trying to pick up the pieces…

She opened her eyes.

She stared for a long moment at the Persian-style metal lantern that hung from the centre of the high ceiling. She'd seen this light fixture before.

Dropping her gaze to floor level, she took in the rest of the bedroom's furnishings.

A rosewood chest of drawers stood next to an oriental dressing screen. Paper-and-bamboo blinds hung in the window, not doing very much to block the daylight from the room. Esther knew this place, and her heart skipped a beat as she realised where she was. She turned her head. She was alone in the bed this time. That was different. A peek under the bedsheets revealed that only her trousers, boots and socks were missing; the rest of her clothes were still on her. That was different too. Maybe when she'd nose-dived off the wagon, she hadn't landed quite as badly as she'd feared.

With a groan, she pushed herself from under the sheets. She couldn't quite bring herself to stand, so she sat on the edge of the bed and took a few steadying breaths. As promised, the headache rolled forward and her head began to pound. Her stomach lurched queasily.

"Leaving already?"

She jumped at the sound of a woman's voice behind her. She turned to see Triona standing in the doorway in a set of hospital scrubs, that pixie smile Esther had spent the last six weeks thinking about playing about her lips. Triona, with her soft, sultry Irish accent. Triona, who'd scribbled her name and phone number in blue marker on her cast two months ago, and whom Esther had thought about ringing every day since. Triona, who had somehow managed to hijack a corner of her brain ever since she'd set Esther's broken arm in plaster. It was almost as if Esther had needed a new addiction after she'd kicked the booze, and that addiction had come in the form of an obsession over a sexy Irish nurse with azure blue eyes and a dimpled smile. And she wasn't even gay!

"Don't worry," Triona told her, "I didn't take advantage of you. I slept on the couch. You could barely talk when we got you out of that toilet stall."

Esther groaned again and rubbed a hand over her face.

Triona crossed the room. She set a glass of fizzing orange liquid and a couple of white pills on the dresser.

"Vitamin C and paracetamol," the nurse explained. "Figured you'd need a kick-start this morning. How are you feeling?"

"Like a pig shat in my head."

Triona laughed then, a beautiful lilting sound that, unlikely as it seemed in the circumstances, actually made Esther feel degrees better to hear.

"*Withnail and I,*" the nurse said. "God, I haven't seen that flick in absolute ages. At least we know you have good taste in movies. There's some hope for you yet." She studied Esther for a moment, her expression a mix of concern and amusement. "Your jeans are in the bathroom. It's the first door on the left, in case you've forgotten. I threw them on a quick wash last night, but they've been hanging over the radiator so they might be dry by now. I managed to get most of the vomit off your boots too, although they'll be damp for a while yet."

"God, I'm so sorry."

Triona chuckled. "Don't worry about it," she replied. "I see far worse in my job." She headed for the door again. "Get that drink and those pills into you and come down to the kitchen when you feel ready. There are towels in the bathroom cabinet if you want to have a shower first."

Esther did as she was told, swallowing the painkillers and washing them down with the fizzing liquid. Her stomach was already doing somersaults, so she made herself take the drink in three quick gulps and steeled herself when it all threatened to come back up. Breathing slowly and steadily, she focused on a piece of oriental artwork on the wall. She was practiced at this routine: a few minutes of resilience now, hold it down, and it would start working within the half hour.

Only when she was sure that the pills were going to stay in her stomach did she attempt to get to her feet. The room spun nauseatingly, but she took her time as she made her way gingerly out to the hall. The sound of pans clattering and the murmur of a radio station drifted up from the kitchen below, along with the smell of frying bacon. Esther's stomach offered her a moment of confusion, growling with hunger and threatening to toss out its contents all at the same time. She hurried into the bathroom and closed the door.

The bathroom was clean but cluttered, with make-up and creams and lotions packed onto every available surface. A hairdryer lay abandoned on the floor near the door.

Esther spotted her jeans, slung over a towel-rack radiator next to the sink. She closed her eyes and suppressed another groan, as the memory of throwing up all over herself at the nightclub came back to her without warning. She'd been laughing at something, but she couldn't remember what. Had there been somebody talking to her through the stall door? Had there been somebody in the toilet stall with her? It was no good; most of the evening was lost to her now.

She did her best to freshen herself up, showering quickly, and drying herself off with a fluffy, lavender-scented towel from the cabinet. By the time she pulled on her jeans, her head had stopped spinning and her stomach had settled.

Down in the kitchen, Triona was pushing scrambled eggs around a pan while she hummed along to a tune on the radio. When the toaster popped, she turned and spotted Esther standing in the doorway. She smiled her dimpled smile.

"Hey, you look better," she announced brightly. "How's the head now?"

"Better, thanks."

Triona nodded towards a stool by the breakfast bar, where there were two places already set—two plates with a pair of fried half-tomatoes on each, a dish full of bacon and a rack of toast. Two jugs sat nearby, one with orange juice and one with ice water.

"You hungry?" Triona asked.

Esther sat. "I can't decide."

The nurse laughed as she brought over the pan and divided the eggs, pushing a portion onto each plate. "Not quite the Full Irish," she said apologetically. "I had limited supplies in the fridge." She hesitated. "Sorry, you're not vegan or anything, are you?"

Esther shook her head, then regretted the movement. She let out a slow breath.

"Oh good," Triona said with relief, not seeming to notice Esther's sudden discomfort. "My da swears a Full Irish Breakfast cures the worst of hangovers." She lifted a small silver pot from the cooker hob. "Coffee?"

"Yes, please," Esther replied, eager to get her first dose of caffeine in. She was going to need several to get her through today.

The music on the radio switched, from whatever upbeat pop song Triona had been humming along to, to a mellower tune. Esther was glad of the change.

Once she'd poured the coffee, Triona sat across from Esther and took some bacon from the dish.

"Help yourself to whatever you feel like," she said, as she tucked in.

The bacon did smell good. Esther's stomach rumbled, the hunger pangs getting the better of the queasiness, and she decided it was worth the risk. She started on the eggs, small forkfuls to begin with.

"So… your cast's off, I see," Triona said. "How's your arm?"

Esther nodded. "Good, thank you."

"At least now you can honestly say you lost my number," she said, grinning to show there was no spite in the remark, only a playful amusement. Playful amusement seemed to be Triona's default state of being.

"I'm sorry," Esther replied. "I… I did think about ringing you. I thought about it a lot. I mean *a lot*. But… I'm not… I'm not gay, Triona. I thought if I called you, it might be… I don't know—unfair, maybe? Like I was leading you on or something."

Triona shrugged. "I don't mind. I wasn't gay either, until I was."

Esther must have looked puzzled.

Triona smiled wistfully. "When I was fifteen I was in love with a boy in my class," she explained. "Dara Boyle. He was gorgeous. I mean, literally, drop-dead, you know? He played guitar in a rock band. His bandmates thought they were all God's gift, but not Dara. He was quiet and sensitive, and I preferred that. Not to mention he was far better-looking than any of the rest of them.

"We used to hang out and listen to the band rehearse. Me and my friends, I mean. Proper little gaggle of teen groupies, we were. Finn's da had this massive house, with a garage that was nearly as big as our whole downstairs.

Sorry: Finn was the lead singer; he wasn't very good at singing but the fella had plenty of confidence, I'll give him that. Anyways, we all used to gather on Saturdays to listen to them rehearse. Rehearse! As if they were going to be getting gigs in clubs or bars at fifteen!" She clucked and rolled her eyes, smiling at the silliness of it all. "I was mad about Dara. Proper head-over-heels, like. Dragged my friends along to Finn's house every Saturday to watch them play. I even started practicing my old tin whistle, if you can credit it! Like I was one of *The Corrs* or something and might get to join the band. How sad was I?" She guffawed at her own naivety.

"You play the tin whistle?" Esther asked.

Triona laughed. "I know! Irish girl plays the tin whistle. Cliché or what? I do. Well, I did. It's been a while. But forget the tin whistle. It's not important. I never summoned the courage to suggest playing with them, thank God!

"Anyways, one Saturday me and a few of the girls showed up at Finn's, and wouldn't you know it, we'd been pipped to the post this time! Finn and the drummer Jamie were a year ahead and they'd invited some girls from an older year group to come and listen. There was a girl there. Niamh Doherty was her name. She was seventeen, and she was all over Dara. My Dara."

Triona was giving plenty of dramatic expression to her narrative; it helped take Esther's mind off her hangover.

"You'd think I'd be jealous, wouldn't you? Me, head over heels as I was and all?" She shrugged. "Nah. Not at all. It was like something blossomed in me. Something I guess I'd kind of always known was there, but was maybe trying to ignore. A niggle. Well, when I saw Niamh

Doherty, I tell you, it was far from a niggle! I couldn't stop staring. If Dara was drop-dead gorgeous, then Niamh was climb-back-out-of-the-grave gorgeous. I can still see her standing there, her black hair and blue eyes. This perfect set of freckles across her nose. Dara paled in comparison. I realised then, without a doubt, that I was more into girls. No more pretending to myself that I wasn't. And I was totally in love with Niamh. I got to know her, made excuses to hang out with her. I think she felt a bit sorry for me because, my friends being the gossipers they were, she realised I had a crush on Dara. She ended up with Dara in the end. Of course, she never realised that I didn't care about Dara by that stage, I just wanted to be close to her.

"Not that she was gay, or bi, or anything. She wasn't. Sadly." She sighed. "But I'd had my epiphany. Although I completely failed to learn the lesson about torturing myself over women who aren't interested." Her smile became a little less amused and a little more vulnerable as she added, "Guess I've never really learned that lesson."

They ate their breakfasts in silence for a minute, and then Esther asked, "How did you—sorry, tell me to shut up if I'm being nosy—but how did you… tell people? Friends and family?"

Triona shrugged. "This is rural Ireland we're talking about," she replied. "Place might have come on a bit in recent years but, let me tell you, back then I wasn't going around chatting about it. And I didn't tell my parents till years later, when I was going to college here. I went home for Christmas holidays. Waited a couple of days after Stephen's Day to tell them, because I wasn't sure how they'd take it."

"How did they take it?"

Triona smiled, not amused this time but a touch sadly. "My da was great, fair play to him. My ma… not so much." She picked at her breakfast for a moment. Shrugged. "Rural Ireland. Very Catholic family on my ma's side. My uncle's a priest. I guess I was lucky to get good support from one parent, at least. Some of my gay friends here didn't even have that. Some of them…" She shook her head. "Let's just say bad families can really fuck you up. And it's all luck really, where you end up coming from, where you live, where you go to school… Are you okay, Esther?"

Esther had frozen, a forkful of bacon halfway to her mouth. Triona's words had triggered memories of her own childhood with Hannah, and thinking about school had made her think about the Riddell case—and Belfield Grammar. *Where you end up coming from… where you go to school…* Why hadn't she thought of going there before now?

And then something on the radio caught her attention. It was the top-of-the-hour news bulletin. Esther set down her fork and went over to it. She turned up the volume.

"…missing in London for almost two months has been named as Gary Hetherington, a financial trader based in the City of London. A spokesperson for the London Metropolitan Police has confirmed that Mister Hetherington's death is being treated as suspicious at this time, and that a murder investigation has been launched. They've appealed for anyone with any information to come forward."

Esther turned to Triona. "Is my phone…?"

The nurse pointed to where some coats and bags hung from a set of pegs on the back of the kitchen door. Esther spotted her coat and leather handbag among them. She rummaged through both until she found her mobile. It was dead. Shit.

"You can use mine," Triona offered, sliding her phone across the breakfast bar towards Esther.

Esther thanked her and quickly dialled the number for the police switchboard.

"London Met switchboard, please," she told the operator. "Yes, I'm a police officer."

There was a click and a dial tone. Another switchboard operator, asking for the extension or the name of the person she was looking for. She didn't have his extension with her.

"Detective Constable Pierce Goddard, please," she replied, hoping he was at his desk.

"DC Goddard," came the gravelly voice at the other end.

"Pierce? Pierce, it's Esther Penman, the DS from Belfield CID. I spoke to you a couple of days ago about Gary Hetherington? I just heard the news."

"Esther, yeah, I tried to ring you but just kept getting your voicemail."

"Sorry, my battery died and I haven't been in the office this morning."

"Well, it's our boy Gary alright, and looks like murder. We found him last night, but only verified the identity this morning. Post-mortem is scheduled for tomorrow."

"Do we know what happened to him?"

"Been dead awhile," Goddard replied. "A week or so at least, but it's been pretty cold these last few weeks and… well, there's bruising still visible around the neck. Looks to me like he's been strangled."

Esther stood in silence for a long moment. *Strangled.*

"Esther?" Goddard's voice on the phone brought her back to herself.

She blinked. "Hi, yes, Pierce, do you think I could attend the post-mortem? I think our murders might be linked."

Goddard cleared his throat. "I'll have to check with the SIO, but if you think the killings are connected then, yeah, I'd say so. I'll find out and give you a shout later, let you know what she says. It'll be the Westminster mortuary. I'll forward the time as soon as I know it."

Esther hung up, then glanced at Triona. "You mind if I make one more call?"

The Irishwoman was sitting with her elbows on the countertop, chin resting on her fists, watching her with exaggerated interest. "Absolutely," she replied. "You're very sexy when you're in work mode."

Esther blushed. "You mean compared to drunken-slob-throwing-up-all-over-herself mode?" she said, as she dialled a number she knew by heart.

Triona laughed her sparkling laugh; it really was a magical sound, that laugh.

Esther put the phone to her ear, but Jared didn't pick up. She checked her watch. He was probably in one of the morning meetings. The call went through to his voicemail. She left a quick message, letting him know about the Hetherington development and that she was going to hear back from the Met later about attending the autopsy tomorrow. She quickly added that her phone was out of battery and that she wouldn't be in until about lunchtime because she had a lead to chase up, but she'd fill him in on the details when she got back to the station.

She hung up and handed the phone to Triona. "I'm so sorry," she said. "I have to go. Thank you so much for breakfast… and for everything. Really. I'm sorry for making such a dick of myself last night."

Triona shrugged, still smiling. "Don't worry about it," she said.

Esther grabbed her bag and coat. She thanked Triona again, apologised once more, and was about to slip out the door when she spotted the notepad and pen on the counter next to her. After a moment's pause, she picked up the pen and jotted her name and phone number on the pad. She looked up, blushing, to see Triona smiling happily at her.

"You want mine again?" the nurse asked.

Esther shook her head. "I stared at it for six weeks," she told her. "I know it by heart."

Triona's smile widened and Esther's cheeks grew hotter. She murmured goodbye and slipped out the door.

20

ALL HIGH SCHOOLS smelled the same. Esther had been through enough of them in her youth to form a confident opinion on the matter. It was an unpleasant smell, a lingering hint of industrial-strength cleaner mixed with the faint odour of sweaty teenagers. And the hallways all had that same oppressive hush when classes were on. Or maybe it was only Esther who associated that silence with oppressiveness, after all her days of arriving late to class.

It was the final week before the Christmas holidays. A squat plastic tree with mismatched baubles and multicoloured lights stood in the empty reception area, across from a trophy cabinet that had been framed with tinsel. Someone had given the fire-extinguisher in the corner a scarf of tinsel too; a health and safety inspector would probably have a conniption about that.

Esther had been relieved to find Jean was already away to work when she'd arrived home. She'd changed quickly into a fresh set of clothes and boots. Her aunt had been so proud of Esther's efforts at quitting alcohol that Esther didn't think she would be able to face her disappointment. Not that Jean would be anything other than supportive. But Esther was disappointed enough in herself as it was; she wasn't ready to admit her defeat to anyone else just yet.

Her boots were a lost cause, stained and smelling of vomit despite Triona's soaking them and leaving them to air overnight. They'd had to go in the bin, carefully hidden under some garbage bags. Esther had chosen a pair of black boots to wear instead. They were a little dressier, with higher heels, but they'd have to do until she could get her hands on another pair of practical brown Ropers.

She hadn't lingered too long at the house, changing quickly and driving straight to Belfield Grammar, the high school that linked Carlton Riddell, Mark Sterling and Gary Hetherington. She wasn't entirely sure what she was looking for, but it was clearly a thread worth tugging at.

The school secretary was sitting at her desk nearby, tapping away at her computer. She'd offered Esther a seat and some tea or coffee while she waited. Apparently the principal, Ms Fredericks, was addressing a group of Year Elevens and would be back shortly. Esther had politely declined the offer. It wasn't that she couldn't do with another coffee right now—caffeine and paracetamol being her go-to-guys the morning after a night before—but she was pretty confident any coffee would be instant coffee and she wasn't sure she could stomach that right now. She was still feeling pretty lousy, and didn't want to offend the sweet little school secretary, a round, rosy-cheeked woman who'd given her name as Dorothy Long.

Feeling restless, Esther had declined the offer of a seat too, choosing instead to examine the framed photos on the walls and the awards in the trophy cabinet. The restlessness was a result of too many latent memories rising up. Here she was again, worried that a shrewd head teacher was about to sniff out the guilt of her late-night misadventures, no matter the shower and half-can of deodorant she'd used, or the minty chewing gum she was chewing vigorously as she studied class photos and framed student awards.

A distant click of stiletto heels on the plastic-tiled floors grew louder, announcing the arrival of Ms Fredericks. Esther deposited her gum in a nearby trashcan and glanced at Dorothy. The secretary suddenly looked flustered, straightening papers on her desk and giving Esther an apologetic smile. This only added to Esther's sense of unease.

"Dorothy, have you collated the first term reports for the Year Elevens yet?" Ms Fredericks snapped as she whisked into the reception area. "I should have preferred to have them *before* my talk about the GCSE's this morning."

"Y-yes, Miss Fredericks," Dorothy announced, half-standing out of her seat with a sheaf of papers in her hand. "And Miss Fredericks? Um, there's a policewoman here looking to speak with you."

Ms Fredericks turned, an alarmed look on her face. This helped settle Esther's nerves. She wasn't a wayward schoolgirl anymore. She was a 'policewoman'. *What are you guilty of Ms Fredericks?* she thought, as she sized the principal up.

Esther took an instant dislike to Ms Fredericks, if only because of how the woman spoke to her secretary. The principal was young. Mid-to-late twenties. Her blonde hair was scraped back in an efficient bun, and her pencil skirt matched her tailored suit jacket. Her heels were four inches—glossy black with open toes—and her legs were waxed and tanned. She wore tastefully applied make-up and small, subtle diamond earrings, as well as an engagement ring with a much bigger diamond on it. Ms Fredericks wouldn't look out of place at some high-rolling board meeting in the City of London, rather than managing a grammar school in Belfield. A career woman, perhaps, with an eye on the upper offices of the Education Department…

Esther gave her a tight smile. "Hello, Miss Fredericks, my name is Esther Penman. I'm a detective with Belfield CID. Would it be possible to have a quick word?"

"Is this about a student?" Fredericks asked, eyes still wide.

"Past students," Esther replied.

"Well, of course then," the principal said. She looked relieved to learn that the issue was a historic one. "Come ahead into my office. Has Dorothy offered you something to drink?"

Esther smiled at Dorothy. "Yes, she has, but I'm fine, thank you."

"Dorothy, a green tea for me, please," the principal ordered, as she opened the door to her office and gestured for Esther to precede her.

"So… past students?" Fredericks asked, settling down behind her desk and gesturing for Esther to take one of the chairs facing it. "Is this something that happened on school grounds? How far back are we talking?"

"It'll be the year that graduated with Mark Sterling, Gary Hetherington and Carlton Riddell."

Fredericks frowned as she gave her computer mouse a little shake to bring the screen back to life. "Why do those names sound familiar?" she murmured.

"Possibly you've heard them on the news recently," Esther replied. "Gary Hetherington's body was found last night in London. He'd been missing for several weeks. And Carlton Riddell is the man whose body was found here in Belfield five days ago. I'm investigating his murder."

Fredericks looked at Esther, eyes wide again and one hand rising reflexively to her throat. Esther felt a touch of spiteful pleasure at knocking a little of the haughtiness out of the woman, if only for a moment.

"You think this has something to do with Belfield Grammar?" the principal asked in a hushed voice, even though the door to her office was firmly closed.

"I don't know, ma'am," Esther replied. "I'm looking into any link I can find. I'm led to believe Carlton Riddell and Gary Hetherington attended this school together. As did Mark Sterling. I'd like to take a look at whatever records you have from their years here. Yearbook photos, notes about any incidents they were involved in, that kind of thing."

Ms Fredericks blinked a few times, then gave herself a little shake and nodded. She went back to clicking through items on her computer. "Do you know what year they graduated, or even roughly how far back you're looking to go?"

"Ten years or so," Esther replied. "I don't know the exact year."

The principal frowned. "Our records going back that far will be fairly elementary. My predecessors hadn't quite embraced the concept of digital technology, I'm afraid. Computer records for ten years ago will be the basic stuff only. Personal details, parent contacts and graduation records. Any year-to-year notes and teacher comments would have been hardcopy files… and they're probably gone by now. We're not obliged to keep data like that for more than six years."

There was a tap at the door.

"Come," Fredericks commanded.

Dorothy Long appeared with the principal's green tea. It was on a small tray, with a plate of biscuits next to it. There was also a glass of water for Esther.

"Just in case you get thirsty," the secretary murmured to her, as she set the tray down on the desk within easy reach of both women. Esther smiled her thanks, and the secretary slipped out again.

Fredericks seemed hardly to have noticed. She was still frowning at her computer screen, tapping entries on her keyboard as she searched through her records.

A bell rang and Esther was taken back on a tide of memories as the hush that had hung like a blanket over the school turned into a wave of noise. Chatter and laughter. The slamming of locker doors. The rumble of hundreds of pairs of feet moving from one classroom to the next. Even through the closed door of the principal's office, the sound was all-pervasive. A moment later, the same electronic bell rang twice and the sounds faded again.

"Okay," Ms Fredericks announced at last, sitting back, "unfortunately it's as I suspected. Basic personal records only for that year group. But I can confirm that Masters Hetherington, Riddell and Sterling were in the same class."

"Could I get the class list? And the year group?"

Fredericks lifted her tea, blew on it and took a sip. She pursed her lips. "I would need an official data request form. Data protection, you see…"

Esther nodded. "Not a problem." She fished into her

handbag and pulled out one of a sheaf of blank data request forms that she had learned long ago not to leave the office without. "And a yearbook, if you have anything like that," she added, as she scribbled her contact details and the official investigation reference number onto the form. "Something with pictures?"

She signed the form and passed it over the desk to Ms Fredericks, who glanced at it perfunctorily before slipping it into a documents tray. She stood, her tea still in hand.

"I'll have Dorothy check the file room to see if we have any yearbooks going back that far," she said. "And I'll print out the information I have here for you now."

The principal took her tea with her. Outside in the secretary's office, Esther heard her tell Dorothy to check for yearbooks for the year in question. The older woman sounded a little taken aback and repeated the year to the principal as though surprised.

"Yes, Dorothy, can you fetch them, please?" Fredericks snapped impatiently. Then she dropped her voice, but not low enough that Esther didn't catch her next remark. "Let's get that detective what she wants and get her out of here. I don't want the school developing a reputation."

The secretary stammered a flustered agreement. Esther heard her scurry away, and then the printer began to whirr and groan as Fredericks printed out the details she'd found on her computer.

When she returned to the office, she handed the pages to Esther. As promised, they were fairly basic.

"Dorothy is looking to see if there are any yearbooks now," the principal told her as she took her seat again. "Is there anything else I can help you with today, Detective?"

Esther considered the question as she put the pages into

her bag.

"How long have you worked here, Miss Fredericks?" she asked.

The principal set her tea down and drew herself up slightly, as though preparing to defend herself. "This is my second year as head of Belfield Grammar. Before this I worked as a deputy head at a school in Coventry."

"What about your secretary, Dorothy Long? How long has she worked here? Do you know?"

The woman frowned and pursed her lips again. "I believe she's been here quite a while. Thirty years, she might have said. Which has its drawbacks, of course. I think Dorothy struggles with our new software. And computers generally. I suppose you get used to doing things a certain way, and after a while everything changes and, well, it can be hard for older people to keep up. Still, I couldn't bring myself to let her go."

There was a terrible condescension in her voice as she said it. Esther really didn't like Ms Fredericks.

A tap at the door announced the secretary's return. She was clutching a yearbook and looking rather nervous. No wonder, Esther thought, with a bitch like Fredericks as her boss.

"I-is this what you're looking for?" Dorothy asked, passing the book to Esther, who stood to receive it.

It was a typical high school yearbook, with sections dedicated to drama productions, sporting events and academic awards. There were plenty of carefully arranged photos with groups of students beaming at the camera. Here and there a proud parent or a dutifully smiling teacher stood alongside.

A team photograph for the senior rugby squad caught

Esther's eye. She quickly found her two victims among the faces, frozen in time as boys. Gary Hetherington and Carlton Riddell, standing in their rugby kits, middle of the back row, smiling on a sunny day with the school's rugby pitch in the background. A silver trophy sat on the grass in front of Hetherington, who was front and centre. A balding coach stood to one side. Esther searched the list of names printed below the photo. *Coach J. Tindall.*

"Tindall," Esther said. "Does he still work here?"

Fredericks looked at her blankly, but Dorothy sighed and shook her head.

"I'm afraid Jack Tindall had a heart attack during the Easter break five years ago," she said. "So sad. The students were very upset. Coach Tindall was such a popular member of the staff."

"You remember any of these boys?" Esther asked, spinning the book so Dorothy could see it. "Gary Hetherington, or Carlton Riddell?"

Dorothy seemed to blanch a little at the photo. She quickly shook her head. "Oh, there have been so many students through here down the years, I can't remember them all." She turned to the principal. "Will there be anything else, Miss Fredericks?"

"No, Dorothy, thank you, that will be all for the moment."

Esther watched the secretary go, considering her reaction to the photo. She looked down at the yearbook and flicked through the pages. She came to the double-page spreads at the back of the book, where rows of small portraits of each student from every year group lined the pages. They were in alphabetical order, so Gary Hetherington was about halfway down his year group's page, with Carlton Riddell and Mark Sterling both on the bottom row. Sterling looked a little more clean-cut than he did now.

"You can take that with you, Detective," Fredericks said, "if you can see your way to returning it when you're done?"

Esther nodded. "Thank you. I will." Her eyes settled on the names at the bottom, the ones with no portraits. There were three of them. "What happened to these kids' photos?" she asked.

Fredericks shrugged. "No-shows, I imagine," she said dismissively. "We try to put aside two days for the photographer, in case anyone is sick, but there are some students who don't make it in for either session. Every year group has its share of unreliable ones."

Esther bit her tongue as she realised that she would have been one of the 'unreliable ones', as Ms Fredericks put it. A name without a photo. That would have been Esther Penman. Never an A-student. Not on any sports teams. No awards. She'd have been a footnote too.

"Will that be all, Detective?" Fredericks didn't bother to conceal her impatience this time. She was clearly keen to see the back of her.

Esther offered her a polite smile. "For the moment, Miss Fredericks. Thank you for your help."

As Esther emerged from the principal's office, Dorothy Long half-rose out of her seat again, but when she saw that Fredericks was still sitting at her desk, she sat back down. Poor woman was so jumpy. Esther gave her a sympathetic smile and thanked her for all her help, then she headed for the exit with the yearbook under one arm.

* * *

Back at Belfield Central Police Station, Esther murmured a "thank you" to a uniformed officer who held the door for her. Her hands were full, with her handbag slung over one shoulder, the Belfield Grammar yearbook in one hand and her fifth coffee of the day in the other.

When she got to the CID floor, the first person she saw was DCI Brian Small. He was about to step into his office when he turned and locked eyes with her. He stared at her icily for a moment, his florid face flushing a darker shade. Esther felt the greasy fingers of self-doubt curl around her heart. The moment seemed to last an eternity, before the DCI finally shook his head, stepped into his office and closed the door.

Esther hurried between the desks to the sergeants' office. Caroline Mulhern was there, flicking through the pages of a case file and muttering to herself.

"Doesn't anybody learn how to spell properly at school anymore?" she grumbled by way of greeting, as Esther sat down at her own desk. "I swear, the grammar in these statements is shocking!"

"Good morning to you too, Caroline," Esther replied. "Just send it back with a big red F on top and see how the officer deals with that."

Caroline chuckled, a husky smoker's chortle, and continued sifting through the documents and jotting notes on a legal pad.

Esther logged into her computer and saw that she'd already received an email from Pierce Goddard. She read through it quickly. Gary Hetherington's autopsy was confirmed for ten a.m. tomorrow and the Senior Investigating Officer, a DCI called Andrea Greene, had agreed to allow Esther and Jared to be there, but she wanted Esther to bring along a copy of the Belfield investigation file too, as a kind of quid pro quo.

Esther picked up the phone and dialled through to Goddard's extension in London.

"DC Goddard."

"Pierce, it's Esther again. Just got your email, ta. Is your DCI looking a sit-down meeting with me and my DI, or does she just want a copy of our notes so far?"

"Just an outline and the main notes," he replied. "I think she wants to sift through what you guys have. See whether the link is strong enough to join the investigations, and then figure out who should take the lead."

"Take the lead?" Esther murmured, frowning.

"Yeah. Guess she thinks if it's the same suspect then there should only be one team dealing with the lot. Might be a secondment opportunity in it for you."

Esther gave a noncommittal grunt in response. "I'll give her a summary of what we have," she told him.

"You coming to the PM tomorrow?"

"We'll be there."

"Great. See you tomorrow."

Esther hung up. She had a growing sense that these murders were linked, but she definitely didn't like the idea of DCI Greene reallocating her investigation to a team in London. And she wasn't under any illusions as to which police force would take the lead if the powers-that-be decided to merge the investigations. She'd have to provide a briefing document on what they had, but maybe she could tweak the emphasis on a few things in her outlining summary…

"Is Jared in?"

"Think he's in his office," Caroline replied, without looking up from her work.

Esther used the big photocopier in the main office to make an A3 copy of the double-spread of portraits from the high school yearbook. She left the yearbook in her desk drawer and then crossed the CID floor to Jared's office. As she did so she noticed that DCI Small had closed the blinds on his internal window, the one that overlooked the open-plan detectives' workroom.

"Come in," Jared called when she rapped his door.

"We have a post-mortem in London tomorrow morning," Esther announced as she stepped into his office.

"We do?"

Jared didn't seem fazed by the announcement. She knew he was used to her running the show. She also knew it was why she was his favourite sergeant; she did all the work.

"Gary Hetherington," she explained. "He's been found dead in London. Murdered. Looks like he was strangled too. I need to prep a summary of our investigation and compile a copy of the investigation notes for the DCI in London who's running the case. The risk is she might decide the two cases are linked and take over both."

He shrugged. "That's okay. Less work for us."

Esther grimaced. "Always looking on the bright side, aren't you, Detective Inspector Wilcox?" She shook her head. "I'd like to keep control of our enquiry. I'll write up what we've got, but summarise it in a way that might keep the Met off our backs for a bit."

Jared frowned. "Don't hide anything."

"Creative emphasis only. Scout's honour," she replied,

three fingers raised in salute.

He grunted and nodded towards his screen. "I've got something for your summary here," he said. "DNA results are back on Riddell. No matches from the database."

"Nothing at all?" Esther asked.

"There's plenty of forensics," he said. "On his coat and under his fingernails. Looks like we've got a good profile of our killer's DNA. He's just not known to police."

"Not yet," Esther replied. "That's a good result, though. For when we get our hands on the suspect."

"Gotta find him first."

"We'll find him," she said. "We'll find him, and we'll solve our case *and* London's case before they have a chance to steal it from us." She smiled and winked as she headed for the door. "I'll drive in the morning," she added over her shoulder on her way out. "Be ready to go at six!"

21

Hi, my name is Esther, and I'm an alcoholic. It's been… it's been eighteen hours since my last drink.

There are no gasps or murmurs, just an understanding silence. Someone nods sympathetically. There is no judgement here.

Last time I stood here and spoke, I was at fifty-one days. That's more than seven weeks. Seven whole weeks. But now it's eighteen hours. Less than one whole day.

She looks at her feet and takes a deep breath to stiffen her resolve. She is not close to tears, but she is deflated, and she needs to take a moment to pull herself together.

When she looks up again at the faces around her, she speaks with a determination that surprises even her.

It's eighteen hours and counting. That's the better way to look at it.

Eighteen hours and counting. Going up all the time.

And I'm going to get to fifty-one days again. I'm going to get to fifty-one days and get past it this time.

There are nods and encouraging noises from the gathering. Many of those watching smile, gaining a little strength of their own from her words. Reverend Thomas claps his hands, and everyone joins in. This is a bit overwhelming for Esther and she sits down quickly. Blushing in embarrassment, but buoyed by the response, she is happy that she overcame the weaker part of her that wanted to hide from her failure and avoid this meeting.

She is happy that she made herself come here tonight.

* * *

Esther opened the front door as quietly as she could, trying not to make a sound as she slipped inside.

"Esther? Is that you, love?"

She cursed quietly to herself when she spotted the light on in the kitchen. It was after ten p.m. and the house had been in darkness from the front. She had deliberately stayed away this evening, grabbing dinner at a pizza joint halfway between the police station and the community hall where Reverend Thomas held his AA meetings. She'd been avoiding her aunt all day, dodging her calls with quick messages to say she was busy and would be home later.

No avoiding her now.

"It's me," Esther called back, pausing to figure out how to play this. She wondered if Jean had somehow figured out what had happened, somehow intuited last night's binge. She sighed as she pulled off her winter coat, hanging coat and handbag on the stand next to the stairs before heading to the kitchen. She was braced for a rebuke or a look of disappointment.

But when she stepped into the little kitchen, she found Jean sitting with a shoebox full of glossy photographs and a pile of old-fashioned photo envelopes in front of her. There were strips of developed negatives scattered across the table too. Her aunt was the one who looked guilty. She gave Esther a teary smile.

"I'm being a bit silly," she said, as Esther came over and shooed one of the tabbies out of the way so she could sit down next to her aunt and examine the pile of photos. "I was clearing out the wardrobe in the spare room," Jean went on, "to give you a bit more space. Let you get some more of your clothes out of those suitcases. I came across this old box full of pictures from when you were small. I'm getting all nostalgic. Must be my old age."

"Oh, Jean, stop it," Esther muttered affectionately. "People think we're sisters when we're out and about together."

Jean laughed and leaned over to rest her head on Esther's shoulder for a moment. "Not true," she said, then straightened and wiped her eyes. "But thank you."

Esther sifted through some of the glossy three-by-four-inch prints. Pictures of her as a baby in Hannah's arms. Hannah looking happy and… *motherly*, which was not a word Esther had ever associated with her mother. There were pictures of Hannah and Jean together, hugging and smiling, and ones of Esther as a chubby toddler, building sandcastles on a beach, sitting on a swing in a playground, straddling a tricycle in a hallway. There was a photo of her in a primary school uniform too, one of her earlier schools. In all of them she seemed happy: smiling, laughing, playing. It was so odd for her to see herself like that; Esther couldn't remember feeling that happy as a child. But then, all of these photos were either taken by Jean or they had Jean in them. Her aunt had been a force of stability in her early childhood, and Hannah was noticeably absent from many of them.

And then something caught Esther's eye. Her heart quickened as she reached out and lifted a photograph that sat half-hidden among a stack of the earliest prints. It was one of the few pictures with both Hannah and Jean in it together. Her aunt and mother were with a man, sitting next to a barbecue in someone's back yard. Her mother had her arms around the man's neck, and they were all smiling for the camera.

"Who's that?" Esther asked, and she heard the breathlessness in her own voice as she said it.

Jean saw what she was looking at and suddenly went very still. Esther turned to her. Jean wasn't smiling now. Her eyes flickered between the photograph and Esther, and from the expression on her aunt's face, Esther could guess the answer.

"Is this… this is my father, isn't it?"

Her aunt nodded slowly. "There are probably not too many photos of him here. This might be the only one."

She glanced from the picture to Esther and scrutinised her niece for a long moment. Esther knew what her aunt was thinking. Many of these photos showed Hannah posing with various men, but there was only one photograph with this man.

"How did you know?" Jean asked.

"There was a man at the cemetery the other day," she said. "He was watching me while I was standing at Mum's grave." The man in the photo was thinner and younger, with darker hair, but there was no mistaking him, despite the passage of time. This was the man from the cemetery.

"Are you okay, love?" Jean asked. She reached out and put a hand gently on Esther's arm.

Esther nodded, but the truth was that she wasn't all that sure *how* she felt. Conflicted? Curious? She'd thought about her father over the years. Of course she had. Growing up, she'd known nothing about him. When she was younger she had constructed fantasies, fantasies in which he was heroic and handsome, strong and wise, wanting to meet her but unable to find her. She'd only ever had one real father-figure when she was young, and his appearance in her life had been reduced to a cameo by her mother's bad habits. Big Mike, a police inspector Hannah had dated when Esther was a teenager. It had been her mother's longest spell of sobriety. But she'd fucked it up in the end, as always. Ever since then, Esther had associated Mike—and police generally, she supposed—with that stolen period of happiness in a childhood dominated by chaos and misery. Before Mike, she'd only had her imaginary fathers, constructed from scraps of TV and movie characters. And after Mike… well, as she'd grown older she had just pushed the whole thing away. Stopped wondering. Stopped imagining.

And now here he was, staring out of an old photograph at her.

And she'd chased him around a graveyard five days ago.

Jean cleared her throat. "His name is Travis," she said, watching Esther carefully now. "Travis Somerville. He was an actor. Not a very successful one. At least, that's what he was doing during his short, fairly disastrous appearance in your mother's life. He was from London originally, and I guess that's where he probably scuttled back to after…" She hesitated. "Afterwards."

She studied Esther for a moment.

"They were never good for one another, your mother and him, so I can't say I was all that put out to hear he'd vanished one night, about four months into her pregnancy. Your mother was devastated, of course. I'm not saying that he drove her to become who she was. Not entirely. Hannah had always been wild. Always been into drink and… and the harder stuff. It's how they met. Some crazy party, full of drugs and all sorts. They were quite alike that way. But I think… I think it might have been what really sent her over the edge, his leaving like that. I think she really believed he would stay. I tried to warn her he wouldn't. I could see him getting uncomfortable. I could see it coming a mile off. But she wouldn't hear it. Thought I was just jealous. Typical Hannah." She shook her head again. "No, I never thought they were good for each other. Or to each other. If he'd stayed… God, it might actually have been worse, if you can believe that."

Jean fixed her niece with a flat look.

"His disappearance may well have been the better thing," she said softly, as she gave Esther's arm a sympathetic squeeze.

Esther stared back down at the picture of her father. It was so odd, having an image of him at last.

"Was that his real name?" Esther asked. "Travis Somerville?"

Jean shrugged. "Not sure. Hannah was too upset to go looking for him, and I… I thought she was better off with him out of the picture. I thought I could help her raise you. Thought she might settle down. That lasted all of… I don't know, a year, maybe. Your mum… she was who she was."

Esther nodded, but said nothing. She was wondering if the name was real, and if it might be enough to go on…

"You want a cup of tea?" Jean asked at last, after they had sat in silence for a full minute. She rose from the table and went to stick the kettle on.

"No, thanks," Esther replied. "Early start in the morning." She stood up from the table. "Have to drive to London first thing."

"Oh, a trip to London?" Jean said, taking a cup down from the cupboard. "Sounds fun."

"Not really. We have an autopsy to go to."

"Oh."

"The Met has a murder victim who might be linked to our investigation," Esther explained. "We're going down there to swap notes."

Her aunt gave a dramatic little shiver. "I don't know how you do it, Esther, love. Must be gruesome."

Esther frowned and shook her head. She never really got what everyone's hang-up about dead bodies was. Not dead strangers, anyway. They were just bodies. Just meat and bones. Maybe it was the exposure of the job that had conditioned her to feel indifferent, because most cops she knew felt the same way. A corpse was just a corpse. There was nothing mystical or horrifying about it. Unless the poor sod had been dead for several weeks, in which case the smell alone was horrifying, and somehow managed to linger in your nose for hours after you left the scene…

"It's just work," she told her aunt with a shrug. "I didn't know the guy."

Jean grimaced. "Even not knowing him, I'm not sure I'd have the stomach to go looking at things like that."

"You get used to it, I guess." She ran a thumb along the edge of the photograph in her hand. "You mind if I keep this?" she asked.

Jean nodded. "Of course." She tried to make it sound blasé, but Esther could see a hint of concern in her expression.

Esther forced a smile. "Well… goodnight, then," she said.

"Goodnight, love."

Esther left as the kettle began to boil. She went upstairs to her room, where she sat on the edge of her bed and stared for a long time at the photo of her mother and father, together, smiling for the camera.

22

DOROTHY LONG STEPPED back to scrutinise the Christmas tree. The decorations still weren't spread quite as evenly as she would have liked. The lights were okay this time, thank goodness, because unwinding that cable and rearranging it again would have been a right pain in the behind. After a moment's consideration, she decided that there was too much gold tinsel near the top and too many red baubles along the left-hand side. She stepped forward, made a few adjustments and stepped back again. She nodded to herself, pleased with the result.

She hadn't been paying much attention to the news on the television set behind her, but when she heard the anchor-man say a familiar name, she set aside her festive chore.

"... Gary Hetherington, originally from Belfield, was discovered dead in an abandoned warehouse near London's Docklands. Police are treating the death as suspicious and have appealed for anyone with information to contact them."

Dorothy stood stock-still as the newscaster moved on to another story. Then she set down the box of tiny reindeer she had been about to add to the tree, picked up the remote control and turned off the television. Another one. Two young men from Belfield Grammar found dead within a week. How odd.

She was trying to ignore the twisting worry in her gut. She had been putting it off. She had been procrastinating. Dithering and dodging like a right doodle-head. She glanced at the ceiling. The faint sound of stereo music was coming from his room.

Dorothy had long ago given up on the idea that Edwin might meet a nice girl. Long given up on her dream of grandchildren. He had always been an awkward boy, her Edwin, and never one for close friends. In fact, he'd never really had very many friends at all. And the socially awkward boy had turned into a socially awkward man. Edwin did little beyond going to work—stacking shelves at a big DIY chain store—and coming home again, to play video games and paint tiny figurines of historical soldiers. His room was full of tiny armies, cavalry and cannoneers and infantry units, all expertly painted. She loved her son dearly, and told herself many a time that a mother could do far worse than have a boy who didn't socialise much. Edwin had never been in trouble with the police and had never been into alcohol or drugs. And besides, she would have someone to look after her as she got older; Edwin's father had died when he was very young—so young that he didn't really remember Tom at all—and her only other relation was a sister in Canada who hadn't been home in about ten years.

Dorothy took a deep breath and steeled herself. She couldn't put it off any longer. She'd been thinking about this all day, ever since that policewoman had called at the school. Those boys she'd been asking about—Carlton Riddell and Gary Hetherington—they had been in Edwin's year at Belfield Grammar. She remembered them. They'd been on the rugby team that had done so well. Got up to plenty of mischief too, as she recalled. She was convinced poor Edwin had been the focus of their attentions once or twice.

She began making her way up the stairs to his room.

Odd as Edwin was, he'd been acting even more oddly in recent weeks. More withdrawn, and home later than usual some nights too. But all her gentle enquiries about where he'd been were met with surly grunts. Edwin wasn't surly. Quiet, yes, but never surly. Something was wrong, and it was clear that he was not going to volunteer anything without a bit of prodding. Perhaps he'd heard about Carlton. Belfield wasn't a big city, after all, and although he certainly hadn't been friends with the Riddell boy, murder was still a shocking business, especially if it was someone you knew, even from your school days. She would bring up the policewoman's visit with him and see what kind of a reaction she got.

She stopped at the door to his room, closed as usual, and tapped tentatively.

"Edwin?"

No answer. She knocked again, a little more loudly this time.

When she got no response, she turned the handle and stuck her head inside.

"Edwin?"

The light was on, but he wasn't in. The noise was his radio alarm clock. He must have forgotten to switch it off this morning.

She crossed the room, picking up clothes that had been left lying in piles on the carpet as she went, and turned off the radio. In the sudden silence, she scanned the room. It looked much the same as it always had: the posters of dragons and knights on the walls, the shelves of books and painstakingly painted miniatures, the desk covered in comic books and half-painted model soldiers. His computer screen was black, but the PC tower under the desk was humming as if it was still running. There was a half-eaten pizza on a plate and a couple of tea-stained mugs. The air in the room was thick with a musky fug.

She pushed open the window to let some fresh air in, despite the chill outside. Shifting the laundry to her left arm, she began collecting the dirty crockery.

It was true that Edwin didn't like her being in his room, but who would keep the place tidy if she didn't come in here once in a while? He never moaned about her clearing his plates or collecting his washing, did he?

He must be on a late shift. Perhaps she ought to pick him up from work one of these days; that way, he wouldn't be able to avoid her questions on the ride home, and she would get some answers.

Again, she felt that niggling worry in her gut.

Tomorrow, maybe. After all, there was all this laundry to get done first.

She'd pick him up tomorrow.

23

LONDON TWICE IN one week was twice too often as far as Jared was concerned. Having battled their way through Brent Cross, and struggled southward around Hyde Park, they'd eventually managed to get to the Westminster Mortuary just in time for the post-mortem of Gary Hetherington. Jared was just glad it was Esther who'd been driving this time and not him.

Normally he'd have slept through at least some of the journey. Instead, he had found himself sneaking sidelong glances at her all the way from Belfield. But there were no awkward conversations this time round. She seemed to have pulled herself out of her slump.

He knew she'd been drinking. Not last night, he was fairly sure, but definitely the night before. It had been close to midday yesterday by the time she'd shown up at the station, and she had spent all afternoon alternating between guzzling coffee and chewing gum. Most people probably wouldn't have noticed, but Jared had known Esther for too long not to recognise when she was having a morning-after-the-night-before, and yesterday had been a morning-after kind of day. She'd fallen off the wagon.

Not that he was in any position to criticise, a man who'd never had the guts to climb onto the damn wagon in the first place. Still, he felt for her. She'd been doing so well. He resolved not to mention it. Not yet. Binning the booze had been all Esther. There'd been no interventions, nobody else nudging her towards it. And Christ knew he was no great influence. When he finally realised she was serious and had kicked the drink, he had done his best to remain quietly supportive, and he got the sense that quiet was exactly how he should remain now. So they had discussed the case on the drive south instead, and Esther had told him about her trip to Belfield Grammar. She'd shown him the photocopied spread of the year group featuring Hetherington, Riddell and Sterling. She was convinced there was something in it. Jared wasn't so sure. He wondered if maybe she was floundering a bit after the disappointment of the Steiner arrest, grasping at any random link. Her summary for the London DCI seemed to underline the tenuousness of it all, and Jared wondered at the fact that she hadn't noticed that herself. But Esther had a good instinct most of the time, so he had decided to leave it for the moment. Let her run her leads and see where it got them.

After hours of driving, they'd finally turned down Regency Street and into the back carpark of the forensic mortuary, where they'd met Esther's contact, a detective called Pierce Goddard, and his boss, Detective Chief Inspector Andrea Greene. DCI Greene was a beautiful, buxom redhead in her late forties, and the first glimpse of her made Jared wish he'd put in a bit more of an effort this morning, instead of throwing on his usual rumpled suit and tie.

All four detectives were standing around the body of Gary Hetherington now, along with the pathologist and his mortuary assistant. Hetherington's body lay uncovered, waiting to be cut open. His skin was grey, but the body had been relatively well-preserved by the winter cold. Greene was studying the photos Esther had given her. The book of glossy prints showed Carlton Riddell lying on the slab in the Belfield mortuary, just as Hetherington lay here now. She was looking at close-ups of the injuries to his neck. There was no mistaking the similarities.

"Not conclusive, obviously," Greene remarked, as she glanced from the photos to the body on the table. "We'll not make any decisions until the full report comes back. In the meantime, Pierce will continue to liaise with your team, Jared, if you're in agreement?"

Jared cleared his throat and nodded. He felt the heat rising to his cheeks as he realised he'd been staring at the DCI's face—admiring the sweep of her eyebrows, her bright blue eyes and her high cheek bones—while she'd been considering the two sets of injuries which might turn out to be a link between their murder enquiries. She seemed not to have noticed, or at least chose to ignore the attention. She handed the photobook to Goddard, who tucked it into the brown folder Esther had given him, which contained copies of the Riddell case notes and the summary of the investigation she'd put together last night. The London DCI had scanned it in the carpark before coming in.

"We'll stay in touch and keep each other apprised of our progress," Greene said decisively. "Agreed?"

Jared nodded. "Yes, ma'am."

He glanced at Esther, who seemed to relax a little. If keeping London out of the Belfield investigation had been her intention, then her summary seemed to have done the trick.

DCI Greene turned to the pathologist. "Professor? Are you ready to proceed?"

The pathologist, a little bird of a man in his early sixties, ducked his head in response, and the detectives all stepped out to the gallery to let him set to work on the body.

"Start recording, please," the old man told his assistant, who pressed a button on a video camera to capture the procedure. "Time is ten forty-six a.m., Thursday, December nineteenth. Recommencement of the physical post-mortem examination of Gary Hetherington, having concluded the external examination and photographing of the subject, including contusion injuries to the neck and throat, we now move on to the internal examination…"

Jared headed for the doors. It wasn't that he was squeamish, not after all his years as a homicide detective. No, it was just that his staying to watch another dead man get carved up on a slab in a mortuary wouldn't be of benefit to anyone here, and certainly not the pathologist, who would talk them through his findings when he was done. Besides, what he *really* needed was a smoke. Esther was a bit of a Nazi about smoking in her car, and he was well below his daily intake of nicotine for this time of the morning.

Outside, he found a low red-brick wall to sit on, conveniently screened from the street by two gleaming black mortuary vans. He took a long, satisfying draw on his cigarette and listened to the background noise of the city—

the rumble of traffic, the chatter and clatter of pedestrians, the distant honk of horns. As he exhaled, he felt a tension he didn't know he'd been carrying ease.

The leafless branches above him rustled in the icy northern breeze, and he pulled his coat tighter around himself. He felt the cold more than he used to these days.

"Old-fashioned smoking, I see."

Jared turned to see Pierce Goddard strolling out of the mortuary building. The younger detective was sucking on one of those vaping devices, producing a big, thick cloud that hung about him when he exhaled. He lifted the contraption, indicating it as he said: "You never think of switching?"

Jared shrugged. "Why swap one thing for the other? That stuff can't be good for you either."

Goddard seemed to appraise the vaper. "Less tar, though. No tar, I think."

Jared just shrugged again.

"Listen, Guv," Goddard said, "I've had a chat with the DCI and she's happy for me to take you to Hetherington's apartment, if you and DS Penman need to take a look at it. It's been processed and all, but… well, who knows? Fresh pair of eyes couldn't hurt, eh?"

Jared hesitated, then nodded. "A fine idea," he said. The truth was, he'd like to get the hell out of the capital as soon as possible, but since they were here, they might as well make the most of it. And he knew Esther would want to take Goddard up on the offer.

As if his thought were a summons, Esther appeared at the mortuary doors and strolled over to join them. He watched as Goddard suddenly straightened a little and repeated his offer to her. Jared smirked, suddenly understanding why the offer had been made. The way Goddard stared at Esther, becoming more tongue-tied and red-faced as he talked, made his interest obvious. If Esther noticed, she gave no indication. She had that effect on young men. Jared wasn't sure if it was those cat-like green-blue eyes of hers, or the way she looked at you with them. She was a stunner, there was no mistake. Luckily, he was immune to her charms by now. He'd seen Esther at her worst, as well as her best, and he looked at her too much like a daughter now to see her the way young Goddard was seeing her. Poor idiot. He was yammering something about the case, growing more awkward while Esther scrutinised him. He was young for a detective, early twenties, with expertly mussed black hair and a layer of that carefully crafted stubble that was so fashionable these days. Esther would chew him up and spit him out if he let her. Another one of her victims. The thought reminded Jared of their trip to Stansted. He decided to interrupt the show.

"Does DCI Greene need you to remain for the results of the PM?" he asked, stubbing out his cigarette and hoisting himself off the brick wall.

Goddard ceased his babbling and turned. "Um, no, Guv. She's going to wait on and have a chat with the pathologist herself afterwards. She has Bethany with her to take notes and seize exhibits."

Bethany must have been one of the other detectives who'd waited in the gallery while he and Esther had conferred with Goddard and DCI Greene. Jared figured it was unlikely that the internal exam was going to provide them with anything useful. The external injuries appeared to be similar to the injuries inflicted on Carlton Riddell. That's what they'd come to confirm, and now that they'd done it, they might as well get on with whatever else they needed to do here. Hopefully, that way, they wouldn't have to come back.

"Well, then, what do you say we head over to Hetherington's apartment now?" Jared suggested. "We'll collect a copy of the post-mortem summary later, or you can send it on up to us at Belfield Central afterwards."

Esther nodded, and Goddard caught her nod and quickly followed suit.

"Yeah, whatever suits you, Guv. I'll go let the DCI know."

Esther gave Jared a querying look as Goddard hurried back inside.

"Seen enough autopsies," Jared muttered. "Let's get what we need and get back on the road."

Esther smirked. "If you say so. Guv."

Jared chuckled.

* * *

Esther tried not to let the stress of driving through London show on her face as she fought her way east towards Gary Hetherington's apartment in the City. Pierce Goddard sat in the front passenger seat, performing the role of navigator. He talked them through his work on the investigation in between calling out directions. Esther was only half-listening to the chatter about his work, willing him to give her the directions a little sooner each time, but she heard enough to murmur a 'yes, please' when he offered to provide a copy of all his witness details.

Her hands tightened on the steering wheel when a cyclist, nipping up her nearside, suddenly swerved out in front of her to avoid a cabbie who was pulling out from the kerb. She didn't even have time to hit the horn. She let out a deep breath as her heart slowed again, zoning out from Goddard's flow of chatter. Somehow, he'd moved on to the topic of nightlife spots in central London. She concentrated on switching lanes as he called out another turn. Made herself loosen her grip on the wheel. She should have asked him to drive.

It took over half an hour, cutting across Lambeth and Newington and crossing Tower Bridge, and her back and armpits were damp with sweat by the time they arrived. Goddard directed her to an underground carpark that serviced Hetherington's apartment building. An elderly parking attendant in a hi-viz coat tipped his flat cap to Goddard when the detective flashed his warrant card. The old man flipped a switch to raise the barrier and down they went.

Esther soon forgot about her aching knuckles and sweaty pits as they descended into a concrete-pillared cavern filled with millions of pounds worth of luxury cars—although she did start sweating again when she had to back into a spot between a Lamborghini sports car and a monstrous Bentley.

As they crossed the parking lot to the elevators, Goddard pointed out a black Ferrari convertible.

"That's Hetherington's Portofino," he told them. "We've run the plates with our traffic camera team for the weeks prior to his disappearance, but it looks like it pretty much just sat here the whole time. Probably just for trips home or out the country. Driving's not really the best way to get around London if you live in the City."

"Tell me about it," Esther muttered.

They headed to the tenth floor and Goddard let them into the apartment. It had the stale smell of a place unaired for several weeks. One wall of the vast living space was floor-to-ceiling glass, offering an impressive view of the Shard and Tower Bridge to the south. Neat and tidy, the place had that unlived-in feeling, like a showroom.

"This was how you guys found it?" Esther asked.

Goddard nodded. "Pretty much."

"And he lived alone?" she asked.

"The ex-girlfriend has a place over in Shepherd's Bush," he told her. He pointed to the sheet of names and phone numbers he'd handed to Jared on the drive. "Portia Spencer. She's top of your list there."

Goddard had said the apartment had been processed twice—a full search when Hetherington became a high-risk misper and a forensic run-through after he was found dead—but Esther slipped on a pair of nitrile gloves out of habit as she stepped into the kitchen, a tastefully designed haven of marble and chrome, spacious and uncluttered. She began pulling the drawers out, one by one, while Jared went to search the living area. A lot of the drawers were empty, and those that weren't held nothing unusual: cutlery and tea towels, biros, half a roll of sticky-tape, takeaway menus. After a glance through the cupboards and the fridge-freezer—which was blessedly bare—Esther went to the bedroom. She checked the bedside table first, but again it held nothing out of the ordinary: a blister pack of over-the-counter painkillers, a couple of expensive watches and two paperback books. War novels. No handwritten notes, no diaries, no journals.

She crossed the room to the giant wardrobe, which contained an impressive selection of expensive-looking suits, tailored shirts and silk ties, everything carefully and neatly arranged.

"Did he have a cleaner?" Esther called out.

"No cleaner," Goddard replied. He had followed her to the bedroom and was standing in the doorway. "Just kind of a neat freak, I think."

It didn't take them long to realise that they weren't going to find anything of use.

The three of them came together again in the living room, standing in front of the huge glass wall to take in the view of the Thames's south bank and the London skyline.

Jared handed Esther the list of witnesses and she glanced over it. It wasn't very long. Top of the list, as Goddard had mentioned, was Portia Spencer, ex-girlfriend. Below that, Brad Kendall, Hetherington's boss at Kendall & Co., Financial Management. A few neighbours' names at the bottom, with notes to the side of each outlining that none of them seemed to know Hetherington well at all. She asked Goddard about those.

"Yeah, not much community spirit in this building," he replied. "All seem like young high-fliers. Career people. Bit like Gary himself, I guess. None of them really seem to know each other at all, or care much. Was a pain in the backside trying to get hold of them at first. They're all lawyers and financial consultants and that type of thing. Spend all day at the office. I've noted some of their office contacts there, but you'd be wasting your time with them, I reckon."

Esther's eyes settled on the last entry on his list.

"Bolster Fitness?" she read aloud.

"Turns out our friend Gary was a bit of a gym addict," Goddard told them. "That's actually how he and Portia met. She's a bit of a gym bunny herself." He smirked. "You'll know what I mean when you meet her. She says the break-up was amicable, but Hetherington switched gyms all the same. Bolster's all the way up in Islington, so he went more than a mile out of his way to avoid her."

The DC checked his watch.

"Unfortunately, we gotta wrap this little walk-through up, I'm afraid," he said, sounding genuinely regretful. "I've a couple of witness interviews lined up for this afternoon. An old case the CPS have been breaking my balls about. Really gotta get them squared away. You guys be okay with that list? I can take the Tube back to the station. It'll be quicker. Let you guys get on with your follow-ups."

"Of course," Jared replied. "You've been a great help, Pierce. Thank you."

"No problem, Guv."

They followed him from the apartment, down to the lobby and out onto the street. Once outside, he hesitated. His eyes lingered on Esther for a moment.

"Are you planning on staying in London tonight?" he asked, a touch of colour rising to his cheeks. "I know a couple of nice spots. If you want, I could show you guys around the town."

"No, we have to get back to Belfield tonight," she replied simply. Thoughts of DCI Small came racing into her mind and she had to crush the insane notion that Goddard had somehow heard about her 'reputation'. The sudden reminder made her angry; she had to school her features and soften her voice. "But thank you for all your help today, Pierce. I really appreciate it."

Goddard smiled through his disappointment. "Anytime. Give me a call. Glad to help."

Esther and Jared stood outside the front of the apartment building, watching Goddard hurry across the road and away towards the nearest Tube station. It was cold today, the sky bright and the air crisp. Patches of frost still lingered on the grass in the park across the street, a quaint little spot bounded by freshly painted Victorian railings. Esther could tell that it would be a beautiful, leafy oasis in the summer. The whole neighbourhood was steeped in affluence. She wondered if Gary Hetherington had enjoyed any of it, or whether he had become oblivious to the trappings of wealth in the end, as so many rich people seemed to become.

"Let's make some calls," Jared said at last, nodding towards the list in Esther's hand. "See if we can meet a couple of these people and get back to Belfield sooner rather than later."

"I'll ring the ex," she replied. "You can try his boss."

They thumbed the numbers into their respective phones as they headed back towards the building's underground carpark.

Portia Spencer picked up after the first ring.

"Hello?"

"Is this Portia Spencer?" Esther asked.

"Yes," came the reply. "Who's this?"

"My name is Esther Penman. I'm a detective with Belfield police. I'm investigating a case linked to the murder of Gary Hetherington. I'm in London today, and I was wondering if it might be possible to grab a few minutes of your time. Would that be okay?"

A hesitation on the other end of the line, then: "The

detectives were here just yesterday, asking questions."

"They were detectives investigating Gary's death," Esther replied gently. "I'm investigating another case. A man who was killed in Gary's hometown. Someone Gary went to school with. Would it be okay to come and speak with you today? If you feel up to it?"

"Yes… yes, that's fine," came the unsteady reply. "I'm at home. Can you come to my flat?"

"We can do that," Esther replied, smiling and mouthing a 'thank you' to the old parking attendant as he admitted them back into the underground lot. "I got your address from our London colleagues. We can be there"—she checked her watch—"about half twelve? Would that suit?"

"Yes, that's… that's fine."

"Thanks, Portia. We'll see you then." Esther hung up.

Jared had stopped short. "I'm sorry, hold on," he was saying, "you're breaking up, hang on." He waved at Esther to indicate that he was losing signal and started moving back up to the street. She nodded and went to get the car.

When she pulled up outside a couple of minutes later, Jared was still on the phone. The grimace he wore as he sat into the car told her he was not having as easy a time of it as she'd had with Portia.

"Well, as soon as possible, if you can," he said, to whoever was on the other end, "we're only here today. Yes. I appreciate that, thank you," he added, not sounding all that appreciative, and definitely not looking it, as he hung up and tossed his phone into the central console. "You'd think I was trying to get an interview with the bloody King, for Christ's sake," he growled.

"No luck?" she asked, as she keyed Portia Spencer's Shepherd's Bush address into her own phone. When she pulled out into the traffic, the app's robotic voice began to dictate directions.

"Apparently Mister Kendall is very busy," Jared grumbled. "Secretary couldn't promise a meeting today, but she's going to ring us back later."

"Well, we have Miss Portia Spencer waiting for us," Esther replied. "So let's go see what the gym-bunny ex-girlfriend can tell us."

24

PORTIA SPENCER'S APARTMENT was blessedly short on Christmas tat. A small tree on the kitchen counter was her only concession to the season. The woman herself, on the other hand, was *all* tat, as far as Esther could see, with her peroxide-blonde hair, her mahogany skin, and teeth so white Esther wouldn't be surprised to learn they glowed in the dark. Talking to her was an irritating task. She chewed gum constantly and overused the work 'like'. Squeezed into luminous purple lycra that accentuated her sculpted curves, the woman was indeed a 'gym bunny', as Pierce Goddard had called her.

A set of light weights and a training mat were laid out on the ground in front of the TV. Whether it was a semi-permanent feature or they had interrupted a workout, Esther couldn't tell, but given the outfit, she figured it was the latter.

The woman sat across from them on the second of a pair of cream leather couches—her whole apartment was a blend of carefully contrasted shades of cream and magnolia—dabbing at eyes that were red from crying. She must have touched up her makeup in the time it took them to get from the street to her apartment door, because her mascara was still applied perfectly. But in spite of her efforts on the cosmetic front, she seemed genuinely upset when she spoke about Gary Hetherington. Esther had paid close attention, trying to read her emotions whenever she spoke. Jared certainly wasn't going to notice anything, that was for sure, since he couldn't stop staring at her big plastic boobs. They looked ridiculous, Esther thought. Like big, tanned balloons. Men were idiots.

"I just couldn't believe it, like, you know?" Portia was telling them. "He was so… *fit!* Gary spent most of his time working his upper body—like, he was fit, he was fast, he was strong, you know? Whoever killed him must have been just as strong. Or there must have been, like, a bunch of them." She took a deep, anguished breath and stood. "Excuse me, a moment."

Jared half-rose as she hurried out. He cast Esther a questioning glance, the suggestion clearly being that Esther might consider following her to see if she was okay. Esther responded with a flat look of her own.

"Sit down, Jared," she murmured. "Just give her a moment."

Jared sat.

"And they're not real, by the way," she added quietly.

Jared frowned at her.

"Seriously," Esther whispered. "Stop staring at them."

He had the decency to blush as Portia returned with a fresh set of tissues and a glass of water.

"I'm so sorry," she said, realising she hadn't offered

them anything. "Can I get you guys some tea or something? I only have herbal infusions, but there's, like, a whole selection."

"No, thank you, ma'am," Jared replied stiffly. "We'll try not to take up too much more of your time."

Esther spoke as the woman returned to her seat. "What about your relationship?" she asked. "Detective Goddard told us you and Gary split up a while ago? When did you last see him?"

"We broke up in July. I didn't see him after that. Sorry, that's not exactly right. I did, just once, when he came by to, like, pick up some stuff he'd left at my flat. That was, um, early August? Yeah. That was the last time I saw him. I told Pierce all of this."

"And the split was amicable, is that right? But Gary still switched gyms?"

"Yeah. It wasn't a messy break-up. Not at all. I've had, like, a lot messier!" She gave a mirthless laugh. "Gary could be jealous. He was a bit intense at the start, but then that kind of faded." She shrugged. "Maybe that was half the problem, you know?" She gave Esther a lopsided smile. "At least when he was jealous, I knew he was into me. But then he got, like, really, *really* into his work. Spent most of his time at the office. That was probably the other half of the problem. I started getting suspicious sometimes. What girl wouldn't, right? Sometimes we'd fight about that. But it was never, like, physical or anything."

"You think he might have been cheating on you?" Esther asked.

Portia shrugged. "I don't know. We were, like, drifting apart by then. Maybe. Maybe not. You know what those financial guys are like, working crazy hours. It was getting so that we were, like, working out in the gym together more than being together-together, you know?"

"Did Gary have any issues with anyone else at the gym?" Esther asked. "Or were there any people he mentioned more often than others? Anyone at work he was having problems with?"

Portia shook her head. "Pierce asked me about that too. I can't think of anyone who had any beef with Gary. Not at my gym anyway. I don't know about, like, other gyms or anything? I don't really know anyone who goes to Bolster Fitness. That's the gym he moved to after we, like, split."

"Did he ever mention the name Carlton Riddell? Or Mark Sterling?" Esther asked.

Portia frowned. "I've never heard those names. Who are they? Are they, like, the suspects?"

"No, ma'am," Esther replied, "just old friends of Gary's. Carlton Riddell is the man who was killed in Belfield a few days ago."

Portia's eyes widened. "Oh, yeah, you said! Is there, like, a serial killer going around or something?"

Esther shook her head. "It's not likely," she replied. The last thing she needed was this woman spouting to the press, or on social media. "We just have to investigate every possibility thoroughly."

Scanning her notes quickly, Esther figured they'd got everything they were going to get from Portia Spencer. Standing, she thanked the woman for her time.

Jared followed suit, careful to keep his eyes squarely on her face as he bid her good day.

When they were back out in the street, Jared checked his phone.

"Anything from Hetherington's old firm yet?" Esther

asked.

He shook his head. "Nothing."

"Let's go pay a visit to Bolster Fitness while we're waiting," she suggested.

* * *

This time they decided to take the Tube. Esther declared she wasn't ready for another round with the London traffic, and they would get there faster on the subway in any case. Jared couldn't blame her, but he didn't relish the idea of trekking through the city either. Every street was wedged with Christmas shoppers, and the Tube just presented its own sort of battle: pushing their way through throngs at underground stations, and trying not to be swept away by the tide of people whenever they stopped to look at the maps on the walls.

All in all, the chaos of the season slowed them down, and it was mid-afternoon when they emerged again from underground. As he climbed the steps to the surface, Jared felt sweaty and exhausted.

They headed west a couple of blocks and found the gym they were looking for wedged between two high street clothing stores, the words Bolster Fitness made out in red lettering on a white backlit sign.

Inside, they were greeted by the sound of clinking weights and the thundering rhythm of treadmills from the floor above, all underscored by thumping dance music. Unlike the clothing stores next door, there wasn't much of a Christmas vibe here; a white plastic tree with red baubles stood in one corner, and a single string of tinsel draped the sign above reception. This was an environment that was entirely alien to Jared. He stared at the glossy covers of the magazines that littered the tables in the reception area, with photos of half-naked men and women showing off their muscular torsos. Magazines with pictures like that had been confined to the top shelf in his day. He pulled his gaze away from them—and the similarly half-clad models advertising sports brands on posters on the walls—and followed Esther as she marched straight up to the counter.

The man behind reception was a tank. He looked like one of those American wrestlers, with a neck wider than his head. He had a sharp crewcut and a thin gold chain hanging out over his size-too-small T-shirt. He eyed Esther and Jared warily as she flashed her warrant card and asked him if he knew a member called Gary Hetherington.

"We have over a thousand members," he replied cagily. "You got, like, a warrant or anything?"

"To ask you if you know someone?" Esther replied tersely. "I don't need a warrant for that. I already know he was a member here. I just wanted to know if you knew him. Or if any of the staff might have known him."

The big receptionist shrugged. "Dunno. Some of the guys do one-on-one training with people, but like I said, we have over a thousand members."

Esther frowned. "You have a list of the staff who do one-on-ones?"

"Up on the wall there," the guy replied, as he nodded towards a framed poster on the wall beside reception. The poster displayed a list of names next to their workout specialisations. "Oh, except for Lewis Treford and Jake Faraday."

Esther, on her way over to examine the poster, froze. She turned back to the receptionist. "Lewis Treford and who?" she asked.

"Jake Faraday," he replied. "Those guys don't work here anymore. We just haven't got around to printing a new list."

Jared watched Esther rummage in her battered leather handbag and pull out a sheet of paper. When she unfolded it, he could see it was the photocopied yearbook page she'd shown him earlier that morning. She stared at the page for a moment.

"Why do they not work here anymore?" she asked, with a sharpness in her voice that made Jared lean in and try to get a better look at the paper in her hands. He hadn't paid much notice to it the first time round. At the top of the page, in cursive script, were the words *Belfield Grammar School Senior Year*, with neat rows of small portrait photographs below.

The receptionist hesitated, glancing about conspiratorially before replying, "Well, Lewis was found going at it with one of his clients in the toilets. Big *no-no* here. Manager sacked him straight away, no meeting or nothing."

"And Faraday?" Esther asked.

Musclehead straightened up and shrugged, clearly disappointed by her lack of interest in the scandal. "Just started slacking off, showing up late, that sort of thing. Turned up drunk once, had to be sent home."

"Does management keep the resumés of former employees?" Esther pressed.

The receptionist frowned. "I'm pretty sure stuff like that needs a warrant."

To Jared's surprise, Esther whipped out another sheet of

paper from her bag. She quickly scribbled some details onto the form and slid it across the counter.

"There," she said. "Official police request form. If you have a resumé or a photo on file, I need a copy of them."

Jared watched the big man study the form uncertainly. He glanced at Esther and back down again, frowning deeply at the paper in his hands as he considered what to do. It almost looked comical. The data request form wasn't a warrant, but muscle-head didn't know that, and faced with Esther's emphatic assuredness, he quickly cracked.

"I'll just go get the manager," he said.

"What is it?" Jared asked Esther, as the receptionist disappeared into a back room. He looked again at the yearbook page in her hands. "Am I missing something here?"

Esther was chewing her lip as she glanced from the photocopy in her hands to the poster on the wall.

"Might be a coincidence," she said, "but I don't think so. Look here."

She spread the yearbook page on the reception counter.

"Carlton Riddell," she said, pointing out the small black-and-white photo of their murder victim as a teenager. Her finger moved a little further along the row to another portrait. "Mark Sterling." The greasy man was much fresher-looking as a teenager. Indicating a third photo halfway up the page, she added, "And here's Gary Hetherington."

Then she slid her finger to the bottom, where the names of children with no photographs were listed.

"A.J. Faraday," she said, as she pointed out the name. "They all went to the same class. There's a link here, Jared."

He nodded towards the poster on the gym wall. "You

think that *that* Faraday is the same as *this* Faraday?" he asked, lowering his voice as a couple of newcomers passed by, swiping their membership cards to get through the turnstile at the end of the counter and disappearing up the stairs beyond. "In a city of ten million?"

"I don't like coincidences," she said, half to herself, as she stared at the names.

Several minutes passed before the manager appeared, her beefy receptionist in tow. She was more professionally dressed in shirt and trousers, but she clearly shared the same interests as Portia Spencer; her teeth gleamed white when she smiled at them, all the brighter against the darkness of a well-tanned face, and there wasn't much spare flesh on her either.

"Officers," she said. "Could I trouble you to show me your identification? Just to keep myself right, you understand." As soon as Jared and Esther had obliged, the woman set a photocopied resumé with a headshot inlay onto the counter and slid it towards them. "Jake Faraday's CV. Is there a problem I need to know about?"

Esther picked up the resumé. "Date of birth works," she muttered to Jared. "And he's listed his high school as Belfield Grammar." She raised her head and addressed the gym manager. "What can you tell us about him?"

The manager shrugged. "Not a whole lot. Jake kept himself to himself. I mean, don't get me wrong, he was nice enough. Friendly. He used to practically live here, either working out or working with clients. He was very dedicated. Really took care of himself. Well, up until about three months ago. That's when the problems started."

"What problems?" Jared asked.

"Missing appointments with customers. Showing up

drunk. His whole attitude, his whole… *personality* seemed to change. I gave him a couple of warnings. Gave him chances. I tried to get him to talk, to tell me if something had happened at home or something, but he was totally defensive. Wouldn't open up. Not even a little bit." She sighed. "I felt bad about it—he'd been such a good employee up to then—but customers began complaining. His head wasn't in the sessions he was doing, and he kept missing shifts. He got a written warning and then…" She shrugged. "And then I had to let him go." Her face creased with concern. "Is he okay? I hope he's not in any trouble?"

Esther ignored the questions. Questions she couldn't answer even if she'd known what the answers were. "When was he let go?" she asked.

"October. Sixteenth or seventeenth, I think it was."

"Have you or any of your staff seen Jake since he left?"

"Not that I know of. I don't think anyone here was really that close with him. Jake was a real private kind of guy. I can ask around, if you like?"

Esther handed over her contact card. "Thank you, I'd really appreciate that. If anything comes up, you can get me on that number or send me an email."

Esther made a note of the manager's details and then they thanked her for her time and left.

According to Faraday's CV, his home address was only a few stations away from where they were, so they decided to check it out. Again, the Tube ride took longer than expected, and when they arrived, they found that Faraday had vacated the pokey little bedsit sometime in October, with no notice given, and three months' rent outstanding. The landlord, who lived on the ground floor of the building, was not particularly helpful. An elderly South Asian man with patchy English, he was only interested in complaining about Faraday's arrears, and demanding that the police get the money back for him. When Esther asked if they could see the apartment, the little man flat-out refused. He had a new tenant, and Faraday hadn't left anything behind apart from debts and unemptied rubbish bins.

They left, Jared feeling drained by the fruitless encounter. Still, exhausted as he was by the exchange, he decided to try Gary Hetherington's old firm one more time.

"It's Detective Inspector Jared Wilcox looking for Brad Kendall again," he told the cheery secretary, as he and Esther worked their way back along the busy streets. "We're not far away at the moment. Would it be possible to call in? We only need a few minutes of his time."

"I'm sorry," the woman chirped. "Mister Kendall is out at meetings for the next two hours. It won't be possible to arrange a meeting today."

Jared bit back a growl. "We're only in London today. Ten minutes is all we need."

"I'm so sorry."

Jared hung up in frustration. Esther was looking at the photo inlay on Jake Faraday's CV. He looked just as big and bulked-up as the gym receptionist, but with a shaved head and dark brows that cast shadows over his eyes. Neither ugly nor handsome, his features had taken on the chiselled look of a man who ate well and worked out often.

Abruptly, Esther folded up the resumé and stuffed it in her bag.

"Well?" she asked him.

He scowled and shook his head. "Kendall can't meet us today. Come on, let's get a train back to the car. I'm sick of London."

Esther didn't raise any argument.

25

ESTHER'S LIGHTS WERE off, but she kept the engine running and her car's heating system turned up against the cold of the December evening. She was in an upmarket suburb on the outskirts of a wealthy commuter town, an hour north of London. Some of the residences were choked with festive lighting, but the house Esther watched was modestly decorated; a wreath hung on the door and a set of white lights were placed evenly around the bulbous evergreen in the front yard. She had parked directly across the road from the house, in the darkness between the streetlamps.

The list of Travis Somervilles she'd compiled from a quick computer search at work had been narrowed down by virtue of age to two potential candidates. She had come here first and struck lucky; when he'd appeared at one of the upstairs windows within minutes of her arrival, Esther had immediately recognised the man from the cemetery. She'd held her breath as he'd looked out into the street, but he'd been staring up the road as though searching for someone and didn't seem to notice her. After a moment, he'd pulled the blinds and disappeared. That was ten minutes ago, and Esther sat here still, unsure what to do.

Why had she come here?

She was still sitting, mulling this over, when a small car pulled up directly in front of Somerville's house and a woman in her twenties got out. She lifted a small boy, about three or four years old, from the back seat.

Somerville's front porch light came on and the man himself reappeared, smiling broadly at the newcomers.

"Grandpa!" the little boy shouted, as he wriggled out of the woman's grasp and raced up the short driveway.

Somerville scooped the boy into his arms, the woman trudging up the drive after him. Still holding the boy in one arm, Somerville gave the woman a quick hug with his free arm, and she kissed his cheek. Then all three of them disappeared inside.

Esther sat for a long time, staring at the house. She tried to ignore the sting in her throat, the weight in her belly like lead. Was that woman her half-sister? Was that her nephew racing up the drive?

She was suddenly waylaid by a dizzying assault of thoughts she hadn't been expecting. She wasn't sure what she *had* been expecting.

Abruptly, she shifted into first gear and pulled out, hardly glancing in her mirrors as she gunned her little Fiat down the street and headed for the nearest motorway.

She drove, her mind racing madly as she hit the highway. She darted in and out of lanes, pressing hard on the accelerator every time a gap opened up. It began to rain, a patter that quickly became a heavy downpour. The wipers flicked across the windscreen, making the lights of the other cars blur and weep.

Her sense of time dimmed, and her mind grew numb as she drove, pushing along the overtake lane for long periods at well over the posted limit.

When the exit for Sarsbury appeared, she ignored it. Instead, she took the next off-ramp, the exit for Belfield. The wipers thudded, the rain drummed, and Esther's mind spun through a whirlwind of thoughts until, ten minutes later, she found herself pulling up outside Triona's house.

She felt strange, her insides tangled and fuzzy. She was not at all certain what she was doing here. Still, she found herself getting out of the car and climbing the steps of the urban terrace.

The rain was pouring down now, and Esther was drenched in moments. She reached the door and watched herself press the doorbell. The chime inside the house seemed to bring her to her senses. What was she doing? What if Triona had company? She was being a fool! She should get in her car and go home.

But just as she was about to turn away, a light came on in the hall. The front door opened. Triona stood there in baggy sweats, a damp towel in one hand, her hair mussed and wet. The nurse's surprised expression was quickly replaced by a look of concern as she pulled the door wider.

"My God, Esther, you're soaked!" she said. "Come in! Quick!"

Esther couldn't find her voice or move of her own accord, and Triona had to take her by the hand and pull her inside. Esther could smell the lingering scent of citrus shampoo.

"Let me get you a dry towel," Triona said.

She disappeared up the stairs and reappeared a moment later with a fluffy white bath towel in her arm.

"Are you okay?" she asked, handing it to Esther.

Esther frowned and opened her mouth to speak, but she couldn't find the words. She wasn't sure she wanted to talk at all.

"Get that jumper off you," Triona said, not unkindly, as she moved closer, "or you'll catch your death."

As Triona helped her out of the sodden sweater, her face came close to Esther's. They both stopped and stared at each other for a long moment. To Esther it felt like an eternity, but it wasn't awkward. They stood there, staring into each other's eyes, until suddenly they weren't staring anymore. Esther dropped the towel as they came together. She couldn't have said who moved first, or who kissed whom. They moved as one. Esther felt Triona's lips meet hers, felt the woman's hands cup her face. Already every part of her was tingling.

Triona grunted as Esther pushed her gently against the wall and kissed her harder, tongue brushing her lips.

When thunder rolled through the sky outside, neither woman noticed. They were already stumbling up the stairs to the bedroom, tugging at each other's clothes. A moment later they gave up and simply stripped off their own clothes.

They were both naked by the time they got to the bedroom. Triona pushed Esther backwards onto the bed and straddled her. Then she leaned down and kissed Esther about as tenderly as Esther had ever been kissed. Esther panted softly as the nurse moved to her neck, slipped her tongue into her ear, then made her way down her body, kissing her nipples, sliding the tip of her tongue into her navel. Esther heard herself whimper as the woman worked her way down further still…

When Triona moved between her legs, Esther felt an explosion of pleasure that rippled from her groin out through her whole body, from her forehead to the tips of her toes. She was unable to control the gasps and moans that escaped her then, as Triona kissed and fingered and nuzzled.

Esther realised that she couldn't remember the last time she'd had sober sex. It was incredible.

As Triona tended to her, Esther came, again and again and again…

26

THE THUNDERSTORM HAD lasted only a few minutes, but fat raindrops still fell from the carpark's floodlights, hitting the roof of Dorothy's car with loud, intermittent *thunks*. The place was almost empty, the light from those towering floodlamps glimmering wetly on the stretches of empty tarmac.

She'd pulled up as close as she could to the sprawling hardware store that dominated this end of the retail park, but she hadn't pulled right up to the doors; it might be closing time, with barely a dozen cars in a lot that could hold hundreds, but she couldn't bring herself to park in the disabled bays right outside the front. It would have felt wrong.

There was a brief flurry of movement now that the rain had ceased: some last-minute shoppers, hauling straggly Christmas trees to their cars; a couple of employees slipping away a few minutes early. Some of the lights went out in the store itself. An older member of staff emerged. He rolled the shutter halfway down and then ducked back inside again.

Determined as Dorothy had been to do this earlier, she wasn't feeling at all confident about it now. She just wasn't the confrontational type. Never had been. She was considering again the wisdom of her plan when, a moment later, as the rest of the staff began to leave, she spotted him.

While other employees filed out in pairs or small groups, Edwin shuffled out alone. As always, his head was down, his shoulders hunched against a world he only ever seemed to half-occupy while the rest of him drifted in some dreamworld. Abruptly he stopped and looked out across the carpark as if searching for someone. His eyes slid over her car without recognising it, before he turned and began to trudge away once more. He hadn't even noticed her. But then, why would he? She never picked him up from work.

She tapped the horn and flashed her lights.

Edwin stopped and stared, looking confused for a moment, before starting towards her.

"Mum," he exclaimed as he sat into the car, "what are you doing here?"

Dorothy started the engine and began a lugubrious manoeuvre to back out of the parking space, even though the ones in front of her and all around her were empty. She would be the first to admit that she was not the most confident driver; perpetually nervous about hitting something—or some*one*—every journey was stressful. That was why, for example, she always did her shopping early in the morning; a busy supermarket carpark was enough to undo her.

"We've been missing each other the past few days, like ships in the night," she replied, as she wrestled the gearstick into first and juddered towards the exit, "and I've been wanting to talk to you about something."

Edwin suddenly seemed uneasy. Some subtle shift in his bearing tickled Dorothy's senses. It was enough to confirm for her that something was off. She pulled out onto the main road and picked up a bit of speed. There was nowhere for him to go, and she was determined to get to the bottom of whatever was going on.

"You must have heard the news?" she said. "About those boys, those old classmates of yours? Carlton and Gary? They were in your year at school. On the rugby team. You remember?"

Edwin was staring straight ahead. He'd grown rigid, his lips clamped shut, his face pale.

"Edwin? Are you okay?" she asked anxiously. "It's just… you've been so quiet recently! You're worrying me."

That's when she realised he was crying. He was shaking, and silent tears were rolling down his cheeks.

Shocked by her son's behaviour, Dorothy pulled over quickly, ignoring the blast of a horn from the car behind. She unbuckled her belt and reached out to put her arms around him. He didn't resist.

"Oh, Edwin, love!" she cried. "What is it? What is it, love?"

She was so shaken by his sudden breakdown that tears were springing up in her own eyes too. She hadn't seen Edwin cry since he was a child, and there was something terribly unsettling about it.

"Edwin! What is it?"

Edwin sucked in a deep breath, as if he'd been underwater a long time and was only now coming up for air.

"Something's happened, Mum," he said, coughing out

sobs. "Something bad. Something very bad."

"Oh, Edwin!"

They both sat there in Dorothy's car at the side of the road, clinging to each other and letting the tears roll, while Edwin pulled himself together enough to speak.

And then he told his mother everything.

27

MARK STERLING'S HEAD was as cloudy as his sitting room, steeped in the mellowing fog of weed he'd secured for himself earlier that day. He'd sold what he needed to sell. Selling weed was easy in the Drakehill estate, as long as you didn't run into the Petrauskas. Those bastards were big and thick and they didn't like anyone muscling in on their turf. Thankfully, the Lithuanian brothers hadn't been anywhere in sight today, and Mark had taken his tidy little cash profit and come home to smoke the rest and chill.

He'd had a message from Vicky yesterday. She had wanted to meet him at that café she'd mentioned. Berta's. She'd said it was urgent, but he'd been in Manchester getting his stash, so they'd settled on tomorrow morning. Not too early. Mark didn't do early, although he *was* looking forward to seeing her again. He was hoping she might wear something tight and revealing like last time…

At first, he thought he imagined the soft rap at his apartment door. But when he heard it a second time, he cursed softly to himself. Gloria. She was becoming a right pain in the ass. No wonder her husband was away so much. Mark was pretty sure illicit love affairs weren't supposed to involve quite so much nagging. Still, she was a good shag, and she could be pretty wild in bed, doing things he wouldn't have thought of, or wouldn't have had the courage to suggest. It was true she was a few years older than him, but she'd been a hell of an education so far…

Mark realised he was getting hard. Smiling to himself, he decided a visit from Gloria might not be so bad after all. As long as she kept her mouth shut. Well, maybe not that… but as long as she didn't talk too much…

Still smiling, he heaved himself off the sofa and shuffled from the living room.

But when he pulled open the front door, the smile slid queasily from his face…

It wasn't the size of the man standing in his doorway that made Mark's guts twist into a knot, although it was difficult not to notice the huge chest and shoulders straining against the hooded top. No. It was the eyes. Mark recognised the eyes straight away.

"Holy shit, Alfie-boy!" he stammered breathlessly. "Shit, man, you've grown!"

He tried to make the exclamation sound witty, or friendly. But Mark Sterling had never been friendly to Alfie Faraday. It wouldn't wash now.

As Faraday took a step forward, Mark panicked.

"Stop!" he shouted. "Wait!"

He tried to shove the door closed, but Faraday simply reached out and grabbed hold of the rickety thing. His arm was roped in muscle. When the bulked-up monster that used to be Little Alfie pushed, Mark could feel huge strength behind the effort. Could feel his own strength deserting him.

With a cry, he suddenly let go. Turning, he fled to the kitchen and shoved the door closed behind him. He lunged across the room to the outer door that led to the fire escape.

Betsy, dozing under the kitchen table, raised her head in alarm at the sudden intrusion, but if Mark had been hoping for some kind of canine defence, the black Lab gave no indication she was about to oblige. She whined and yelped, but didn't even get out of her basket.

He wrenched open the door to the fire escape and plunged down the stairs, almost tumbling headlong to the ground when he slipped on the icy metal steps. Grasping hold of the handrail, he risked a glance over his shoulder. The mellowing calm of the cannabis was gone now, and his heart hammered even faster when he saw the hulking shadow emerge from the kitchen doorway onto the metal platform above.

The fire escape led out into a rear carpark—a narrow, trash-littered place full of weeds and potholes. Dim orange streetlamps from the nearby road did little to dispel the gloom, and it was more from memory than observation that Mark managed to avoid any of the broken concrete bollards that separated the yard from the green beyond. He felt a stitch forming in his side and a dull pain in his chest as he staggered out onto the grass, ankle-high and already covered in frost. Although he couldn't see them in the darkness, he knew there was a stand of trees at the far end of the green, and streets of houses beyond. If he could make it that far…

He cried out when he slipped on a patch of mud, blind panic setting in as he crashed to the ground.

Scrambling back to his feet, he watched Faraday come

pounding towards him. He had no time to react. Faraday struck out, hard, and Mark went tumbling to the ground once more.

The combined effects of the drugs and his newfound terror made Mark's thoughts writhe like eels, too slippery to grasp. He was caked in cold mud and had a searing pain in his side from his frantic dash. Confused and petrified, he called out to his assailant.

"Alfie, stop! A.J., *please! Stop!*"

It was no use. He felt another blow to his head. It sent stars across his vision. He tried to rise to his feet again, but the whole world was spinning. Iron-strong fingers seized his throat and began to squeeze. Flailing desperately now, Mark lashed out at the shadowy figure straddling him. But it was as if Faraday couldn't feel him. It was like trying to punch an oak tree for all the good it did.

The last of Mark's strength was leaching out of him as those fingers tightened around his neck. His lungs burned for air that wouldn't come. He kicked desperately, but his legs seemed to have lost all power. He wasn't even sure they moved. Desolation filled him. The world began to grow dark as the pain, so intense a moment ago, abruptly began to fade.

Just before Mark drifted away completely, just as his mind became buoyed on an incoming tide of acceptance, Faraday leaned forward and looked into his eyes one last time.

All trace of the scared little schoolboy that Mark Sterling remembered was gone, and he wondered at how he had recognised those eyes at all. Because despite the gaunt face and the bulky frame, it was Alfred Faraday's eyes that had changed the most. Cold eyes. Dark eyes. The eyes of a killer.

Faraday said nothing, just stared… until Mark Sterling's world went black.

28

THE LIGHT WAS barely touching the sky when Esther crept up to the front door of her aunt's house. She felt a little like she was floating. She wasn't drunk—she hadn't had a drop—but she felt that tickly thrill she usually associated with alcohol. Slipping the key into the lock, she pushed the door open gently, then winced at the click that seemed to echo in the silent hallway as she closed it behind her.

To her dismay, the upstairs hall light came on and Jean appeared at the top of the stairs, pulling on her robe. Her face was tight with concern.

"Esther! Goodness, are you okay?"

"I'm fine, Jean. I'm good actually."

She smiled, going for reassurance, but it only seemed to make Jean even more anxious.

Her aunt hurried down the stairs on slippered feet, with no concerns about either of her feline friends prowling down the steps in front of her. Was it only Esther who found the creatures' company on stairs so treacherous?

As she came closer, Esther got the impression her aunt was searching for the smell of alcohol.

"Don't worry," she told her. "No drink. Honest."

Jean's countenance softened a little in the half-light and, not smelling anything, she relaxed visibly.

"Oh good," she said. "I'm so glad. Maybe I don't tell you often enough how proud I am of you for kicking that stuff. It's more than your mum was able to do." She frowned. "Where were you? Did something happen at work?"

Esther shook her head. "I've… I've met someone. I was with someone. I'm sorry, I didn't see your messages until late and I didn't think you'd still be up."

Jean managed a smile then. "Don't be silly. It's not you who should be sorry, it's me. You're a grown woman. You don't need an old aunt like me fussing over your whereabouts. I should have trusted you more."

Esther felt a stab of guilt. Jean didn't know about her lapse yet.

"Well, is he handsome?" her aunt teased. "Is it someone from work?"

She hesitated. Made a quick decision. "She works in the hospital, actually. She's a nurse."

Jean hadn't been expecting that. Her eyes widened fractionally, but she broke into a warm smile again quickly enough. "I'm glad, Esther," she said, reaching out and giving her niece's arm an affectionate squeeze. "You deserve a bit of happiness in your life. Long overdue, I'd say."

"Thanks, Jean."

She wasn't going to pretend her aunt's acceptance didn't help. She still harboured a trace of anxiety, even now.

Esther wasn't sure how well she would be able to pull off cool and relaxed when she was in public with Triona, and she was worried Triona would notice. The thought dampened her good mood a little.

"What about a warm cup of tea?" Jean asked, shuffling away towards the kitchen without waiting for a response. "It's so cold out these days! You must be half-frozen!"

Esther followed, but hung in the kitchen doorway while her aunt filled the kettle and took two mugs down from the cupboard.

"I went to see him," Esther said.

Jean stopped and turned.

"Travis," Esther explained. "I looked him up. He lives in a small town about an hour north of London. He has a family."

Concern flitted across her aunt's face again. She sat down at the table, while the kettle came to the boil and clicked off, unnoticed.

"What happened?" she asked.

Esther stepped into the kitchen, taking the mugs off Jean to finish making the tea. "I didn't speak to him or anything. Just saw him. I think he lives alone, but a woman about my age arrived at the house with a small boy. The boy called him 'grandpa', so I assume the woman is his daughter. Or daughter-in-law, maybe." She set a cup of tea in front of Jean and sat down across the table from her. "I just stayed in my car and watched them. Hugging, smiling. Like a perfectly normal family."

Esther took a sip of tea. Jean seemed to have forgotten her own cup. She was watching Esther carefully, searching her face for something.

"And how did seeing him make you feel?" she asked.

Esther frowned. "I don't know how I felt. I felt lots of things. Too many things. I thought about going up and knocking the door. Thought about why I wanted to do it… and then I realised I didn't. I have my own family." She looked at Jean. "You're my family. All the family I need."

Jean gave Esther a grateful smile and reached out and squeezed her hand. Esther squeezed back. They sipped their tea in silence for a moment, before Jean spoke again.

"How did he seem?" she asked.

Esther thought about the little boy wrapping his arms around Travis Somerville. Thought about the smile that split the man's face as he scooped the child up.

"He seemed happy," Esther said.

Jean nodded, turning back to her tea, giving no indication how she felt about that.

29

JARED TRIED TO ignore the laughing and clowning around in the main office outside. Some of the more festive-minded detectives were trying to assemble an artificial Christmas tree that the premises manager had located in one of the old storerooms. They seemed to have managed to distract the entire office with their struggles, but he didn't want to dampen the good mood, so he left them to it. They'd get the thing put together and be back to work soon enough.

He focused on the report in front of him instead. He'd received the email, flagged as high priority, from Carl Etebo at their CSI department that morning. A follow-up phone call had confirmed it; Jared liked to hear a thing straight from the horse's mouth, so to speak, since reports from fingerprint and forensic labs were always very technical. In his experience, getting a straight answer was best accomplished by speaking directly to someone who could explain it in plain English to an old codger like him.

The report contained a breakthrough in the Riddell case: an eyelash plucked from the clothing Gary Hetherington had been wearing when his body was found was a DNA match for the skin cells they'd scraped from under Carlton Riddell's fingernails. As far as Jared was concerned, it was a clear indication that both men had been killed by the same person. Problem was, they still didn't have a match on the police database; Riddell's killer had never been arrested in the UK. Once they had the perpetrator detained, a simple DNA swab would solve both murders in one go, but first they needed to find the perpetrator…

Jared looked up at the sound of a knock on his door. Detective Chief Inspector Brian Small poked his head in. "You have a moment, Jared?"

"Sir," Jared said as he stood—an old habit from back when the police followed something of a military etiquette—but the DCI waved his hands for him to sit back down. "If it's about the noise in the office, sir, I was going to give them another ten minutes or so to get that tree together and then get them back to their desks…"

Small looked confused for a moment, before he realised that Jared was referring to the Christmas tree construction project outside. He smiled and shook his head.

"No, Jared, that's fine. Let them enjoy themselves. Been working hard this year. Let them have an hour or two to relax a bit. It's Christmas, after all." His smile faded as he crossed the room and looked out the window, into the yard below. "No, it was, um… DS Penman I was looking to speak to you about."

"Oh?"

Small appeared to choose his words carefully. "I wanted to talk to you about possibly taking her off the big cases for a while and putting her on admin duties. I think it might be better to take some pressure off her, with all that's happened to her recently. The Peter Darren case. Her mother dying. I'm not sure giving her a big workload—a high-profile case—was entirely the best thing. She's been rather… I don't know, unsettled recently, have you noticed? She seems to be struggling with whatever's going on in her head. I'm wondering if she's fully got a grip on reality sometimes. Seems a bit delusional." He waved the comment away with an added, "I'm sure it's the stress."

Jared realised his mouth was moving but he wasn't making any sounds. He cleared his throat and tried again.

"I'm not actually sure admin duties are what's best for Esther." He felt his brow furrow. "Delusional?"

Sure, Esther had been a bit withdrawn lately, and she could be prickly at the best of times, but he'd never known her to be *delusional.*

"I'm just concerned about her welfare, you understand, Jared," Small said. "Perhaps a transfer to a quieter station might be in order? Maybe give her time to slow down a bit, take it a bit easier. I think it might be just what she needs right now. I know Esther may not agree, but maybe she's not the best judge of that at the moment."

"The best judge of what?"

The DCI spun around at the sound of Esther's voice. He had such a startled look on his face that Jared might have laughed if he wasn't still stunned by the suggestion of sending her away. She stood in the doorway, the sound of her approach having been drowned out by the noise outside. When Small locked eyes with her, Jared could see the colour drain from his face.

She regarded the DCI coldly, and Jared wondered how

much she'd heard. She switched her gaze to Jared. "I'm not the best judge of what?" she asked.

Small answered, trying to regain some poise but failing pretty miserably. He clearly hadn't been expecting the confrontation, and he was agitated. He licked his lips nervously. "Of your own best interests, Esther. At work, I mean. I was just saying to DI Wilcox that perhaps you should slow down for a bit. Get a little break at one of the quieter stations for a few months."

Esther shook her head. "No, sir. Thank you. I'm quite happy where I am."

Small smiled weakly. "It's not really a request, DS Penman." He tried to put some authority in his voice, but under Esther's frosty stare, it fell flat. Jared wasn't sure where this dynamic was coming from, but he was happy that Esther was winning the battle of wills. He did not want to lose her.

"I'm not moving, sir," Esther replied, her voice as icy as her stare. "Is this because I'm not as easy as you'd heard? You want me moved? Feeling awkward after our last encounter?"

And suddenly the penny dropped. Jared thought about how out-of-sorts she'd been recently. He turned to the DCI and watched as the man's face went from pale to bright red.

"Don't you dare cast accusations at me," he spluttered, angry and embarrassed—but wilting visibly in the face of Esther's stony demeanour. With a glance at Jared, he realised he was being studied from both angles and changed tack, quickly and clumsily; he shook his head and gave an awkward laugh. "I'm just thinking about your welfare, Esther, that's all!"

"Well, sir, you needn't," she replied. "I am happy to

remain where I am, working with DI Wilcox and retaining my caseload. And I can assure you that my judgement on the matter is perfectly sound. Is that all?"

The DCI looked wrung-out, his cheeks still flushed pink. He drew himself up and nodded, trying to give the impression that the decision was his.

"Well," he said, breathing out heavily, "if that's how you feel, then… fine." He turned to Jared. "Just be sure to keep an eye on her, Jared, going forward. Make sure she's not… overworked."

"Yes, sir," Jared replied.

With that, Brian Small nodded to them both and stepped quickly from the room. Jared looked at Esther.

"What was that about?" he asked.

"Don't worry about it."

"You sure?" he replied. "Nothing you want to file an official complaint about?"

She shook her head. "No."

He hesitated, but her expression told him to drop it, so he changed the subject.

"We've had a report back from Carl at CSI," he told her, passing the report across the desk to her. "An eyelash on Hetherington's clothing is a match for the scrapings under Riddell's fingernails."

She took the sheet and sat on the edge of his desk as she scanned it quickly.

"I knew it," she said. "And Mark Sterling is involved somehow too. It's got something to do with that class—their year group at Belfield Grammar. We need to track down this guy Faraday."

"Prime suspect?"

"Could be. We get our hands on him and a simple

buccal swab will tell us. If it's a match, we solve two cases in one go." She grinned. "We just gotta beat the Met to him."

There was something about Esther this morning, Jared thought. In spite of the encounter with the DCI she seemed… *breezier* than she had in a long time.

"You seem in good spirits today," he remarked, leaning back in his chair.

Still smiling, she looked thoughtful for a moment. "Yeah, I am," she said. "Slept well, I guess."

She slipped off his desk and headed for the door.

"Why don't we start going through PNC," she suggested. "Let's see what we can dig up on Faraday, and go hunting for our prime suspect…"

"Roger that," he replied with a smile. He was probably the only police inspector in the world who liked taking orders from his sergeant.

As they set to work, Jared decided to get two of their best technical-research detectives—John Peters and Brenda Wallis—to help. Esther phoned the principal of Belfield Grammar and got a date of birth and guardian details for Jake Faraday, although according to school records he was registered as *Alfred* Jacob Faraday. The date of birth tallied with the CV from Bolster Fitness, but despite half an hour of scouring outside sources, John and Brenda dug up very little on either 'Jake' or 'Alfred Jacob' Faraday. There was no social media apart from an outdated ad for personal training at Bolster Fitness from a couple of years ago. And he was only linked to one report on the Police National Computer, a report concerning the non-suspicious death of a Rhonda Faraday ten years prior. Rhonda had been Faraday's grandmother, and sole guardian according to the school records. Her death was put down as the result of a long-term terminal illness. The address for that report was the same as the one on the school records, a place called Milltown Row, an old social housing development in the south part of the city. The latest entry on the police system for this same address was from three years ago. A report of anti-social behaviour, called in by a woman named Elizabeth Parkes. That could be an indication the property had changed hands, but it wasn't conclusive. Ms Parkes might live with Faraday, or the call-taker might have logged the wrong address. There was only one sure way to find out…

"The entries are so old," Esther mused as she flicked through the database printouts on the way to the car. "Could be this Parkes woman moved in and the Faradays are long gone."

"Well, if Brenda and John can't find anything, it's usually because there's nothing there to find."

As Jared said the words, he glanced across at the two detectives who were climbing into an unmarked Ford on the far side of the yard. Brenda and John were going to shadow them to the address, then cover the rear of the property during the door-knock.

"And there's always an outside chance he might still be there," he said, as they reached their unmarked car and sat in. "He and the Parkes woman might be linked."

"True," Esther replied, pulling on her seatbelt. "We could have our man in custody and charged by teatime. Think how impressed DCI Greene would be."

She gave him a sly sideways glance, and he felt his cheeks reddening. He started the car. Her positive mood seemed unshakeable this morning.

Jared rolled out of the station yard, followed by Peters and Wallis in their dark Ford. They slipped through the streets of Belfield in tandem, cutting through the centre of town. The place was filled to bursting with Christmas shoppers. It was just about as busy as Jared had ever seen it. The weather had improved too. It was still overcast, but at least it was dry.

It took them twenty minutes to get to Milltown Row. The old suburb was almost empty of people at this time of the morning. A primary school sat on the corner at the far end of the street, its windows protected by grills, its tall fence topped with rusted barbed wire. The noise of break-time drifted out from the yard, the shrieks and laughter of small children at play. Litter dotted a nearby green, where a solitary old man walked an ageing mutt.

Jared pulled up to the kerb outside Faraday's address, a bleak, pebbledash house overlooking the green. He watched John and Brenda park at the end of the street. They got out of the car and walked towards the rear alley. He gave them a minute to get into position and then tapped the button on his radio handset.

"You two in place?" he asked.

He'd chosen a radio channel no one else was using, so he hadn't ascribed callsigns; with only him and Brenda carrying radios, there was no confusion about who was talking to whom.

"*In place*," came Brenda's voice. "*Clear view of the rear windows. There's an elderly female in the kitchen. Blue dressing gown. Doing dishes. Didn't you say this guy's grandmother was dead?*"

"Yeah," Jared replied. "This woman might be our Elizabeth Parkes."

He glanced at Esther, who shrugged.

"Let's go find out," she said.

Jared followed Esther to the front door, peering through the living room window as she rang the doorbell. Inside, the place was clean and tidy, and full of old-fashioned things. A row of porcelain ornaments lined the mantelpiece, with more in a glass-fronted cabinet beyond. A set of *Hello!* magazines were stacked neatly on the coffee table in the centre of the room.

A shrill bell rang in the distance, and the shouts and laughter of the children faded. Break time was over.

"*She's heading out of the kitchen,*" Brenda told them through the radio.

"Roger," Jared replied.

A moment later the front door was opened by a suspicious-looking woman in her late sixties or seventies. She pulled her blue dressing gown tighter around herself.

"Can I help you?" she asked.

Esther produced her warrant card. "Police, madam. We're looking for a man named Alfred—or Jake—Faraday. Does he live here?"

The woman frowned. "No, officer, I'm sorry. The Faraday boy moved out of here ten years ago, after his grandmother died. That's when I moved in."

"Can I ask your name, if you don't mind?"

"Elizabeth Parkes. Is anything the matter?"

"We're just looking to speak to Mister Faraday," Esther replied. "Did he leave a forwarding address, or do you have any way of getting in contact with him?"

Elizabeth Parkes shook her head apologetically. "I'm sorry, no. I didn't really know the Faradays all that well."

Jared glanced around the neighbourhood. "Anyone hereabouts you think might be able to help us find him?"

The woman thought for a moment, but then shook her head again. "They weren't very sociable people." She indicated the house on the left. "Missus Norman used to speak about Rhonda Faraday, but she's just been moved to a care home, not two months past, and I really don't think she'd be able to help. Not with her dementia as severe as it is."

"You know the name of the care home?"

"Cloverhill."

Esther jotted the name down, then nodded toward the house on the other side. "And the people who live there?"

"Students," she replied, with a grimace. "But if you want to knock their door and warn them about noisy parties, I wouldn't mind one bit."

Esther offered her a sympathetic smile. "I'll mention it to our neighbourhood team. Hopefully we can get someone in uniform to call out and have a chat."

The woman nodded. "Thank you. Sorry I can't be of any more help."

She closed the door, and they headed back to their vehicle. Jared lifted the radio and hit the transmit button. "That's a negative. Let's head back to base."

"*Yes-yes, received,*" came Brenda's reply.

"Back to the drawing board," he said to Esther, as they sat into the car.

"We've still got a name, at least," Esther replied, undaunted. "A prime suspect. That's a big step forward. We'll track him down. We could try this Norman woman over at Cloverhill."

"Sounds like a bit of a long shot, from what Elizabeth Parkes said."

"Well, Faraday can't hide forever. Let's go through that

yearbook. We speak to enough people, we'll get a handle on what his links are to Hetherington and Riddell. And we should go speak to Mark Sterling again, although I'd prefer to be able to exert a bit more pressure on him this time."

"Meaning?"

Esther grimaced. "Meaning I want to be able to put handcuffs on him and take him down to the station."

Jared started the engine. "We might need to dig up some probable cause for that."

"Didn't we get some intel about drugs when we asked for that background check on him?"

He nodded as he pulled out and headed back towards Belfield Central. "Nothing huge. Seems he's trying to nibble a bit of business off the Petrauskas in Drakehill." He shrugged. "There wasn't much, but it might be enough for a warrant."

"Let's go over it again," Esther said decisively. "Get the ball rolling on a warrant application."

"Sounds like a plan."

* * *

The dry weather didn't last. A cold winter rain had started to fall by the time Esther and Jared arrived back at the station. They had to race across the yard to the front doors to avoid getting soaked.

It was lunchtime and the enquiry office was full. People sat or stood about, waiting to be dealt with for everything from passport applications to traffic tickets.

As Esther and Jared crossed the waiting area, the enquiry

assistant tapped at the glass that screened her from the public. It was Pat, a woman of indeterminate age who had been working at Belfield Central for many years, long before Esther joined. She waved them over.

"Woman over there asked to speak to you personally, Esther," Pat told her. "Been waiting half an hour. Came in with that young man."

Esther turned and immediately recognised the secretary from Belfield Grammar School, Dorothy Long. Mrs Long recognised her too. She half-rose from her seat, the young man at her side glancing nervously towards the reception desk as she did so. He looked kind of familiar to Esther, and both he and Dorothy appeared worried about something. Or frightened. Esther suddenly got the sense that whatever it was Dorothy Long wanted to speak to her about, it was something important.

"Thank you, Pat," Esther said. "Are any of the interview rooms free?"

Pat nodded to the door at the far end. "Number four is empty."

Esther gestured for Jared to accompany her, then crossed the room to speak with her visitor.

"Hello, Missus Long," Esther said, smiling and doing her best to put the nervous woman at her ease. "This is Detective Inspector Jared Wilcox. I understand you wanted to see me? Would it be okay if Jared sat in with us?"

Dorothy nodded. Then she turned to the young man. On closer inspection, Esther realised he wasn't as young as he first appeared; he just carried himself like a teenager. The feeling of having seen him before grew stronger.

"This is my son, Edwin," Dorothy said. "Stand up, Edwin," she whispered.

Edwin stood, but kept his eyes on the ground for the most part.

Edwin Long.

Abruptly, Esther realised where she'd seen his face before. Not just the face, but the name; she'd been looking at that name for days, never having put it together with Dorothy's surname. The yearbook. Edwin Long was part of Carlton Riddell's senior year at Belfield Grammar.

Edwin seemed to sense Esther's eyes on him. He looked up at her, and immediately blushed from his neck to the roots of his hair. He swallowed, and quickly dropped his gaze to the floor again. He was shifting from foot to foot now, every inch the anxious teenager, for all he was in his late twenties.

"You want to talk to me too, Edwin?" Esther asked.

Edwin flinched at the sound of his name on her lips, but he nodded. "Yes."

Esther saw that Dorothy's eyes had filled with tears as she regarded her son. Quickly, Esther ushered them toward the interview room. "Let's speak privately," she said.

Jared too had picked up on the dynamic of the encounter; he stepped forward and held open the door for them.

30

ONCE THE FOUR of them were settled around the table in the interview room, and Esther had fetched a cup of tea for Dorothy and a glass of water for her son, Edwin told them his story. He told them about his final year at Belfield Grammar. And his good friend A.J. Faraday.

Alfred Jacob Faraday lived with his grandmother on Milltown Row—Esther shared a look with Jared when she heard the name of the street they'd visited that morning—and he never spoke about his parents. People said his mother had committed suicide when he was very young, and he'd never known his father. Neither A.J. nor Edwin were particularly popular in school. Edwin, face reddening, owned to the fact that he still wasn't popular. Dorothy, eyes moist, reached out to pat his forearm.

"I knew I was a geek," Edwin went on, "but A.J.… A.J. never really seemed to get that there was a social order. Never understood that we were the… at the bottom of it. The bullying didn't seem to faze him either. Until it did."

Edwin told them how, at the other end of the spectrum, at the top of the social ladder, were the rich and the beautiful of Belfield Grammar. The rugby players, the prettiest girls, the children of the most affluent Belfielders. Students like Gary Hetherington, Carlton Riddell, Mark Sterling and Vicky Ellsmith. Those four were the heart of the in-crowd in their final years at the school, inseparable, a clique all unto themselves. Gary was the rugby captain. He'd dated Vicky throughout most of their time at high school, as far as Edwin could remember, but the relationship was a stormy one, prone to the odd dramatic, short-term break-up. It was like being an extra in some weird, real-world soap opera whenever the two of them fell out during termtime. But even though they were on-off, everyone knew they were crazy about each other. Everyone except A.J.

"A.J. was obsessed with Vicky," Edwin said, shaking his head, eyes glued to the surface of the table as he related his story. "He worshipped the ground she walked on. All because she smiled at him in Second Year. I tried to get him to see that she wasn't interested in nerds like us, but I was never very forceful about it. Didn't want to hurt his feelings. He never got it. He thought he was in love. I mean, I kinda get it. She was *really* pretty. Really pretty and really popular, and when she was nice she was… she was lovely. But she had a nasty streak. And A.J. learned all about it on the night of our Spring Formal in Final Year."

Edwin fell silent. His fingers were knotted together atop the table, his knuckles white.

"What happened on the night of the Spring Formal, Edwin?" Esther asked gently, coaxing him out of his silence.

Edwin clenched his jaw before he spoke. "A few weeks before the night of the ball, Vicky and Gary had one of their big blow-outs. The whole school knew about it. Gary had even asked a different girl to the dance. It was the scandal of the year. Vicky was obviously upset about it all, and A.J. thought it was his chance. Idiot asked her to go to the formal with him. And she said yes." He shook his head. "I told him it wasn't a good idea. Gary wasn't going to just be okay with A.J. bringing his girlfriend to the social occasion of the year. But A.J. wouldn't listen. Said they'd broken up. As if their break-ups ever lasted longer than a week.

"I mean, he was the captain of the rugby team for God's sakes, and A.J. was just… A.J. was just one of us. The geek squad. The social pariahs. I knew something was off, but A.J. turned a deaf ear. Wouldn't listen, and had no time for me after that." He sighed. "And I wasn't the only one who saw what Vicky was doing. Some of the other guys, the guys we would hang around with sometimes, they told A.J. too. They said she was using him. But A.J. got real angry and just shut us all out. For those two weeks, between him asking Vicky out and the night of the formal, we hardly saw him."

Edwin was quiet for a long moment, brow creased at some troubling memory. "It was a few days before the formal when I saw them together again. Vicky and Gary, I mean. They were behind the bleachers on the rugby pitch. Real close. Looked like they were making up to me, if you know what I mean. I went to tell A.J., even though he'd been a real shithead to me and the others—"

Dorothy made a tutting sound and Edwin apologised for swearing. Esther said it didn't matter and to please go on.

"I guess maybe I wasn't as sympathetic as I could have been," he continued. "Maybe I was thinking 'I-told-you-so'. Maybe part of me wanted to get back at him for basically ditching me and our mates for this… this *girl.* I told him what I'd seen, and he was real crabby about it, but eventually he agreed to come down to the football fields. Of course, when we got there Vicky was sitting on the bleachers on her own and Gary was gone. A.J. never admitted he might suspect something, but I guess there was something playing on his mind because he just went straight to Vicky and asked her about it. She was all weird and defensive. I couldn't understand how A.J. couldn't see what I saw, that she and Gary were comfortable together, like they were made for each other. A.J. was just so awkward around her. Vicky… I didn't get why she wouldn't just come right out and tell him, why she kept stringing him along. I didn't realise why until after the night of the formal. Gary must really have gotten into her head that day. He clearly had some screwed-up hold on her. That's the only explanation I can think of, because I don't think Vicky would have done it on her own." His brow creased further. "No, I don't think it was her idea at all."

He lapsed into silence again, staring down at his clasped hands. Esther could see from the rise and fall of his shoulders that he was breathing nervously.

"What wasn't her idea?" she asked gently. She suddenly had the feeling that Edwin Long held the key to this whole case, and that he was about to reveal the link between Carlton Riddell, Gary Hetherington, Mark Sterling and their prime suspect, A.J. Faraday.

"How could anyone have known Gary was so jealous?" Edwin asked, his voice catching now, his lips trembling as he fought back tears. "He hid it so well. Why would anyone like Gary Hetherington be jealous of a nerd like A.J.? But he was. He really was. Otherwise, he wouldn't have convinced the others to go along with his plan."

Edwin looked up then, eyes glistening with tears. There was an edge to his voice when he spoke again. A flicker of anger.

"It was Gary's plan. He might not have come up with the idea; probably got it from Mark—Sterling was always a bit of a snake—but it was Gary who made it happen. I'm sure of it."

"What did they do?" Esther asked, sensing the need to nudge Edwin to get to the point. She could see that the memory was hurting him.

"Vicky helped make it happen," he said. "That's what A.J. finally realised afterwards, after it was too late: that he'd been duped the whole time."

He took a deep breath, his anger subsiding as he related the story of what happened on the night of the Spring Formal…

"I only know some of it. From what little A.J. told me, and what I figured out myself from rumours and stuff.

"During the dance, Vicky led A.J. out to the rugby fields, out to the bleachers. She started taking her clothes off and told him to do the same. A.J. did, of course, probably only too eager. And once he was naked, the rest of them jumped him."

"Who?" Jared asked.

"Gary, Mark, Carlton. They'd been hiding in the bleachers, waiting for Vicky to lead him out. Mark filmed the whole thing. A.J. never told me everything, but whatever they did, it changed him. What I do know is that they stole his clothes and just left him there. Black eyes, broken nose, naked. I'm not sure how long he'd been there when I found him. Probably half an hour. He was crying, but he didn't want any cops, didn't want to talk about it. I got him some spare shorts and jerseys from the sports hall stores and took him home."

Edwin shook his head. "If that had been the end of it, it would have been bad enough, but it wasn't. They started blackmailing him. Mark did, anyway."

"Sterling?" Jared asked.

Edwin nodded. "Said he had a video of A.J. hopping about in front of Vicky with his… with his bits out, and he was going to send it to the whole school. It wasn't much—a hundred quid, I think—but it was a lot for A.J. A.J. lived with his gran and they really didn't have much money. I told A.J. to go to the police, but he was so embarrassed… he begged me to help. I gave him fifty. I know I should have just gone to the police myself, but back then… I couldn't do it to him. You should have seen him. He was so stressed. Completely beside himself.

"Of course, a month later, they asked for more. If his gran hadn't died a couple of days later, I don't know what might have happened, or how much they'd have tried to squeeze out of him. But once the funeral was over… well, A.J. just left school. Called by my house to say he was leaving town for a while, didn't tell me where he was going, and that was it. That was the last I saw or heard from him." Edwin took a deep breath. "Until two weeks ago."

Esther leaned forward. Two weeks ago. Just before Carlton Riddell was murdered.

"I didn't recognise him at first," Edwin went on. "He was huge. All bulk and muscles, like he'd spent every day since he left Belfield working out in a gym. He told me he was having money trouble and he needed somewhere to crash for a few days, asked if I could help him out. I suggested my house, but he didn't want my mum to see him, so I told him I could sneak him into a room in the warehouse at the hardware store where I work. I brought him food and locked him in at night, then got him out and away in the morning before any of the other staff arrived for work. A few days became *most* days. I was worried about getting caught. I asked him how long he was going to stay, and he said he just had a couple of people to visit but it would be over soon." Edwin looked up at Esther. "Those were the words he used. It would be 'over'."

"Did he say anything to you about where he's been going during the day?" Jared asked. "What he's been doing?"

Edwin was silent for a long time, and when he spoke at last, it was almost a whisper. "He didn't tell me anything." Esther saw a tear roll down his cheek. When he raised his face again, he wore an imploring expression. "I didn't know what he was doing," he said, almost choking on a sob. "I didn't know. I didn't know about Gary or Carlton! I didn't know what he was doing!"

There were tears in Dorothy's eyes too as she made hushing noises and put an arm around her son. He didn't resist.

Esther looked at Jared. She could see that he was thinking exactly the same thing she was. They had their killer.

"Does A.J. have access to a vehicle, Edwin?" she asked. "Have you seen him driving anything?"

Edwin nodded. "A red van. He parks up at night in front of the store before closing time."

"Did you happen to catch the registration number?" she asked. "Or would you be able to tell us the make or model?"

Edwin shook his head. "I didn't really pay any attention.

Sorry."

"That's okay, Edwin," she said gently, hiding her frustration. "What about any other people? Has he ever been with anyone else when you've seen him?"

Again, Edwin shook his head. "No. I think that's why he came to me. I don't think he has anyone else to go to."

"What about a phone? Did he give you a number to contact him?"

Another shake of the head. "I don't remember him having a phone anytime I saw him. Just a duffle bag with some clothes and a sleeping bag. I think he was sleeping in the van before he came to me. But then it got so cold recently…"

"Will he be there tonight?" Esther asked. "At the hardware store?"

"I don't know. He's been there most nights, parked up in the van, waiting, but not every night. He didn't show up last night."

"I was there to pick up Edwin last night," Dorothy put in. "Maybe he saw me. I don't remember seeing a red van, although if I'm honest I wasn't really looking."

"What about this video?" Jared asked. "Did any of them ever use it? Has it appeared on the internet or anything?"

Edwin shook his head. "Not that I know of."

"You don't know if they were still blackmailing him after he left?" he asked. "Could they still be blackmailing him now?"

"I doubt it," Edwin said bitterly. "I think A.J. disappeared right after his gran's funeral so he could get away from them. And he *proper* disappeared. If he didn't tell *me* where he was going, I seriously doubt he would have told *them*. You can't blackmail someone you can't get a hold of, can you? As for the video… I don't know that anyone else has ever seen it. No one at school mentioned it before the end of term, so I guess they kept it a secret after all." He shrugged. "Maybe they still have it, who knows?"

Esther took a page from her jotter and passed it across the table along with a pen. "We're going to need contact numbers for both of you," she said, as she stood and pulled her coat on. Jared followed suit. "Go home, carry on your day as normal," she went on. "If A.J. makes *any* type of contact with *either* of you, you need to let us know straight away. Nine-nine-nine. I'll give you a reference number to give to the call-handler, and you'll need to tell them your location and any information you have for us as quickly as possible. Stress that it's an emergency, give them my name, and tell them they need to contact me immediately."

Edwin and Dorothy both sat straighter, eyes widening at the sudden urgency in Esther's voice.

"Are you due to go in to work today, Edwin?" Esther asked.

"I-I was going to call in sick," he stammered.

"Please don't," she said. "What time does A.J. usually show up in his van?"

"I-I don't really know," Edwin replied, as he jotted his number on the page and slid it across so his mother could do the same. "Until last night he was just there, waiting when I knocked off shift."

"And what time will that be tonight?"

"It's Friday, so nine o'clock tonight."

"We'll be with you before then," Esther told him.

"Who?"

"Police," she replied. "Lots of police."

31

"IT ALL FITS," Esther told Jared, as they hurried through the yard back to the car. The rain had stopped by the time they'd seen Dorothy and Edwin out of the station with repeated assurances that they would be in touch soon, and repeated instructions to ring if Faraday made any kind of contact at all. "A.J. Faraday is taking revenge on his high school bullies."

"Bit extreme, don't you think?" Jared asked, a little out of breath from his effort to keep up with her. She was practically running. "After all this time, I mean?"

"Something's triggered it," Esther replied. "Judging by the timelines, I'm guessing it's Gary Hetherington showing up at Faraday's gym in London. Dragging up all the old memories. Invading the new life he made for himself, just when he thought he was leaving it all behind. Maybe there was some kind of confrontation. Maybe he started getting blackmailed all over again. I don't know. Whatever it was, it's sent him over the edge. If Edwin is to be believed,

Faraday has completely transformed. Sounds like he's probably used a hell of a lot of anabolic steroids. Bigger muscles, shorter fuse."

"Where are we going?" Jared asked as they reached the car.

Esther had gone to the driver's side and held out her hand for the keys. He passed them across the roof to her. She unlocked the car and they sat in.

"If it *is* Faraday, then he has two targets left," Esther replied as she started the engine. "Mark Sterling and Vicky Ellsmith. We need to get to them and warn them. And find out more about this video."

"We'll definitely need a warrant if we want to go looking for videos," he cautioned her.

Esther didn't reply. She pulled out her phone and dialled, putting it to her ear as she tugged her seat belt on. "Derek! I need you to run checks on Vicky Ellsmith. Current address, contact numbers, whatever you can find. Then I need you to go straight out to her, wherever she is. We have a suspect. We think he's going to kill again and she might be one of his targets." She gave a brief outline of Edwin's story, then told him to drop everything else and get to Vicky ASAP.

She hung up and tucked her phone away.

"Let's go speak to Mark Sterling again," she said to Jared, as she shifted the car into gear and set off, "and see if we can't dodge the warrant issue with a little street craft."

By the time they pulled up to Mark Sterling's building fifteen minutes later, Jared had managed to get Despatch to divert a uniform crew to meet them. Esther hardly gave the two officers time to climb out of their liveried car. Darting up the weed-choked path, she opened the front door with a hard shove and bounded up the stairs. The uniform officers were hot on her heels, Jared a little further back.

When she got to the third floor, Esther rapped smartly on the door to Mark Sterling's apartment. There was no answer. She knocked again, listening for any sound from within. That was when she noticed the fresh boot mark near the bottom of the door.

"Mister Sterling?" she called, knocking for a third time. "Mark? It's the police. Open up, please. It's urgent!"

She pressed an ear to the door. She heard something then. The dog. It was whining.

"Fuck this," she muttered. She stepped back and landed a well-aimed kick high against the latch side of the door. It rattled in its frame, but didn't come free. She kicked again. There was a bit more give this time.

"Let me, Sarge," said one of the uniformed officers. He was a big lad, so Esther nodded and stepped back to let him have a go. The officer braced himself and ran at the door with his shoulder. It gave way immediately, and he stumbled into the corridor beyond.

Esther was straight in after him. They all began shouting, identifying themselves as police as they went from room to room.

It was Esther who opened the door to the kitchen and found him. He lay flat on his back, his eyes bulging and glazed, his clothes caked in mud. Mark Sterling hadn't been the swarthiest of men when he was alive, but his deathly pallor made the mottled bruising around his throat stand out all the more. As she opened the door, the old greying Labrador struggled lugubriously to its feet. It had been lying next to its master, and Esther said a silent prayer of thanks that the animal hadn't started eating him yet.

The big uniform officer appeared at her shoulder as the dog shuffled heavily towards them.

"Take the dog out," she ordered. "And call this in on the radio. Let Despatch know we've got a murder scene here."

The officer grimaced at the sight of the dead body, then turned his attention to the dog. He patted it tentatively at first, then gave it a friendly scratch behind the ear before he was confident enough to take it by the collar and lead it away. It was his colleague who made the transmission, letting despatchers in the control room know they'd found a body and were establishing a crime scene.

Esther studied the kitchen from the threshold. A trail of blood and dirt ran from Sterling's body to the back door. She picked her way carefully across the kitchen, keeping to the edge of the room to preserve whatever footprints the CSI officers might lift from the greasy linoleum. Pulling on her gloves, she tested the back door and found it to be unlocked. She opened it wide and saw that it led onto a fire escape. Metal steps ran down to a yard and a row of derelict garages below. There was a grassy field at the end of the yard. Despite the recent rain, she could still see traces of dirt and blood on the landing and steps.

The second uniform officer was hovering on the other side of the kitchen. He was much younger than his colleague, and his face was pale as he stared at the dead body.

"You," Esther addressed him, "go downstairs and secure the bottom of this fire escape. It's part of our scene. Are there more units coming?"

He nodded. "Yes, ma'am."

"Good," she said. "We'll need the whole apartment

secured and that yard down below cordoned off. Tell Despatch I need a search team here, to check the green and the trees over there."

The boy stammered another "yes, ma'am" and hurried away.

Jared appeared as Esther closed the outer door and carefully picked her way back across the kitchen, retracing her steps as best as she could. The bigger uniform officer was standing at the front door to the apartment, the dog lying placidly at his feet as he filled out a crime scene logbook. He got what details he needed from Esther and Jared, and Esther made sure to repeat the instructions she'd given to his younger colleague. The older officer seemed the more competent of the two, having already tasked the dog warden for the pooch, and Esther wanted to be sure the whole scene was processed properly.

"We need to get to Vicky Ellsmith," she said to Jared, as they hurried down the stairs to the ground floor. She took out her phone and dialled Derek Grant's number again.

"Sergeant?"

"Derek, did you find anything on Vicky Ellsmith yet? We need to get to her *now*."

"I've found her," Derek replied, and Esther breathed a sigh of relief. "Took a bit of digging. She's married. Her name's Mansfield now, and she lives in the Hills. We're just about to head out there now."

"Okay, use blue lights and step on it! Mark Sterling's dead. Strangled like the others. Send DI Wilcox and me the address. We'll see you there!"

She burst through the building's front door and started running to the car, Jared hurrying along behind her. Hopping into the driver's seat, she started the engine. She was gunning the motor down the street before Jared even had his door fully closed, hitting the blue lights and sirens as she reached the main road.

It was late afternoon and already growing dark. With less than a week to Christmas, the roads were packed with holiday shoppers and Esther had to bully her way past queues of cars. She straddled the central line, forcing the traffic apart as she worked her way steadily towards the northern suburbs.

Jared updated Despatch over the phone while she drove, and by the time they arrived at the Mansfield residence there was a host of liveried police cars converging on it, their flickering blue lights bright in the gathering dusk.

Esther killed the horns, but she left her blue lights on so that none of the uniform officers would try to stop her as she raced down the broad boulevard and swung in through the gates of Vicky Mansfield-nee-Ellsmith's house. When she saw one of the other CID cars in the drive next to a black Porsche, she killed the blues, and her speed.

As she pulled up, she spotted Derek Grant and Liz Fellowes standing in the doorway, talking to a tall, bespectacled man with silver-grey hair. He was wearing a tux and glossy black dress shoes.

"… telling you I haven't been able to get hold of her all day," the tall man was saying, managing to sound both condescending and worried at the same time. "I have no idea where she is. And now you are here, and all these police cars are here, and it is *quite* clear that something serious is going on, and I would very much appreciate it if you would tell me what that is! She is *my wife*, for God's sake!"

Grant gave Esther a questioning look as she and Jared approached. "Skipper? This is Mister Tobias Mansfield.

Vicky Mansfield's husband."

"Mister Mansfield," Esther said, taking in his manner and expression, and quickly concluding that the only way to deal with a man like him would be to oblige him—and hammer him with a sharp, no-nonsense briefing. "We have reason to believe your wife may be in danger. We are investigating a number of murders linked to her old school, Belfield Grammar. There have been three people killed already, and all of them are linked to Vicky's old class. It is crucial that we speak to her as soon as possible. Have you any idea where she might be this afternoon?"

That seemed to take a little of the aristocratic wind out of the man. He had grown visibly paler as Esther spoke.

"N-no, I-I've been telling the detective here, I haven't heard from her all day," he stammered. "I was at work until lunchtime, and she wasn't here when I got home. I've been ringing her, but her mobile phone seems to be off. I expected her to be here. We have an engagement at City Hall tonight, and I thought she'd be getting ready."

"She was here when you left for work?" Esther asked.

"Yes."

"And she didn't mention any plans for the day?"

He shook his head. "No. She was just making coffee… and… I can't even remember what we talked about. Trivial morning chitchat. I can't remember."

Esther was scanning the front of the house. "Have you any CCTV?"

Mansfield looked dismayed. "No. Just an alarm system. No cameras."

"Might she have made any appointments for this City Hall thing tonight?" Liz Fellowes asked, gesturing to Mansfield's tuxedo. "A hair salon, or something?"

The man frowned. "Probably. But she usually writes it in the calendar, and there's nothing there. I checked when I got home."

"Is there any particular salon or stylist she would normally use?" Fellowes pressed, notebook and pen at the ready.

Mansfield's brow knit in concentration; he was evidently struggling to lift a name from his memory.

"Gloria!" he exclaimed suddenly. "Yes, that's her name. Gloria Fanning! Gloria does her hair. And her nails!"

Esther glanced at the black Porsche. "What kind of car does she drive, and is it here?" she asked.

Mansfield shook his head. "A red Cayenne. It's gone."

"Do you know the licence plate number?" Grant asked.

Mansfield's face scrunched up again. "Starts with F. F-five-two… drat, five-two-p-something."

Esther turned to Grant. "Get someone at base to run a wildcard search with those details," she directed. "We'll narrow it down more quickly than searching for registration documents. Send the result to the traffic camera department straight away. You and Liz get to Gloria Fanning's salon, wherever it is. If Vicky's there, or she's stopped somewhere in between, keep her in situ until we get to her. And get as much info from the Fanning woman as possible, in case she's gone somewhere else."

Mansfield was growing fearful again as he listened to Esther rattling out instructions to Grant. "Is she really in serious danger?" he asked. "Is there anything I can do?"

Esther nodded to him. "Yes. Keep your phone on. Keep trying to ring her. And give her mobile number to Detective Grant here. We can run some triangulation checks, see where she last used it. We're going to leave a couple of officers here with you until we get hold of her. If you hear from her, or if you get through to her, you let them know straight away, do you understand?"

Mansfield nodded. "Y-yes, of course. Of course."

Jared was issuing his own instructions to Liz Fellowes, to get crews arranged to check for CCTV in the area and start going house to house. Grant was taking down Vicky's mobile number from Mansfield.

Esther turned and stared out over the city. Her mind churned. Sterling dead, Vicky missing, not answering her phone… She suddenly had a horrible, sinking feeling that Faraday had already got his hands on her…

The clouds had broken and the moon was out now, full and bright. She stared at the long moonlit lawn, and it made her think of another scene, a scene in her mind's eye. A grassy pitch, by moonlight…

Suddenly, she realised where they needed to go. If Faraday had already taken Vicky, Esther knew it wouldn't be a simple killing. Not after what Edwin Long had told them. This was something Faraday had been building up to…

"Jared," she called, already heading for the car. "Jared, I know where he'll take her!"

The DI finished issuing instructions and began lumbering after her.

Tobias Mansfield looked panicked. "Take her? What?" He turned to Grant. "What does she mean?"

Esther didn't wait to hear Grant's reply. She yanked open the car door and sat in. Fishing out the scrap of paper with Edwin Long's number on it, she dialled, switching her phone to speaker as she set it in the central console. She started the engine. Jared looked perplexed as he sat in on the passenger side. The phone rang once, twice, three times…

"Hello?" came the tentative voice on the other end.

"Edwin!" Esther exclaimed, as she executed a messy five-point turn. "Edwin, where *exactly* did Vicky lead A.J. on the night of the Spring Formal?"

32

VICKY'S BREATH FOGGED in the night air as she panted, rapid white puffs that dissolved on the breeze. She was shivering, and goosebumps pebbled her bare skin. Her hands and feet had gone numb.

She'd known where she was—understood the significance of the place—the moment she'd woken. She was suspended from the bleachers, the coarse rope cutting into her wrists whenever she twisted or moved. Her toes grazed the turf, allowing her just enough purchase to take the weight off her shoulders now and again, whenever the ache became unbearable. Every scrap of her clothing had been cut from her body. It lay in an untidy pile nearby.

Changed as he was, he was still the same in some ways. She could see the frightened little boy from her youth in the musclebound monster he'd turned himself into. Pleading and sobbing, she had tried to appeal to that boy, but the monster was prevailing.

She watched him now through her blur of tears. The moon was full and bright overhead, but his face was lit by the iPad in his hands, giving his dark-browed countenance a demonic under-glow. She could hear the tinny voices from the video he was playing back. A video she knew only too well. She recognised her own voice, and it made her sob again.

"I'm so sorry, Alfie," she cried. "I was a total bitch back then! I know that! I'm so sorry for what we did to you."

"Hush," he replied. "This is the best bit."

She shivered and cried. She closed her eyes, reliving the moment as she listened to it. The moment that had played out right here, right on this very spot, ten years ago. The moment that had changed a young man's life forever…

Her breasts were bare, and Alfie's eyes were round. She'd slipped the dress straps off her shoulders and pushed it down to her waist. The summer breeze grazed her nipples, making them stand out hard. She felt terribly exposed. She wanted this over with as fast as possible. She already had her doubts about this plan. But Gary had wanted it. And she had long since realised that there was very little Gary asked for that she wouldn't do. He was like a drug. She loved the way people stared at them whenever they went out together. She knew she was hot, but Gary was like a movie star, with his chiselled jaw, laughing eyes and big shoulders. She spotted him now, creeping out from behind the bleachers, and decided she could maybe tweak his jealousy a touch more before it was over. Make him realise what he'd missed out on for the past few weeks.

She made to push her dress the rest of the way down and hesitated, pouting at Alfie.

"You too, Alfie," she teased. "I want to see your cute little ass. I'm not getting naked all by myself."

Alfie, who'd been frozen in place, gaping at her, suddenly burst into motion. He hauled his jacket off and tossed it to the ground. Pulled his shirt over his head without even taking the time to undo the buttons.

As the skinny boy scrambled to pull his trousers off, Vicky spotted the other two emerging along with Gary. Carlton and Mark. That fucker Mark had his phone out! He was filming it! Quickly, Vicky pulled her dress back up, covering her breasts once more. She'd seen Mark directing the phone at her before he'd turned it on Alfie. That slimy shit had videoed her with her tits out! She'd take his head off after this was over. Or, better yet, she'd have Gary do it!

As Alfie tugged his trousers down over his feet, he noticed that Vicky had hoisted her dress up. He paused, looking confused. And that's when Gary and Carlton fell on him. Laughing and whooping, Carlton grabbed Alfie's trousers, puddled as they were around his ankles, and hauled on them, pulling the boy's feet from under him. Alfie's face was a picture of horrified shock as he fell. Carlton didn't let go; he began dragging Alfie along the grass by the trousers, which were still caught around his shoes. Mark was running alongside, filming it all on his phone as the two of them laughed drunkenly.

"Look at his tiny little cock!" Mark shouted. "No loss, Vicky! You'd not even have felt it!"

Gary was standing to one side as Carlton finally managed to tug Alfie's trousers free. Alfie made a futile effort to snatch them back, but Gary stepped in and landed a well-aimed punch to his gut, winding him and sending the smaller boy tumbling to the ground again.

Carlton began gathering up the rest of Alfie's clothes while Gary thumped him a few more times.

Vicky had experienced a little thrill, a rush of adrenalin, when Gary first approached, his face a dark storm. Was it power she felt at having aroused such anger in him, such jealousy? Gary Hetherington was adored by every girl in the school. And why not? He was gorgeous.

Vicky loved that he was hers. That tart Bethany wasn't good enough for him. He only went with her to get back at Vicky. Vicky knew Gary was hers, truly. And she loved it. She never tired of feeling his big arms around her, or running her fingers over his broad shoulders in public, knowing he was hers. Everyone else wanted him, but Gary Hetherington was hers.

That feeling started to fade, though, as she watched him land blow after blow on weedy little Alfie Faraday.

"Stop it, Gary," she heard herself say.

Either he hadn't heard, or he was ignoring her, because he punched the smaller boy again, and again and again. Alfie was cowering now, curled in a tight ball so that Gary had to grab a fistful of hair and wrench his head back in order to hit him.

"Gary, STOP!"

Her shriek cut through the air, silencing everyone and stilling Gary's hand. He looked up then, his face slackening as if he was waking from a trance.

On the ground, Alfie was sprawled face-down, wheezing and spluttering, a pitiful reed of a thing, his bare buttocks shining white in the moonlight.

Mark finally lowered his phone…

Faraday chortled mirthlessly as he set the iPad down.

"A touch of remorse at the end there, Vicky?" he asked. "A touch of guilt?"

"Alfie, please!" she sobbed. She shuddered, shaking uncontrollably now, whether from the cold or the fear, she couldn't tell anymore. Her teeth chattered and her jaw ached as she pleaded with him. "Please! I'm sorry! We were just stupid kids!"

He made a face. "It didn't stop there, though, did it, Vicky?" he said. He pulled a phone from his pocket. "Let's see if I can find it… Ah, here it is: 'If you don't want clips of your skinny little cock passed around the school, leave an envelope with a hundred pounds in my locker before Friday afternoon. MS.'" Faraday shook his head.

"I'm sorry, Alfie" It was barely a whisper now, the fear and despair rolling through her body in numbing waves. "I didn't know he'd sent that. I'm so sorry."

"No," Faraday said suddenly, his voice ice. "You're not sorry. Not yet. But you will be."

He reached down and lifted a dark length of metal from a big, black holdall near his feet. He unscrewed bits of it, extended it out, and she saw that it was a camera tripod. Two more tripods from the bag were topped by a pair of portable lamps. He pointed them at her, switched them on, and she flinched, squinting in the sudden brightness.

"Now it's your turn to be filmed, Vicky," he said, removing a high-grade digital video camera from the bag and fixing it in place atop the tripod, its glass eyeball trained on her naked form. "And I can guarantee you this video will go further than any school. This will go out to the whole world. Maybe I'll even let you live long enough to see it sent."

He advanced on her then, a flick-knife materialising in one hand, its blade glinting in the lamplights.

Vicky gathered her breath and screamed.

33

VICKY MANSFIELD'S CAR was found within ten minutes of the APB being sent out, thanks to a beady-eyed patrolman covering the northern ward of the city. The red Porsche Cayenne was parked up, locked and secure, in the shady corner of a parking lot that served a set of beauty salons and boutique drapery stores. An overturned shopping bag from one of the clothing stores lay on the tarmac behind the SUV.

CCTV from the small shopping centre didn't cover much of the carpark, but it did show Vicky leaving the mall carrying the bag in question. Although she appeared outwardly relaxed, displaying no visible signs of distress, the clock on the footage told the officers on scene that this last sighting of her was over two hours old. With no sign of her since then, the obvious inference from the discarded shopping bag and dress was that she had been abducted. At a request from Esther and Jared, the officers had cordoned off half the parking lot and sent for CSI. The technicians would process it and gather whatever evidence they could, but Esther was pinning all her hopes now on finding Vicky *here*, at Belfield Grammar.

She hadn't seen this part of the grounds during her last visit. The dormitory wing of Belfield's most prestigious grammar school was one of the oldest buildings in the county. It lay behind the modern wing, next to the school's sprawling sports fields. During term time it housed up to a hundred borders, but this close to Christmas the place was empty, the narrow, leaded windows all dark. Gargoyles lining the rooftop stared down blankly at the urgent scene in the carpark below, where liveried patrol cars were parked haphazardly, and a small host of uniform officers were pulling on their yellow coats and lifting heavy, high-powered flashlights from the trunks of their vehicles. A uniform sergeant was barking orders, mustering them for Esther's briefing. They knew they were about to take part in an urgent search operation for a missing woman, but so far they knew little more than that.

Jared came off the phone as Esther surveyed the scene.

"That's air support scrambling a chopper for us now," he told her. "Should be here within ten minutes. Despatch are trying to contact the school's caretaker as we speak."

"What about a dog callsign?"

He shook his head. "Tied up with something on the motorway. They'll divert as soon as they can."

Esther looked down at the screen of her own phone, studying a satellite view of the school grounds. It was clear they were going to need that helicopter; the terrain was challenging, to say the least. The nineteenth century school had an extensive set of playing fields and forested grounds to the north. The rugby pitch with the bleachers that Edwin had told her about was the furthest away, on the northern end. A narrow dirt path led between the other pitches and outbuildings towards it. If she was wrong about where Faraday had taken Vicky, it might take hours to scour the woods around these playing fields, but Esther hoped the arrival of the helicopter would make that task easier; with their heat-sensitive cameras and the trees all winter-bare, it shouldn't be too difficult to spot two solitary humans in the wilderness. She had a niggling feeling that time was already running short. Vicky had been missing for hours and the truth, though she hated to admit it, was that Vicky Mansfield might already be dead.

There was no sign of Faraday's red van, but that didn't mean he hadn't parked it somewhere nearby. If he *had* kidnapped Vicky, they could only hope Esther was right about where he planned to take her. She headed over to the uniform sergeant marshalling the troops.

"That's eight officers," he told her. "Four crews from three districts. That's all Despatch could send right now."

"It'll have to do," she replied. She raised her voice to address the gathering. "Right, ladies and gents, we have a possible abduction. Subject is twenty-eight-year-old Victoria Mansfield. White female, blonde, slim build, five-foot-five. Last seen wearing a cream overcoat, blue jeans and black ankle boots. Possible suspect is an Alfred Jacob Faraday, twenty-seven years. White male, heavily built, muscular, shaved head, five-foot-eight. We're not one hundred per cent sure what he's wearing, but sighted in recent days in a dark tracksuit, dark hooded top. He may have access to a red van, registration unknown."

She turned to the sergeant then, lowering her voice to address him as she showed him the satellite image of the school and surrounding grounds. "I need four officers to head into the woods this side," she told him, indicating the woodland to the east, "and two to check all the carparks and building doors, and then head towards the cricket grounds on the west side. I want two more to head north with me and DI Wilcox."

The sergeant gave a brisk nod and began giving instructions to the search teams.

Esther retrieved her own little flashlight from the car, greeted the two officers who would accompany her and Jared, and then set off down the dirt path towards the northern pitches.

* * *

Vicky didn't bother suppressing a shudder as Faraday traced the edge of his knife across her bare belly. His face was so close that she could smell his breath, rank and sour, and she sensed him inhaling her, breathing her in. He removed the knife briefly, then reapplied it next to her right nipple. His black eyes met hers, and she swallowed another sob and looked away from the murderous hatred she saw there.

"How do you think you would do without nipples, Vicky?" he asked. "You really need them?"

She cried out as his knife pierced the flesh of her right breast. Blood began to flow. But he pulled the blade away quickly, grimacing as if the sight of the wound disgusted him. When she looked at him again, he was glaring at her.

"The others are dead," he said, his voice flat and emotionless. "Gary, Carlton, Mark. You're the last. I wanted you to know that. I want you to know that I killed the others, and I am going to kill you. But before I kill you, I'm going to take what you offered me all those years ago, when you led me out here to be jumped and beaten and humiliated."

With that, he stepped forward and grabbed her roughly by the hips. He twisted her around. She cried out as she felt his hands grasping at her buttocks, his fingers slipping between her legs, pawing her.

And just as her cry faded, they both heard it. The faint thrum of a helicopter, growing louder…

Abruptly, he let her go and hurried over to the spotlights. When he turned them off, plunging them into darkness, Vicky could see flashlights far off among the trees to the south, and the blinking lights of a helicopter amidst the stars in the distance, moving closer.

Faraday moved quickly. He was behind her again, one hand grasping her ponytail and the other pressing the knife to her throat. She stiffened and sucked in a breath through her chattering teeth as the tip of the blade bit into her neck, just below her jaw.

"Scream and they will find you hanging here with your throat cut open," he hissed into her ear.

She couldn't nod. She couldn't move for fear of being cut by the knife, so she stayed perfectly still, perfectly quiet. But hope was blooming in her chest now, despite her captor's threats. Help was coming.

And then he was moving again. The knife came away from her throat and a dirty rag was shoved roughly into her mouth. He used duct tape to complete the makeshift gag before sawing at the rope that held her suspended from the bleachers. A moment later, she crumpled to the ground, too weak to break her fall as the rope gave way. She let out a muffled grunt as she landed, jarring her left knee and hip. Faraday paid no attention. He took hold of her bound wrists and began dragging her roughly across the grass, heedless of the abrasions he was causing to her naked body as he pulled her relentlessly through the darkness, away from the hunters with their flashlights.

34

JARED WAS SWEATING and breathing more heavily than he should have been for what amounted to no more than a brisk walk. He needed to do more exercise, cut down on the cigs and booze.

Esther had been studying her phone before they set out, looking at the layout of the school grounds. She was convinced that the dirt track leading north through a set of derelict outbuildings would bring them to the rugby pitch where the incident had happened all those years ago. Jared was inclined to agree with her that if she was right about Faraday being here, this was the place he would take his hostage, but it was still nothing more than supposition on their part…

It soon became obvious that the track they were following was just about wide enough for a vehicle. All four officers had noticed the fresh tyre marks on the muddy ground already. There was no way to say it was Faraday's van, but it had made Esther and the two uniform officers they'd brought with them pick up their pace all the same. Jared knew they had come too far to go back and get the cars now—they would lose more time than they would gain by doing that, much as Jared would have liked to believe otherwise—so he huffed and mopped his brow and trekked laboriously along behind the three women. Getting old was shit.

He jogged a few paces to catch up again, while the others cast their torchlight across one grass pitch after another, searching the fields for any sign of Vicky Mansfield, A.J. Faraday, or a red van. It was clear that Esther was resting all her hopes on finding Vicky here.

Jared just hoped it wasn't her dead body they found.

* * *

Alfie. *Alfie.*

He hated the sound of that name. Almost as much as he hated the name 'A.J.' He muttered it to himself under his breath as he pulled the driver's door closed, ignoring the muffled whimpers from Vicky in the back. Alfie was someone else, someone he'd left behind long ago. He was different now…

It was harder to convince himself of that, being back here. There was a time, not so long ago, when he wouldn't have believed he would ever come back to Belfield.

But here he was. And had been for weeks.

Driving the streets of his hometown had turned him inside out. He'd driven past his old house on Milltown Row. Seen his old primary school. Driven past Belfield

Grammar, more than once. Many times, in fact. He'd even parked up one day and stared at the main building for over an hour. Reliving memories. Memories he thought he'd cast off. A past he thought he'd escaped.

It had taken time, but A.J. Faraday had become someone else after he left Belfield. Someone he was happy with. He'd reinvented himself, or so he'd believed.

And then that fucker Hetherington had appeared and ruined everything, with a smug wink and a cheeky remark about his 'new look'.

And he'd called him by his old name.

Alfie.

Asked him whether any of his new friends had seen his high-school video…

After that, Jake Faraday's world had collapsed, bit by bit. He was coming to realise that you never truly escaped your past. You dragged it around with you wherever you went, whatever you did.

He glanced over his shoulder at Vicky Ellsmith, bound and gagged on the floor in the back of the van. Maybe it would be better to keep her alive for a few days. He let his eyes linger on her naked form. Maybe he could have more fun with her that way.

He started the engine.

35

THE ROAD CURVED to the right as they moved beyond the football pitches, a narrow drainage ditch running along its western verge and a bank of woodland flanking it to the east. Jared could see a set of rugby posts looming above the trees ahead.

They all froze when they heard the rumble of an engine. One of the uniform officers made a radio transmission, alerting everyone to the presence of a vehicle on the grounds. But no sooner had she let go of her transmit button than there was movement between the trees up ahead, and a van came barrelling around the bend towards them. The headlamps flashed on in a sudden and blinding explosion of light.

Jared stood frozen as Esther and the two officers dived for cover. Later there would be comments about his stoicism, his courage, his daring—or in Esther's opinion, his reckless stupidity—but Jared knew, there and then, that the only reason he wasn't diving for cover alongside the women was because he was totally beat. There was no bravery in it. The vehicle was too close and moving too quickly. There was no point in even trying to get out of the way. So he brought up his torch and pointed it straight at the van.

He was lucky. That's all. His attempt to dazzle the driver worked; the vehicle wobbled and veered around him, slamming into a hump of ground that lined the drainage ditch, where all control was lost. It pitched over and crashed onto its side, skidding across the track and coming to rest in a crunch of metal and glass on the edge of the trees about fifteen yards away.

Jared staggered towards it, scanning for signs of a fire as he approached. He couldn't see any flames. All he could make out through the steam and the vapour of his own breath was the underbelly of the van, its wheels still spinning even as the engine sputtered and cut.

The back doors had fallen open. He crouched down and shone his torch into the dark space within. A rucksack, blankets and lengths of rope were strewn about the interior.

Esther and one of the uniform officers joined him, and the combined light from their torches banished the darkness within completely. A tangle of flesh resolved itself into the shape of a naked woman. Blonde hair, young, with blood running from several cuts and scrapes, her wrists were bound together with nylon rope and there was silver tape across her mouth. She was clearly dazed by the crash.

"Vicky?" Esther called. "Vicky?"

At the sound of her name, Vicky Mansfield blinked and uncurled herself. She began trying to shimmy her way towards them.

Esther was already squeezing past Jared and into the van, followed by the other officer, who threw one of the blankets around Vicky Mansfield's naked form. Esther clambered through to the front, searching the cab.

"He's gone," she shouted back.

Jared turned to the second uniform officer. "Get on the radio. We need a dog unit down here urgently."

Esther was crouching next to Vicky now, tugging the tape from her mouth while the other officer untied the rope at her wrists. The woman gasped and sobbed as the gag came away.

"Vicky, who did this to you?" Esther asked. "Was it A.J.? A.J. Faraday?"

Vicky nodded.

"Is he alone? Vicky, can you tell me if anyone was with him?"

Vicky struggled to get the words out as sobs racked her. "He's-he's alone. He's got a knife."

Jared circled the wreckage. The van's windscreen was shattered, but still in place. The vehicle had landed with the driver's window open and facing the sky.

He aimed his torch at the grass verge on the wooded side of the track. The frosted tufts were overgrown and there were clear footprints. As he raised the light up, Esther appeared next to him, and they both spotted the distant movement at the same time, far in among the trees.

Their suspect was making off through the forest.

Without warning, Esther took to her heels in pursuit.

"Esther, wait!" Jared called. "Wait for the dog!"

But Esther either didn't hear him or chose to ignore him. She was disappearing into the woods, the beam of her flashlight bouncing off the trees.

"Come on!" Jared said to the uniform officer standing nearby. "We need to go with her."

Without waiting to see if she would follow, he began picking his way through the trees after Esther.

* * *

Ignoring the pain in his head, where he'd smacked it against the windscreen in the collision, Jake Faraday raced on through the woods.

He had panicked when he'd seen the cops. And when one of them had dazzled him with their torch, he'd completely lost control of the van. Foolish. He should've kept his cool. Could probably have just run them over if he'd closed his eyes and pressed the accelerator. It had crossed his mind. Why had he flinched from it?

He could hear the helicopter. It was closer now. They'd have infrared and shit like that to track him, if the cop shows on TV were anything to go by. He needed to get off the school grounds and back into the city, fast.

Another glance over his shoulder revealed a flashlight in the distance; he had at least one pursuer.

Pushing through some briars, he snagged his hand on the thorns and cursed aloud, but it didn't slow him any. He willed his legs to pump harder, to go faster.

The routes were coming back to him now, the memories all there, resurfacing like noxious bubbles from a swamp. He knew these woods too well. He'd used them many, many times, having become something of an expert at escaping other students during his early years at Belfield Grammar.

Unwanted as those memories were, they were proving

useful now. He knew exactly where to go to get away…

36

ESTHER CRASHED THROUGH another tangle of undergrowth, the beam of her flashlight dipping and bobbing wildly as she ran. She was desperate not to lose sight of Faraday. Every now and again she would catch a glimpse of his dark shape flitting between the trees.

The forest was winter-dead, the limbs of the ancient oaks and elms rimed with frost. A waning moon cast the whole scene in an eerie blue half-light.

Faraday knew she was behind him. She'd spotted him glancing back at her once as he ran.

Jared's shouts had become distant now, but she wasn't about to slow down and let Faraday get away. He'd killed three people. Vicky Mansfield would have been his fourth if they hadn't interrupted him… No, Esther was determined to get that fucker in handcuffs *tonight!*

Abruptly, she skidded to a halt, grabbing hold of a low-hanging bough with her free hand just in time to stop herself from stumbling down a steep embankment that opened up in front of her without warning. Another sports field.

The helicopter was to the south of her, its searchlight combing the grounds. Esther wished she'd had the presence of mind to bring a radio.

She scanned the moonlit playing field and quickly spotted Faraday's fleeing figure. He was skirting the football pitch, heading towards another dark treeline beyond. They must be nearing the northern boundary of the school grounds by now. What was it that lay to the north? Derelict industrial yards? An old railway site? It was something like that. No time to check. She glanced over her shoulder. Jared's shouts were a good way behind her now, muffled by the trees.

Another glance at Faraday. He was on the far side of the pitch and racing along the edge of the forest. As she watched, he took a sharp turn and darted into the trees and out of sight.

With a muttered curse, she picked her way carefully down the tree-dotted slope and out onto the football field.

As soon as she had her footing on level ground again, she took off, sprinting towards the spot in the treeline where Faraday had disappeared…

* * *

The young officer shouted a warning and her arm shot out, blocking Jared's way. He stumbled to a clumsy halt. They had come to the edge of a steep embankment, where a lonely outlying football pitch made a break in the woods.

He took advantage of the pause in their foot-chase to get

some air into his lungs. He really was getting too old for this caper. His chest was on fire, his legs and arms trembling. The young girl in uniform seemed fine by comparison. Breathing a little heavier maybe, but she looked ready to dart off again at any sign of movement.

But there was no movement. No torch beams in the distance. No sign of either Esther or Faraday. The football pitch was empty, and its worn-out surface was too thin and mottled to hold any discernible tracks in the frost.

As he caught his breath, Jared scanned the surrounding trees for signs of light or movement.

There was nothing.

The embankment ran off to either side of them, a straight line to the east and west. It softened into a shallower incline as it curled around the eastern end of the pitch, where the trees marched along behind rusting, netless goalposts. On the opposite side to where they stood, the scattered woods became thick forest again.

If Esther had doubled back, they would have seen or heard something, he was sure. She was somewhere among the trees out here, but there was no sign of her. Had she caught up with Faraday? Or had Faraday stopped to confront her? Esther was a tough cookie, but the thought of her alone out here, one-on-one against that brute made Jared's heart grow cold in his burning chest. He had to find her.

"Call that chopper over here," he panted to the girl in uniform. "Ask them to scan the woods around this pitch. We'll split up. You go that way." Jared indicated towards the trees to the east. "I'll cross over."

"Yes, Guv," the officer replied. She relayed the command over her radio and set off along the embankment.

Heaving another lungful of air, Jared started down the slope.

37

THE FOREST WAS thicker here, on the other side of the disused football pitch. Esther hadn't caught sight of Faraday since he'd entered this stretch of woods, but she had found a beaten trail leading through the tangle of brambles and winter-brown undergrowth.

When it opened up into a clearing, she paused, struggling to listen past the pounding of blood in her ears and her own heavy breathing. All she could hear was the distant thrum of the police helicopter.

He couldn't be that far ahead of her.

She trained the beam of her flashlight on the ground, scouring the earth for signs of passage. Within seconds, she was rewarded with a glimpse of a footprint in a softer patch of mud. Freshly left, it confirmed he was still heading north. She followed the same direction across the clearing, where she found another trail among the winter weeds, and set off again.

About fifty yards on, the track ended suddenly at a chain-link fence. The industrial yard on the other side was half-lit by orange sodium lamps. Stacks of steel beams and concrete sleepers cast pools of shadow everywhere.

Taking hold of the fence, Esther gave it a good shake. It was strong and tight, with no sign of any gaps in the dirt beneath, and one look at the spiked rollers that ran along the top told her Faraday hadn't gone over it. Judging by the brightness of the steel links, the fence was less than a year old, and Esther suddenly wondered if perhaps there had been a way through here once – and whether that was what Faraday had been banking on. The industrial yard was clearly old; it might have been disused up until recently.

Esther looked one way, then the other. To the east, the forest seemed thicker, the winter scrub already growing right back up against the fence in places. To the west, there was more of a natural gap along the fence-line. The ground was covered in dead foliage and Esther couldn't discern any tracks, but she took a chance and set off west, scanning the chain links for signs of a hole as she went.

The helicopter was louder now. When Esther glanced up, she could see the bright spotlight in the sky to the south. Again, she cursed herself for not bringing a radio.

And then, all of a sudden, she emerged into another clearing and found him.

He stood, squinting against the light from her torch, not ten yards away.

He was a monster. His face was gaunt and flecked with dark stubble, and although his clean-shaven head was bright in the torchlight, his dark, heavy brows cast malevolent shadows over his eyes. Maybe he was only an inch or so taller than her, but at that moment he seemed so much bigger. Almost as wide as he was tall, with arms as thick as her legs, his huge chest heaved breaths that created a shroud of vapour around his head, making him look like a fog-bound demon. Esther's heart, already thumping hard, fluttered at the sight of him, and she felt an instant of profound uncertainty. Why had she raced off on her own? This man could probably crush her skull with his hands. And he had a knife. He held it out to one side, its blade glinting in the torchlight, as if he was getting ready to defend himself.

Or preparing to attack…

The moment stretched as they both stood and stared at one another. Faraday had lifted his free hand to block the light of her torch from his eyes, but he did no more than stare silently at her as he caught his breath.

Esther decided to try to get him talking. If she stalled long enough, the helicopter would find them.

"A.J.?" she asked. "Or is it Jake? Which do you prefer?"

Faraday said nothing. Initially, he seemed to flinch slightly at her words, but the reaction was so subtle it might have been her imagination. He continued to stare at her. The knife in his hand twitched.

"My name's Esther," she told him. "I'm a police officer."

Again, he said nothing. Esther did her best to keep her light trained steadily on him, while her other hand fished in her pocket for her can of pepper spray.

"I know you're upset, A.J." She was proud of how steady her voice sounded, with her heart jackhammering in her chest. "I think you have every right to be upset. What those guys did to you when you were a kid is unforgivable. I understand your anger. I want you to know that I get it."

"How the fuck would you know?" he growled. "How

the *fuck* would you know what it's like?"

He took a step forward. Esther took a step back.

"I can understand your pain," she told him, trying to hide the sudden tremor in her voice. "You should never have had to suffer what they did to you."

Abruptly he laughed, a dry, mirthless sound. "Is that what you think? Well, you're wrong! Of course I should have. I was weak. Pathetic. I did nothing to help myself. What those bastards did that night… it was a gift, in a way. Helped me see—*really* see, for the first time—what a pathetic, useless loser I was."

"No, A.J—"

"*Don't!*" His furious roar silenced her. "Don't stand there and pretend to fucking care! You're like the teachers, just spouting your bullshit, your politically correct garbage, and not meaning one fucking word of it! I *was* a loser! I *was* a creep! Even the fucking teachers didn't like me. No good at sports, no good at maths, no good at fucking anything! No… that was the night I finally realised the truth. And that truth helped me get a fucking grip and make something of myself!"

"And you have," Esther replied. She had taken a firm hold of her pepper spray now, fingering the little cannister so that she had it ready to bring up and deploy in a second. If she could talk him down, though, he might still come willingly. Her handcuffs were in a pouch on her belt below her coat. The pepper spray was a one-shot deal. If it didn't work, or she missed…

Faraday continued to stare at her, the clench in his jaw and the set of his shoulders telling Esther that the talking-down wasn't working yet. He was bracing for a fight.

She tried again.

"I can see that you *have* made something of yourself," she said. "One look at you and anyone can see that. But being a bigger person, a stronger person, is more than just lifting weights at the gym. You need to face down the consequences of your actions. Otherwise, you'll *always* be running."

Another joyless bark of laughter escaped him.

"Is that it?" he asked. "Is that your pitch? You gonna sweet-talk me into a pair of handcuffs, officer?"

And then Esther's heart lurched as he launched himself at her…

* * *

Jared's forward progress was more of a stumble than a run by now, as he pushed his way into thicker undergrowth. He'd found a track of sorts through the patches of briar, and he was sure he'd caught sight of Esther's torch in the distance to the north at one point. It had been a fleeting glimpse, but enough to encourage him onward. He'd called her name then, hoping she'd slow down, but she hadn't, and there'd been no trace of her since.

Abruptly, he came to an empty clearing in the woods and the track disappeared.

"Esther!" he shouted. It was a desperate move, shouting her name in the hope of locating her, but he was starting to feel desperate now. "Esther!"

His chest was on fire and there was a stitch in his side. He leaned over and put his hands on his knees. As much as he wanted to press on, he needed a moment to catch his breath.

The moon emerged from the clouds and that's when he noticed the footprints in the patch of mud. He straightened and wiped his sweaty brow with the back of his hand; despite the cold, he was drenched in perspiration.

"Esther!" he called again. No sound. No sign of her flashlight.

He staggered on.

38

ESTHER BROUGHT THE pepper spray up just in time. As Faraday's knife arced through the air towards her, she dived—aiming and squeezing the nozzle all in one swift movement. She prayed as she fell that the powerful liquid would catch him cleanly in the face.

Landing in the dirt with a grunt, she rolled. She had to keep moving. If the spray took effect, he'd be blinded within seconds, and he would move towards where he'd last seen her. If it didn't…

An angry cry told her that the pepper spray had found its target. Blinded or not, though, Faraday was clearly determined. As Esther scrambled to her feet, she saw him stagger on, swinging wildly with his knife. He was moving towards her flashlight, where she'd dropped it on the ground. It was probably all he could see through the tears.

She went to slip behind him, but as she did so, her boot landed on a dry twig, and it snapped. The sound was clearly audible, even above the thrum of the nearby helicopter.

Faraday spun. He was fast as a snake, knife swiping back and forth as he came at her.

Esther backed up clumsily to avoid the cut of the blade, but as she retreated, her heel caught on a root. She fell, unable to stifle a grunt when she landed on her backside. Faraday heard, and he bore down on her before she could react. Luckily, he was still half-blind from the pepper spray; she was able to twist away as his knife came at her in a violent slash. It found only empty air where she had lain a moment ago.

He kept coming, stabbing his way towards her, and Esther didn't have time to get to her feet. She scrambled away, but he followed, slashing low with his knife. Even stunned and half-blind as he was, his blade found flesh this time, slicing Esther across the side of her calf. She couldn't stifle her cry as she pulled herself backwards, and he lunged towards the sound of her voice. It was at that moment that Esther's hand closed over a fist-sized rock among a drift of dead leaves. She threw it at his charging shape with all her might.

There was a sickening crack. Faraday stumbled. The knife fell from his hand. He almost fell with it, but somehow, incredibly, he continued to stagger forward. Perhaps his vision was clearing, or perhaps it was instinct or just dumb luck, but he landed right on top of her, taking her to the ground and pinning her to the dirt. As he smashed into her, all the air was knocked from Esther's lungs and stars began to dance across her vision.

Faraday started punching.

Esther writhed and dodged.

If his vision had been completely clear, Faraday might have landed a proper blow. As it was, Esther managed to duck the worst of it, her hands reaching out blindly for that fallen rock…

* * *

Jared's stumbling run ended at a chain-link fence. A factory yard lay on the other side. He gripped the links of the fence and rattled it, checking for gaps. It seemed solid. He peered into the shadowy yard beyond, but there was no movement there, and no sound apart from the beating of the helicopter rotor blades in the sky above.

He was exhausted now. He didn't know how much further he could go before he'd collapse completely. He would have called out Esther's name again, but he couldn't gather enough breath to do it.

And then he heard a cry from somewhere among the trees off to his left. Someone in pain.

Esther!

Finding a sudden surge of energy he didn't know he had, Jared turned and raced towards the source of the sound, following a trail that ran along the fence-line to the west, and finding the breath he needed to call out her name again as he went…

39

THE BITCH POLICEWOMAN kept twisting and turning beneath him, slippery as an eel. Barely able to see through the blur of tears, Faraday gasped as he tried to strike her again and his knuckles found a buried stone instead. His face burned like fire and his eyes wouldn't stop streaming, no matter how much he blinked and wiped at them.

But it wasn't enough to stop him. He knew this woman wanted to take him to prison and lock him up forever. He wasn't about to let this skinny bitch decide how he went. He would show her. He would show her that *he* was the one in control. Not just of his own life, but of *her* life now too. She would pay for ruining his plans…

He swung again, caught her a glancing blow this time. She cried out in pain. Her efforts to push him off were futile. He was too big for her. She was like a child beneath him. Abruptly, he stopped swinging and worked his fingers across the fabric of her coat, searching for her throat.

He would show her who was in control.

And then he would finish her.

* * *

Esther pushed against Faraday as hard as she could, but it was like trying to push off a boulder. When his fist caught the side of her head, the pain of it set her ears ringing and sent stars across her vision again. Her twisting slowed long enough for his hands to find her neck. Thick fingers wrapped themselves around her throat and began to squeeze. She suddenly found herself sucking for air that wouldn't come. Her right hand scrabbled frantically among the dead leaves for the rock she'd thrown, while she tried to pry fingers like knots of wood from her throat with her left. But already her vision was starting to go dark, her mind beginning to drift. Her left hand weakened; her right hand slowed its frantic search…

For a fleeting instant, Esther thought she could hear Jared's voice calling her name through the growing ringing in her ears. But the world began drifting away from her, and she wasn't entirely sure it was real…

And then, just as she thought she would pass out, her searching fingers found something. Not the rock. Something else. Her strength was fading, but she managed to find the handle. She gripped it as hard as she could, and with her last scrap of strength, she brought it up, firm and straight, right below Faraday's ribs.

The sound he made was unnerving. A grunt from the very depths of his lungs.

His crushing grip on her throat went slack. As his

fingers came away, Esther gasped, sucking for air like a drowning woman. She felt woozy.

Faraday was looking down at himself, a puzzled expression on his face. He reached down and tried to pull the blade free. A terrible whimpering noise escaped his lips, before he toppled sideways with a grunt, wheezing like a deflating balloon.

The moment his huge weight fell from her, Esther dragged herself backwards and away from him. But her efforts were feeble, and she hardly travelled any distance at all before her strength left her completely. Her head was pounding now, her throat raw and ragged.

He made no move to go after her. When he finally tugged the knife free from his gut, he was shaking uncontrollably, his hands glistening darkly in the pale moonlight. All his attention was fixed on the bloody wound in his stomach. Still, Esther kept a wary eye on him as he pulled himself over to the broad trunk of an oak tree and lay back against it. She wasn't prepared to approach him while he still held that knife. If anything, she needed to get further away from him.

But those thoughts came to her dreamily. All her strength had dissolved and her head was swimming.

She watched as Faraday's gaze rose from the wound and the bloody knife in his hand, watched as his eyes fell upon her once more. There were only a few yards between them, but she couldn't make herself get up and move. Her vision grew darker as she watched him struggle to get up. She knew she should feel alarmed. She knew she should try to escape. But it all felt like a dream now. All Esther wanted to do was sleep.

As Faraday struggled to get to his feet, her world drifted

into darkness…

40

JARED COULDN'T HEAR anything now, apart from the sound of his own clumsy progress through the forest and the drone of the helicopter somewhere nearby.

Then, all of a sudden, he staggered into a moonlit clearing. His thundering heart skipped a beat as his eyes fell on Esther, lying motionless on the ground.

Not far from her, a man lay slumped against a tree. Faraday. He was hunched to one side as if he was about to stand up, but he wasn't moving either. When Jared caught sight of the bloody knife in his hand, he gave an anguished cry and lurched towards Esther's prone form.

Without turning his back on Faraday, Jared dropped to the ground next to Esther. Setting down his torch, he fumbled for her wrist, searching frantically for a pulse. He sagged with relief when she groaned and her eyes fluttered open.

"Esther!" he gasped. "Where did he get you?"

He was searching her clothes for signs of blood. He

found a shallow gash in her jeans over the left calf, but there wasn't nearly as much blood as the slick blade in Faraday's hand suggested there should be.

Esther shook her head slightly, and winced in pain. "It was *me* stabbed *him*," she rasped. "He was choking me. Would've killed me."

"You're not stabbed?" Jared asked, wanting a solid confirmation before he switched his attention to their suspect.

"No," she replied, wincing again as he helped her to sit up. "Just nicked my leg is all."

Once he was satisfied that Esther was not in any immediate danger, Jared turned to Faraday.

Scooping up his flashlight, he carried out a visual search before he approached.

The man was huge. Even slumped under the boughs of a tree, he looked massive, his hooded top straining around the girth of his upper arms and chest. His shaved head shone pale in the torchlight, his eyes set deep in dark hollows beneath a heavy brow. It was clear even before he drew close that Faraday wasn't breathing. The killer's gaunt cheeks were wet with tears, and Jared detected the scent of pepper spray in the air. Close up, he thought he could make out the faint lines of half-healed scratch marks on the man's face.

He directed the flashlight towards the stomach area, where a large patch on the dark fabric of Faraday's hooded top glistened wetly. Both of his hands were coated in sticky red blood. Jared leaned in and placed his fingers on the man's neck, just below the jawline.

"Is he dead?" Esther asked hoarsely.

Jared nodded grimly.

"Yes," he replied. "He's dead."

"Fuck," Esther wheezed.

Jared crossed the clearing and helped Esther get to her feet, pulling her arm over his shoulders so he could take her weight. His own heart rate was returning to something like normal, and although his legs were still aching, the task of keeping Esther on her feet seemed to lend him some newfound strength.

"Let's get you to a doctor," he said. "There's enough uniform officers nearby to take care of Faraday and hold the scene."

Together, they picked their way carefully back the way they'd come.

"I thought I could handle him, Jared," Esther mumbled as they left the clearing. There was a touch of regret in her voice. "I just… I just couldn't let him get away. And now he's dead."

"You did what you had to," he told her. "It's our job to catch the killer. He had a knife. You had a can of pepper spray. Self-defence."

"There'll still be people who want my head for this."

He sighed. "There will." He gave her shoulder a gentle squeeze. "But never forget the fact that you saved a young woman's life tonight. Without you, there'd still have been a dead body on these grounds. But it would've been Vicky Mansfield's. Don't lose sight of that. Don't lose sight of who the bad guy was here."

"Thanks, Jared. You've always got my back."

Jared nodded. "Always."

EPILOGUE

Hello. My name is Esther and I'm an alcoholic. It's been six days since my last drink.

This new update is greeted with murmurs of encouragement.

I had a lapse recently, as some of you know. I spoke about it at the last meeting. But I'm dealing with it the right way.

I've accepted it. I've owned it.

And I still have all those days of achievement from before to build on. That's the way I look at it.

And it's all about one day at a time, right?

Nods and muttered agreements are the response to her question. No judgement. No condemnation. Only support.

Things are looking better now. I've met someone, and it's given me new strength. To try harder, and keep trying.

That's all we can do, I guess. Keep trying.

One day at a time.

* * *

The office was quiet now. It was late afternoon on Christmas Eve and the CID offices were on minimum staffing. Only those people with no last-minute shopping or families to go home to lingered, shuffling papers into files or tapping at computer keyboards. The Christmas tree blinked lonesomely in a shadowy corner, but most of the place was dark and silent. Now and again, the tranquillity was broken by the sirens of a patrol car departing the station yard on an emergency call, but up on the CID floor, things moved slowly and quietly.

Esther stood at the window in her office, staring down the main shopping boulevard towards City Hall, where a Christmas tree in the front plaza stood almost as tall as the building itself. Lights and decorations were strung evenly between lampposts all along the avenue, and City Hall was lit up gaudily for the holiday season. Traffic was heavy, the headlights and taillights adding to the festive glow as the light in the sky faded.

With a small sigh, she returned to her desk and sat down, scanning the last couple of paragraphs of her report. She'd spent the whole day trying to summarise the Faraday case. The DNA under Carlton Riddell's fingernails, together with DNA found on Sterling and the eyelash found on Hetherington, comprehensively linked Faraday to all three murders. But Jared had gone further, knowing that this report could be vital for Esther in the long run. He'd organised a criminal psychologist to add a professional clinical assessment, using what they knew about their serial killer's history.

The psychologist, working off the information available, outlined a clear case of PTSD as a result of the childhood bullying Faraday had suffered. Her theory resonated strongly with Esther's first hunch, outlining a probable nervous breakdown when Hetherington, one of his old tormentors, showed up in London, invading the new life he'd made for himself. This unexpected disruption had knocked Faraday completely off-balance, and once he'd lost his job and home, he'd simply snapped, becoming utterly fixated on his gruesome new cause – a twisted desire for revenge.

Gary Hetherington had been his first victim: strangled, and his body dumped in a disused warehouse on a London dock. According to the psychologist, the emotional aspect of the crimes was evidenced in the manner of each victim's death. All were strangled – a close-up, personal kind of killing. Faraday would have been looking into their eyes when they died. It showed how much the need for vengeance had consumed him.

Esther's team had managed to track the movement of Faraday's van over the last few months. The CCTV that was still available suggested he'd spent weeks living in it after Hetherington's death, plotting his revenge as he drifted back towards Belfield.

As for Vicky Mansfield, her account of what Faraday had done to her before the police arrived was chilling. The psychologist wrote about Faraday harbouring a twisted desire for some kind of sexual revenge against her. There was little doubt he would have killed her too if the police hadn't arrived in time.

Esther had read the psychologist's report with interest, and referenced it heavily in her own summary for the Chief Constable. Given all the media interest, the top brass wanted answers, and wanted them yesterday. The police watchdog, the IOPC, would be looking to cut her to shreds for chasing down Faraday after Vicky had been rescued. And she was sure DCI Small would jump at any chance to suspend her or send her away. But, for the moment, front-page headlines about Vicky Mansfield's rescue, and Jared shifting all the credit Esther's way, meant she had the support of the Police and Crime Commissioner. He'd even mentioned a medal. Esther didn't care about medals; as long as she got to keep her job here in CID, she was happy. Besides, politicians were fickle. They could all turn on her yet. Still, while they were on her side, the DCI wouldn't dare to move against her.

As for Vicky herself, the woman was badly shaken by her ordeal. She had been a tearful mess when Esther visited her in the hospital later that night. She'd confessed everything to Esther and Jared, blubbering about what she and Gary, and Carlton and Mark, had done to Faraday—Alfie, she called him—and swore she didn't know anything about the blackmail afterwards. The woman was a bundle of conflicting emotions, flashing between outrage and anger at her kidnap and assault, to guilt at what she and her friends had done as teenagers, to just a mess of fearful blubbering. It would take her a while to recover, Esther thought. Maybe just in time for Faraday's inquest.

Esther and Jared had called out to Edwin Long the

following day too. He had been quiet and withdrawn when he learned about his old friend's death, and about what he'd done before his death. What he'd been about to do. Esther felt sorry for the young man. He couldn't have known, and she'd told him as much. Told him nobody could have guessed what Alfred Jacob Faraday had become.

With a sigh, she realised she was wiped. She couldn't write any more. Switching off her computer, she grabbed her bag and coat and headed for the door.

As she crossed the main room, saying goodnight to the detectives who were still there and wishing them a happy Christmas, she noticed that the light in Jared's office was still on. She tapped on the door and stepped inside. Her boss looked weary as he glanced up from his computer and gave her a half-smile.

"You could be a make-up artist," he said. "You've covered that shiner like it wasn't even there."

Esther raised a tentative hand to the bruise on her left cheek. "Oh. Yeah. Swelling's gone down." She'd had to apply a liberal amount of foundation to her neck to cover the marks Faraday had left there too.

"No interest in showing off your war wounds then?"

"Don't want to scare any children while I do my Christmas shopping," she replied.

Jared chuckled. "Fair enough."

"On the subject of Christmas," she said, "do you have any plans? I think Jean's been a bit overenthusiastic with the turkey. It's a monster. Even with the neighbours calling over, we'll be fighting our way through turkey sandwiches for a week or more. You care to join us?"

He smiled gratefully, but shook his head. "Samantha has

asked me to call over. For the boys' sake, she said."

Esther knew Jared's marriage was on the ropes after an ill-advised dalliance with a woman from one of the neighbourhood teams. He and his wife had been living apart for a couple of months now, but they hadn't divorced. Not yet.

"Is she softening, do you think?" she asked.

He shrugged. "I'm not getting my hopes up," he replied. "But I'll take it."

Esther nodded and gave him a sympathetic smile. "Good luck. You in Boxing Day?"

"Unfortunately, yes. I drew the short straw."

"Me too. I'll see you then. Merry Christmas, Jared."

"Merry Christmas, Esther."

Esther shrugged into her coat and wrapped a scarf around her neck as she left the station. She stepped out into the bitterly cold evening air. Patches of frost were already forming in the shadows, the wet mud in the gutters rimed with ice, as she began wending her way through throngs of Christmas shoppers.

A group of carol singers had taken up residence outside a department store on one of the pedestrianized streets, and a crowd had gathered to listen. Esther paused there for a moment, studying the faces of the people around her. She spotted a small boy in the crowd. She guessed he was about the same age as her nephew. He was mouthing the words to 'Silent Night' as he watched the carollers, and she experienced a sudden rush of feeling for him—this stranger—a rush of sentiment she wasn't sure she would have felt before her visit to Travis Somerville's house.

She shook her head and moved on.

But even after she left the carol singers and the little boy behind—their voices fading beneath the jingles piped from storefronts up and down the street—the feeling lingered. A warm, tingling, slightly disconcerting sensation deep in her gut.

A couple of blocks further on, Esther stepped into the coffee shop she'd been looking for. All the tables were full, and there was a queue at the counter, but she quickly spotted Triona waving to her from a far corner.

"Hi, how's your cheek?" the nurse asked, as Esther sat down across from her.

"Still tender, but at least I look a little less like Quasimodo now."

Triona laughed, reaching out and squeezing Esther's hand as the waitress arrived to take their order.

After the girl went to get their coffees, Esther took a small, gift-wrapped package from her bag.

"Here," she said to Triona, "I got you something."

The nurse's eyes widened. "A Christmas present?"

"Open it."

"Shouldn't I save it for Christmas morning?"

"I have something else planned for Christmas morning," Esther replied huskily, and blushed in spite of herself.

Triona grinned and ripped the wrapping off unceremoniously, laughing in delight when she saw what was inside.

"*Withnail and I*, Blu-ray Limited Edition. Wow, cool! We should watch this together, over the holidays."

"Let's do that," Esther said, smiling.

Triona leaned over and kissed her, and Esther realised then that she didn't care who saw them.

DON'T MISS the OTHER EXCITING TITLES in the Detective Esther Penman series…

Follow the author on **Amazon** *and* **Bookbub**,
or subscribe to the newsletter at
jkflynn.co.uk
for updates on all new releases & promotional offers!